CW01623261

ZO[illegible]A AND THE DEAD DUTCHMEN

L.G. WILDER

Copyright © L. G. Wilder 2024

The right of L. G. Wilder to be identified as the Author of the Work has been asserted by him in accordance with the Copyright, Designs and Patents Act 1988.

All rights reserved.

No part of this publication may be reproduced, stored in a retrieval system, or transmitted, in any form or by any means without the prior written permission of the Author.

This book is sold subject to the condition that it shall not, by way of trade or otherwise, be lent, re-sold, hired out, or otherwise circulated without the Author's prior consent in any form of binding or cover and without a similar condition including this condition being imposed on the subsequent purchaser.

This novel is a work of fiction. Except in the case of historical fact, the names, characters and incidents it portrays are the work of the Author's imagination and are not to be construed as real. Any resemblance to real persons, living or dead, is purely coincidental.

Independently published.

Paperback:
ISBN 9782959646911

Also available in ebook:
ISBN 9782959646904

www.lgwilder.com

As I finish writing, in autumn 2024, there can be only one possible dedication for this work.
To the courage and resilience of the people of Ukraine, standing firm in the face of horrific aggression.
Slava Ukrayini! Heroyam Slava!
Glory to Ukraine! Glory to the heroes!

PART 1

The Professor

CHAPTER 1

Zoya was curled up on the battered leather sofa in the corner of her boss's office when the shouting started. She jolted awake and glanced at her watch. It was a few minutes after eight a.m., which meant she had managed just under two hours of sleep. She rubbed her fists into her eyes. When she heard the next yell, she pushed herself upright. This time the voice was closer – Major Dobroshtan was advancing down the corridor – and Zoya could make out the words. It was a simple command, repeated.

"Get me Lieutenant Zozulya! Now!"

Zoya was dizzy and her stomach churned unforgivingly, but she moved fast. By the time Dobroshtan slammed the door open – aiming another shout over his shoulder, then falling silent when he spotted Zoya – she was seated to attention in front of his desk. She converted the sweep of her hand through her tousled hair into something approaching a salute. She turned and smiled at her boss, registering his bloodshot eyes and unshaven cheeks, saying good morning without expecting a reply.

If the Major was surprised to discover that the person he had been summoning had already arrived, he hid it well. Perhaps he thought that was how life should naturally work for the head of Odesa's elite Homicide Unit. Alternatively, he was simply too hungover to register the brief glitch that had just occurred in his personal time-space continuum. In any case, he didn't ask and Zoya didn't explain. Instead, he circled the desk and aimed himself heavily and reasonably successfully into his high-backed swivel chair.

Dobroshtan sighed heavily and reached for the bronze desk calendar that stood dead centre of the tabletop. He turned one of the dials to advance the date one day closer to retirement. He raised an eyebrow when he saw the result and turned the calendar towards Zoya. She read that the month was March, the year 2015, the date Friday the thirteenth. She shrugged. They would both, if asked, have denied that they were superstitious. Yet each would have been lying. They were, after all, detectives who dealt with murder in all its sordid and tragic varieties on a daily basis – sometimes superstition was all that got them through the day.

The Major cracked his knuckles, one by one. The sound was loud and ugly. It also signalled the beginning of what Dobroshtan's team had come to call his morning workout. It was a performance that involved snatching up the slim-bladed combat knife he used as a letter opener, raising it to eye level for a moment to admire its brutally efficient form, then slashing it left and right in a long and intricate sequence of cuts and parries. Most days, the imaginary knife fight presented no real danger to anyone but the Major himself. Today was different. Dobroshtan's hands trembled, his movements were uncoordinated, and his gaze fluttered and flickered. As the needle tip of the blade crept closer to Zoya's face, she flexed the powerful muscles of her glutes and quads in case a sudden backward movement was called for. She clenched her toes in her heavy work boots and forced herself not to flinch. She waited to find out how much trouble she was in.

"It's from the Great Patriotic War," Dobroshtan said with a husky but surprisingly steady voice, holding the knife still for a moment. "The truck driver told us his grandfather took it from a retreating SS officer. From his grave most likely, if the grandfather was anything like his grandson."

Although the streets were almost clear of snow, the city had yet to be liberated from the fierce grip of the winter heating season. The cramped office's two cast-iron radiators remained on permanent full blast, leaving a continuous cycle of window opening and closing as the only way to maintain a survivable temperature.

Zoya had chosen to sleep with the dusty panes cracked wide open, so a burst of noise from the street, when it came, sounded out clear and close. Car tyres squealed as they skidded over wet tarmac, and a single, ominously heavy thud followed; or perhaps it was two thuds, close enough together to be almost indistinguishable. A second later they heard the unmistakable crash of metal on metal and a brief crunch of shattering glass.

Dobroshtan's hand froze mid-sweep. His nostrils flared and his head tugged to the right. A crescendo of hoarse yells – men's voices, raised in shock and anger – echoed between the street's close-stacked concrete walls. The Major listened hard.

But his distraction was short-lived. Dobroshtan knew that a road accident, even one outside police headquarters, was the traffic cops' responsibility, not his. He sighed regretfully and his eyes shifted their focus back to Zoya.

"Where were we?" he muttered.

"You were about to tell me about Pasha Four Sticks," Zoya said. "The first case you solved when you joined the force. The long-distance truck driver who used the knife you're currently wielding to murder six victims over a two-year period. Four men and two women, chosen simply because they were the first people he encountered when he entered the city after returning from one of his trips. Sir."

Dobroshtan stared mournfully at Zoya. Eventually she lowered her eyes.

"Thank you, Lieutenant," he said. "I was actually going to inform you that General Negodyaev called me three times over the course of last night. Naturally, he is aware that you have the best arrest record in the unit, yet he is furiously insistent that I fire you. His closing words were 'Either she goes, or you go'. Now, why do you think that is, Lieutenant?"

Zoya didn't reply. She hadn't doubted that the General would call, but she had still been clinging to the slim chance he would have been too embarrassed to share too many of the specifics of the previous evening's incident. The one where Zoya had been called out to a shooting at the prestigious Palladium nightclub on Italiiskyi Boulevard, and in the course of her enquiries had arrested a young woman in a silver-sequinned minidress who seemed to believe she was entitled to depart the crime scene without giving a statement or leaving her name and address.

After which, Zoya had to admit, she had reacted less than professionally when the woman had tried to push her way into her car whilst treating Zoya to two of her least favourite phrases: "Do you know who my father is?", followed by "I'll have you fired if you don't let me leave right now".

The Major's mouth flickered into what might have been a smile, but might also have been a grimace.

"It was Negodyaev's daughter you put in handcuffs," he said. "And the BMW – whose upholstery you doused with the bottle of very expensive tequila she was carrying, and then set on fire – that was apparently a gift from her loving *Papasha* on the spoilt little brat's eighteenth birthday."

Dobroshtan's hand moved up to rub at his forehead. He realised he was still holding the knife. He replaced it on its hardwood stand and rifled through a stack of files on the left side of the desk until he found the one he was looking for. He opened it, moistened the tip of one finger, and began to flick slowly through the pages. It was Zoya's personnel file. He was searching for something Zoya knew he wouldn't find. Hope perhaps, or clarity at least.

Outside, the shouting had been replaced by the wail of sirens approaching from the west. Their volume built, angry and urgent, reaching a peak when the ambulance arrived, before then cutting out. Zoya pictured the scene. The paramedics, underpaid and under-equipped, would struggle out of their ramshackle vehicle. They would curse the cold spring rain as they bent over an anonymous pedestrian's fallen form, assessing and evaluating. Zoya knew they were dedicated men and women who always did their best; who celebrated their successes modestly and joked fatalistically to hide the pain of failure. *Like cops*, she thought – only sometimes these guys arrived in time to save a life, not just to clean up the mess. She wondered if today would be one of those days.

Zoya switched her attention back to Dobroshtan when he began to cough. He had stopped smoking six months ago, though he told anyone who asked that he had probably left it too late. He gulped and massaged the slack skin on his neck as he read out selected passages from the file.

"Lieutenant Zozulya is disrespectful towards authority," he noted, then turned the page.

"She ignores departmental policies and rules whenever she finds it convenient," he continued, and turned again.

"The Lieutenant continues to prioritise her own needs to the complete exclusion of the interests of her fellow officers."

Dobroshtan looked up, hoping perhaps that Zoya would disagree. She didn't. She nodded instead, sympathetically. She knew Dobroshtan's night-time vodka consumption reflected the reality that Zoya's screwups hurt him far more than they hurt her.

Then they were saved. The door of Dobroshtan's office crashed open. The young man who appeared in the doorframe was panting from his sprint up the stairs. He wore a cheap suit without a tie, and one of his hands was stained in blood. Zoya thought his name was Oleg: a recent recruit, straight out of the training academy, and apparently too inexperienced to have realised how fast his career would stall if he allowed himself to be seen as the bearer of bad news.

"It's Captain Trusov," he stammered. "I was on my smoking break, and I saw it all. He walked out between two parked cars, and the Mercedes was going far too fast. He didn't have a chance. The ambulance just got here, but they won't be able to do anything. He was thrown against a tree trunk and his neck snapped like a twig."

The Major sank back into his chair as Oleg retreated. He buried his head in his hands. Zoya sat and waited some more. There didn't seem to be much she could say. It wasn't that she had disliked Trusov, it was just that he was everything she was not. He was politically connected, the youngest son of a senator. He had been promoted when she had not. He was tall and handsome, with a thatch of dark hair that was far glossier than her own. He was a man. All of which explained why the Captain had been the obvious choice when the department had been selected to provide a candidate for an upcoming Interpol secondment, and why Zoya had convinced herself that she hadn't minded in the slightest. Until now, when she wondered who would replace him.

Dobroshtan had picked up the knife again. He stabbed it down at the sheath of papers as he repeated the words. Insubordination. Stab. Disrespect. Stab. Ignores rules. Stab, stab. He had reached the end of the file. The final section, usually ignored, was titled "Linguistic Abilities" and in Zoya's case it covered half a neatly typed page. Dobroshtan aimed one fat finger and skimmed the lines. He looked up, as if he couldn't believe his luck. His face radiated the satisfaction of a man whose problems had suddenly, unexpectedly, been solved. His eyes brightened and his hands stopped shaking.

"Lieutenant Zozulya," he said, "the paperwork I will forward to General Negodyaev following our meeting will reflect your official termination from the Odesa Police Department. You will leave my office before I change my mind and you will report to my assistant. She will handle your visa application. Congratulations, Lieutenant, sometimes bad behaviour really is rewarded."

He glanced again at the desk calendar and this time the twist of his lips was definitely a smile, not a grimace.

"You're Interpol's problem now," he said.

CHAPTER 2

Manchester. Why?

It was a Sunday. Nine days had passed since Zoya's termination, and the wait had given her plenty of time to wonder why Interpol would put their UK office in a mid-sized city somewhere in the north of the country, instead of in the capital. And why, come to that, had they based their global headquarters in Lyon, not in Paris? It was some political thing, Zoya had speculated; or perhaps it came down, as so much did, to arguments over budget allocations. Or, more positively, maybe it was a result of the famed French love for fine cuisine (which she thought would explain Lyon, though she hadn't been so sure about Manchester).

These random thoughts were washed away by the insistent tug on her arm from the wisp of a man who had greeted her in arrivals with a misspelt name board.

"We have to hurry," he said. "There's a dead Dutchman in Woolton."

At least that's what it sounded like. Admittedly, Zoya's head was still woozy after the free drinks she had claimed during her two flights; but, even when she replayed the man's words, she didn't find any better interpretation. Whatever it was he had said, her escort seemed happy and excited.

"Let's go," she said.

He bounced through the terminal with keen poodle steps. He was dressed in brown: light-brown corduroy trousers over square-toed tan leather shoes, scuffed but clean; a darker-brown jacket, with shiny elbows and sleeves that were too long (or arms that were too short). No wedding ring – which explained a lot – centre-parted hair the same colour as the jacket; thick-lensed tortoiseshell spectacles protecting, of course, brown eyes. All of this offset by the pale-pink skin of a face that had clearly dedicated its life to hiding from the sun. He was every Ukrainian's idea of a maths teacher from a small provincial town, and she wondered if the same stereotype applied in England.

"I'm a sta-ti-sti-cian," he said, pronouncing the word very slowly to make sure she understood, "from the University of Manchester. Not a detective. Not originally at least. Interpol had this idea, very smart if you ask me, to recruit some of us to work with them. We've been looking for statistical anomalies, and I found one. Dead Dutch people, there are too many of them. My name's Robin by the way. Professor Robin Rutherford."

They had reached the car: a silver Volkswagen with a dented rear bumper. She allowed him to stow her suitcase, hiding a smile as he strained to lift with two hands what she would have hoisted quite easily with one – she had after all been the Odesa female junior powerlifting champion for two years running, with a 265kg deadlift under her belt. *Chivalry,* she thought, *is alive and stupid.* Next, they performed the obligatory dance as they both headed towards the righthand door, and he apologised twice for not having mentioned that the steering wheel was on the other side. Once seated, he fiddled with the rear-view mirror – in case he had experienced an unexpected growth spurt since he last sat in his own car – then turned the ignition.

"Right. Off we go then Zoya. May I call you Zoya? Or would you prefer Lieutenant Zozulya? And I'm ever so sorry to drag you out like this on your first day, but this is a real coup. It's my first actual crime scene, and local police have been told to wait for us. Liverpool's a bit of a slog to get to, so you just sit back and relax for now."

Zoya leant back with a jaw-straining yawn. She stretched her back and then her legs; carefully, since she didn't want to break anything in her host's car – at least, not on her first day. She decided she liked this Professor Robin Rutherford. He was maybe a bit simple-minded, in the way that many excessively intelligent people were, but he seemed friendly, which made a nice change from the alternately brutal and politically backstabbing Odesa cops she usually dealt with. Bears and foxes, as she categorised them. She closed her eyes and began to sort through her questions.

She wondered why the professor kept on apologising when he had done nothing wrong. She wondered whether Woolton and Liverpool were different places or if one was maybe a district of the other, and which one of them they were going to. She wondered why this Robin seemed so excited to visit a murder scene when she had seen so many over the years. She wondered what a "slog" was. Finally, she wondered how it was possible to have too many dead Dutch men. Then she closed her eyes and drifted away.

*

"Sorry? Zoya?"

A timid voice at her side. He hadn't poked her, which was good. For him. The car had stopped and Zoya's head sagged to the side. She straightened and rubbed at her neck, opening her eyes and seeing very little. The daylight was fading, and the windscreen was smeared with long runnels of rain. Beyond the glass everything was blurred and uncertain. There were yellow streetlamps overhead instead of sunshine, and the strobes of at least two police cars were shooting at them with alternate streaks of blue and red.

Zoya glanced at her watch, which lied that it was 17.05. The time difference meant that in England it was 16.05 on a rainy, late-spring day. She opened the car door and levered herself out. The air was fresh and cool. Her body was stiff, so she squatted and pushed herself up three times to ease the kinks. She lifted her face towards a sprinkle of rainwater then wiped it off with the back of her hand. The nap had banished her hangover before it had a chance to take hold. She felt calm and alert. She looked around.

They were near the bottom of a narrow, sloping street. Parked cars lined strips of pavement; low walls enclosing a series of shrunken and mostly empty gardens. The houses were joined together in two-storey, brick-built steps up the slope. None of this was anything like the picture of Liverpool Zoya had in her mind. Then she realised she had been creating her own image as she went along. She knew the city had a river, so she had placed shops and restaurants on its banks. A port too, so the silhouettes of cranes were sketched against the skyline. In the city centre she had added a few skyscrapers in a concession to possible modernity. And there were the crowds of wandering musicians strumming in the streets, for obvious Beatles-related reasons. In any case, she was reasonably certain there would be more to Liverpool than the drizzle and silence of these huddled, flat little homes. Which meant this had to be Woolton.

Ahead of her the road was closed off by police cars and blue tape. Beyond the tape, white-suited figures were loading equipment into a square-sided van. The forensics team, going home. Zoya marched up the incline, and only then realised she had no identification – other than the Odesa Homicide Unit card she had somehow neglected to hand in – when she reached the first policeman. She paused and waited for Robin to catch up.

"Interpol?" Robin said doubtfully, showing his card.

The police officer was tired and miserable. He had not been allowed inside the house despite the rumours of an interesting crime scene, and the rain hadn't stopped since he had arrived. Then, just when they had been ready to lock the place down and head to the pub, a call had come through. Interpol wanted to take a look. No reason had been given. The team had cursed and waited.

The policeman examined Robin's ID, then surveyed the two arrivals with a clear expression of disbelief. One of them was wide as the proverbial s***house, the other skinny as a pencil. One had decorated a black mid-length coat with a bright-green woollen scarf and an even gaudier pleated skirt, the other had camouflaged himself for nighttime manoeuvres in various shades of mud. One glowered at him with piercing eyes from under thick black eyebrows, the other fidgeted nervously and apologised for being there. And yet this unlikely couple claimed to be with Interpol, who were supposed to be the cream of the cream. The policeman gave up. Glumly, he recorded their names – a Ukrainian somebody and a professor something – and lifted the tape to let them through.

Two detectives were sheltering from the rain inside the half-glass door of the house. One was male and older; one was younger and prettier. *And probably smarter*, Zoya thought. They had both adopted the same pose: leaning back, left leg planted in the worn carpet, right leg bent and propped against the hallway wall. They wore covers over their shoes, but they had taken off their latex gloves whilst they waited. They had been chatting about something – maybe they had been flirting a little to smooth the slow passage of time. They straightened, eyeing the arrivals with professional thoroughness. Then the man grinned.

"Interpol's taken on Laurel and Mrs Hardy then?" he said.

Robin looked puzzled. He thought about it for a moment then he smiled and blushed. Zoya had no idea what the detective meant, so she glared at him just in case. The detective coughed.

"Right," his younger, prettier, probably smarter partner said. "Let's not waste any more time. The deceased is upstairs. Forensics have cleared the scene; they were just about to take the body out. It's all kind of kinky, but we're still not sure why Interpol's interested. Put these on and we'll go on up."

She handed shoe covers to Zoya and Robin and distributed fresh gloves for all of them. Professor Robin Rutherford looked excited and scared. Lieutenant Zoya Zozulya just hoped the corpse hadn't soiled himself or been disembowelled. Those were the worst, and she suddenly remembered she hadn't eaten since the plane – the first one – and it seemed so long ago. She thrust her gloved hands into the deep pockets of her coat and made sure she led the way.

At the bottom of the stairs there was a door to the left. It was thin and insubstantial, but with a lock, meaning it led to a separate apartment, and therefore neighbours that the detectives would have questioned. There was a shabby stripe of blue carpet, with a track of footsteps eroded down the centre, then grey painted wood on the stairs. There was rough wallpaper on the walls, like they had been spattered with woodchips then painted beige. No pictures. The first-floor landing had the same blue carpet, but less worn; and another door, also on the left, this one slightly ajar. It looked newer It looked newer and more solid, and the lock stronger. There was no damage to the door and no scratches on the lock.

Zoya pushed the door and paused. It opened straight into the apartment's living room. Her first impression was that it was painfully bright. An overhead light with a plain white shade and standing lamps in two of the corners were all were switched on, probably by the police team, and their cumulative effect was far too harsh for such a small space. She blinked and forced herself to take in the details.

Immediately to the right of the door was a pine chest of drawers with a bunch of keys on its top. Above the chest, a single dark-blue coat hung from a row of pegs. Two pairs of shoes – brightly coloured trainers and plain black leather office wear – poked out from beneath it. In the centre of the room a white leather sofa and two matching armchairs surrounded a pale-blue carpet with a hexagonal pattern, and ahead of them a flatscreen TV stood on a low glass table. The pieces of furniture were aligned parallel to the walls and at right angles to each other. The remote control was placed so that it bisected one of the corners of the table, pointing off to the right where heavy beige curtains were drawn over windows that would have a view of the street. There were no books, photos or plants. Everything was perfectly tidy and perfectly impersonal – an impression spoiled only by the forensics team's scattered dabs of fingerprint powder.

Zoya realised everyone was blocked behind her. Close to her shoulder, the male detective coughed again.

"He's in the bedroom," he said. "To your left."

And he was. There was a white bedside table with a single drawer next to a double bed, queen-sized, with pale grey sheets and duvet cover. The bed was unwrinkled, with plumped pillows and tight corners. Which was more than you could say for the dead man lunging out of the built-in white laminate wardrobe. He was on his knees, angling forwards, supported by a thin red cord that was tied to the wardrobe's metal clothes rail then looped around his neck. His hands were bound behind his back with a length of the same cord. He wore an unbuttoned white cotton shirt and nothing else. His body was muscular and covered in tattoos. Zoya moved closer, squatting in front of the man. His face was purple and swollen, its bloodshot eyes bulging and calling desperately for help. She saw several old, healed scars on his torso, but no signs of recent injury on either face or body. She glanced down at his groin, then averted her gaze. She thought she shouldn't be unfair; he had probably looked more impressive when he was alive. Finally, she moved to the side and peered closely at the knots on the rope around his neck and his wrists.

"A sex game gone wrong," a voice said from behind her. The male detective. Older and not as smart. "They say the lack of oxygen heightens pleasure, but you know how it is. No pain, no gain. So I'm told. We've seen a few similar cases over the last year or two. Sometimes it's auto-asphyxiation, but we're figuring there had to be someone helping this guy along, since his hands are tied behind his back. There's also traces of coke on the bedside table. But there's no sign of foul play, no forced entry, no struggle and no injuries. Likely his companion was into the same stuff, and he took off when this guy kicked the bucket. We took a statement from the lady downstairs. She's his landlady as well as his neighbour. He moved in just two weeks ago and she was already thinking of asking him to leave. Said he was 'one of them'. That he brought men back to the apartment. Different men, rough-looking, all hours. She was going to complain, but she said she was scared of him. With the tattoos and all. We still need to find the second man, but really at this point it looks like an open-and-shut case."

"But he was Dutch?" Robin asked, a little plaintively.

"That he was. We found his passport and his driver's license in the drawers by the door. His name is De Groot, a Dutch citizen resident in Amsterdam. Not sure why that's relevant though."

"Zank you," Zoya said as she turned to face the detectives, laying on the accent for added effect. "Now ve must go."

She led the way back down the stairs and along the street. At her side Robin was silent and deflated, no doubt a result of his first close-up encounter with an exotically unnatural death. Also, because he had been hoping for murder and was therefore not entirely satisfied with mere sex games. Zoya thought his priorities were exactly the opposite of her own.

They got into the car. As she fastened her seatbelt, Zoya's mind sparked with more questions. She wondered what "kinky" meant and where the bucket was that the dead man had kicked. She wondered how it was that the detective's mangled vowels were so unlike any version of English she had ever heard before. More importantly, she wondered what to do next. She had cleared passport control only three hours ago and already she was faced with the first difficult choice of her Interpol secondment. She could accuse the local police of incompetence. She could accuse them of a cover-up. Or she could keep this between her and Robin for now. She turned to the professor and sighed.

"Tell me about your other dead Dutchmen," she said.

CHAPTER 3

They drove through the drizzle accompanied by the rhythmic flap and squeak of windscreen wipers. Once they reached the motorway, Robin began his account from a point somewhere over a distant horizon where no Dutchmen were yet to be seen. It was what Zoya had been expecting – that, since Robin was both a professor and a man, he would not be able to resist educating her on the finer points of statistical analysis before moving on to what she actually needed to know. She didn't mind. His voice was a soothing background to her own thoughts, and she hoped the chance to go over familiar territory would improve Robin's mood after his recent disappointment. Zoya was kind that way, sometimes. She therefore resisted the temptation to point out that she had a degree in applied mathematics from the University of Kyiv, and instead allowed her mind free rein to trace through the myriad weird and wonderful branches of BDSM fetishes until she reached her final destination – the once-niche, now apparently mainstream, practice of erotic sexual asphyxiation. It was a familiar journey.

In her late twenties, Zoya had discovered that she attracted a certain type of man. It had surprised her at first, until she had taken a moment to inspect her muscular naked form in the mirror. The men themselves could be old or young, wide or skinny, married or single, but they all shared one characteristic: the overwhelming psychological need to be dominated. Whatever the specifics – spanking, whipping, handcuffs and gags, humiliation, or orgasmic delay – it all came down to an unquenchable thirst for subservience. For a while Zoya had gone along with them, out of curiosity more than anything else, and she had supplied carefully measured brutality with indifferent efficiency and no more judgement than if the men had asked for tea instead of coffee. However, it was a phase that hadn't lasted long. Because, in all of this, Zoya had one simple problem. After pulling regular double shifts sifting the worst of the criminal scum from the dark waters of her city, the begging late-night calls to dominate yet another man – whatever his level of guilt or innocence – were far too like bringing her work home with her. And she didn't even get paid overtime.

But, as her father had liked to say before he had drunk himself to death, all knowledge was good knowledge. Firstly, Zoya had realised that if she wanted to be happy, she had better start selecting her men herself rather than waiting to be chosen. And then, as today had demonstrated, she had discovered that sometimes an intimate experience of the darker recesses of human desire made you, if not a better person, at least a better detective.

The small part of Zoya's brain that was still listening to Robin had identified a possible turning point in his lecture. She tuned back in.

"So that, in short, was our methodology," he said. "Once we had that figured out, we adapted our algorithm to identify potential statistically significant variations in death rates and causes of death. We focused on North America and Europe, since that's where we could source the most reliable data sets, however we did include other-country data where it was available. Essentially, not wishing to oversimplify anything here, we fed everything we obtained into a very powerful computer and waited to see what it spat out. What emerged was some really interesting stuff, some of which we could explain and some we couldn't. As an example, across the various countries, we identified several hotspots of death by mercury poisoning, each of which had very different causes. Inuit groups generally had excessive levels due to mercury concentration in whale and seal meat. Then there was a First Nations tribe in Canada that had been exposed to pollution from a local pulp mill. So far so good. But there was also a hotspot in the Galician region of northern Spain, which no one understood – until we passed the information to the local police. They used our findings to identify a doctor who took locum jobs when his colleagues were on vacation, and it turned out he was poisoning elderly patients with mercury from his store of old-fashioned thermometers. He claimed they were mercy killings, but it was still murder. Case solved. Then there was another one: a bizarre anomaly that had us all buzzing for a while. Globally, women are far less likely to kill than men, but the computer was telling us that Swiss women were seven times more likely to commit murder than women in any of the other countries we studied. Eventually we realised it was all down to one woman in Geneva who had developed a grudge against local financial sector workers when she lost her savings, resulting in her taking six of them to bed over the course of a two-year period and shooting them in the head with a small-calibre pistol. It was really quite funny at the time."

"The small population implied an inadequate dataset," Zoya surmised, "leading to exaggerated interpretation of one individual's actions. Sampling errors that were compounded by the unusual number of bankers in the city and a poorly controlled selection of the time period for analysis."

Robin looked across, clearly surprised – either by the rapid improvement of Zoya's English, or by her astute and rather impatient summary.

"Well yes, that was exactly it. But the whole point was to identify a variation and then see if it could be explained. In that sense it was kind of a proof of concept – we found, we explained. But then there were the examples we couldn't figure out."

Finally, Zoya thought, he had reached the Dutchmen. Yet, frustratingly, Robin chose this moment to fall silent. She angled her body towards him and wondered if it was too early in their relationship to punch him in the shoulder. She paused when she saw that his hands were clenched tightly to the steering wheel and that he was staring intensely and a little manically through the windscreen. The rain had developed from the earlier light spatter to a full-blown squall, the windscreen wipers were thrashing desperately from side to side, and Robin seemed to be lost. She gazed up and spotted the road sign at the same moment he did. Manchester – City Centre – 2 Miles – Regent Road/A57. He grunted.

"That's a relief. Bloody rain. Next turnoff. I thought we'd go through the centre so you can get an idea where you are."

"Where I am is that you were about to tell me about the Dutchmen . . ." she reminded him.

"Yes, exactly. It just came up, ten days ago. I've identified that, over the course of the past two months, roughly three times more male Dutch citizens have died outside their country than we would have expected based on the population of the Netherlands as a percentage of the total European Union population. Naturally, after excluding the most obvious deaths from ill health and old age, and after taking into account relevant tourism and travel patterns."

"Which tells us what?" Zoya asked.

"That's the thing. I don't know yet. I'm in the early stages of gathering information on specific deaths to identify any interesting trends. And of course, since we're Interpol, the whole point of this exercise is to identify criminal activity rather than, for example, a health or a social policy issue. But so far I have only one death tagged as a definite murder, and that was a small-time drug dealer in Italy who seems to have upset the local mafia. Unconnected to anything else as far as I can tell. Apart from that, I have a collection of accidents, suicides and unknowns. Which was why I was so hopeful about today's case: with it looking like a potentially suspicious death on home turf, and my actually getting the chance to see the crime scene instead of just reading the police reports."

He had cheered up whilst he was talking, but now that he had reached the same apparent dead end Zoya was worried he would start blubbing. At the same time, he was pointing past her through the car window.

"There you are, the Edwardian. It's where they're putting you up. A taste of luxury to start with. Swimming pool, fitness centre, the works. Don't get too used it though, I understand it's only for two weeks until they find you an apartment."

Robin pulled into the drop-off bay in front of the hotel's main entrance. Above them loomed an overwrought colonial-style building fashioned from pale blocks of stone, with a series of high-arched windows that had courageously shouldered the responsibility of dispensing much-needed light into the gloomy evening.

"I'll leave you to settle in then," Robin said. "And I'll pick you up at eight-thirty tomorrow morning if that's OK."

Zoya thought for a moment. She considered inviting the professor up to her room, but figured he had probably had enough excitement for one day. She didn't want to seem ungrateful though, so she rewarded him for his hospitality with a little parting gift.

"It was a setup," she said. "The guy we saw. There were two things that gave it away: one small, one big. First there were the knots. Men who like to be dominated are very, what's the word, very exact. Very precise. Everything has to be done properly or it ruins the mood. He would want neat knots; well tied, probably even a specific type of knot. What I saw was untidy. Messy. If that's all there was then maybe I could be wrong – people are different after all, maybe this particular guy and his partner didn't care so much – but the big giveaway was the rope. It was too thin. People get confused when they hear about this kind of stuff, because they associate strangling with pain and death. They don't realise that the point for these guys is exactly the opposite. It's not the pain, it's the burst of pleasure in the brain that comes from denial of oxygen. The *temporary* denial. Which in practice means you tighten then loosen, tighten then loosen. That only works if you use something wide – like a soft belt, or maybe a thick rope. And preferably something that doesn't leave marks, since they still have to go to work in the morning. But the rope our dead man had around his neck would have dug in immediately. It would have caused him intense agony, with nothing pleasurable about it at all. This was not a game, nor was it consensual."

"He was murdered," Robin stammered hopefully.

"One hundred percent," Zoya confirmed.

Robin had come back to life. His eyes glistened and he rubbed one hand feverishly over his face. A thought occurred to him. He reached over the back of his seat.

"Listen," he said. "I was going to wait until tomorrow, but why don't I give them to you now? The case files from the other deaths. Everything we've got. Maybe you can get a head start before our meeting with the boss tomorrow?"

He pushed over a bulging black nylon rucksack. Zoya unzipped the top and saw that it was full of cardboard folders, somewhere between twenty and thirty of them.

"No promises," she said. But she did take the bag.

*

At first Zoya was disappointed to discover that the hotel's accommodation was in a modern high-rise annex rather than the stately building she had entered from the street. Until, that was, she opened the door into her temporary oasis. There were mirrors everywhere and an excessive use of gleaming chrome; a toilet she would never have to clean; fancy glass bottles of soap and shampoo with a brand name she hadn't heard of; plus a glistening bathtub – and she didn't like to think when she had last had a bath.

She ordered fillet steak and fries from the room service menu, two portions. She checked the minibar for vodka then called down again for extra supplies. She stared at Robin's bag and decided it could wait till tomorrow. She had more important things to research.

She discovered that Woolton was indeed a suburb of Liverpool. And that it was apparently one of the richest areas of the city, although she hadn't seen much sign of its wealth whilst they were there. Next, she went onto YouTube and searched for videos highlighting different English regional accents. She started with Liverpool and understood why the detective had spoken so strangely. She moved on to Manchester and practiced that for a while, so that she would be able to blend in with the natives. She discovered that the first accent was called "scouse" and the second was "Manc". She learnt what "kicked the bucket" meant and memorised all the local idioms she could find.

The steaks came. They were juicy and tasty, albeit too small. As she ate, she remembered what the detective had said when he saw her and Robin. She tried some variants of the possible spelling. Lorel. Lorrel. Ardy. Hardly. There it was. Laurel. And. Hardy. She started watching. She laughed so much she almost choked on a chunk of steak. She laughed so much she didn't notice she had finished half the bottle of vodka. She laughed so much that the hotel switchboard was soon overwhelmed with frenzied complaints from the other occupants of her floor of the building. When the bellboy – apologies, more apologies – knocked on her door, she pulled herself together and figured it was time to rest.

She thought it had been a good first day in England: her strange-but-sweet professor; dead Dutchmen; a murder, covered up; Laurel and Mrs Hardy. She wished she could call her brother and tell him all about it. Instead, she stretched out on starched sheets with her tablet at her side, wishing herself goodnight and putting on the one thing that she knew would tip her into sleep – her favourite Disney movie. Her eyes grew heavy, and she drifted as *Frozen* soothed her buzzing thoughts with its syrup-sweet lyrics.

Let it go, she told herself, *let it go. Don't hold it back anymore! Sleep.*

CHAPTER 4

It was Monday 23 March. Which meant she had a new boss.

Opening skirmishes had gone satisfactorily. When Zoya was introduced to a broad and handsome man in a stylish suit, whose appearance and name suggested Moroccan or Algerian heritage, she had kicked off proceedings with a respectful *Salam aleykoum*. Director of the Interpol United Kingdom National Central Bureau, Rashid Tahiri, had countered by declaring he was as French as they came, and that like any true *fils de la République* he had fought his way out of the poverty-stricken ninety-third arrondissement before rising to the heady heights of the Sorbonne. Spotting Zoya's momentary distraction as she absorbed his geographical references, he had snuck past her defences by confessing his love of Tolstoy and quoting the opening lines of *Anna Karenina* at her. *A bold tactic*, she had thought, *quoting Russian classics at a Ukrainian*. And, in any case, family happiness seemed irrelevant to matters at hand – plus his Russian accent was atrocious. Zoya had considered mentioning her love for the famous Belgian detective Hercule Poirot, but instead had kept it simple and spent the next five minutes of their get-to-know-you chat switching her accent at random intervals between native Slavic villainy and recently acquired Mancunian cheekiness, much to Tahiri's evident confusion.

Once they had both accepted that their sparring opponent was no pushover, they got down to business.

"About your partner," Tahiri said. "He's a little obsessive, with this thing about—"

"About the Dutchmen." Zoya completed his sentence in revenge for not having been informed in advance that Robin was supposed to be her partner.

"It's some bureaucrat's crazy idea," Tahiri continued, "that since Interpol's role is coordination and information gathering rather than solving specific criminal cases, it should be us leading the way in leveraging the information technology age and expanding the role of artificial intelligence in police work. The reality is that at the same time that our officers are overworked trying to source intelligence on actual criminal activity – international organised crime gangs, drug running and money laundering for example – we have a team of academics forced on us to invent problems that don't really exist."

He saw that Zoya was about to interrupt and held up a hand to stop her.

"I've already given the professor considerable leeway," he continued, "so all I'm asking from you now is that you calm him down and convince him to apply his mind to something more useful. Then, as soon as anything new comes up, I'll make sure you're involved."

Zoya had already begun to think there was at least some merit in Robin's approach, but after the irritation of Tahiri's outstretched palm she didn't feel like arguing the point. She was about to report her conclusions from the preceding day's excursion to Liverpool when their meeting was interrupted. Tahiri's assistant had blown into his office on a cloud of Opium. The perfume, not the drug.

"It's Robin," the assistant said. "Professor Rutherford, I mean."

The woman glanced at Zoya, unsure how much she should say in front of their new recruit. She moved closer and whispered her message in her boss's ear.

He stood, and they both left the room.

*

Zoya's day had started early, since her body was still an hour ahead of local time. She had taken the lift to the hotel's basement gym and loaded every dumbbell plate they had in stock onto the bar, achieving a total load that was just about sufficient for a light morning workout. After spending ten minutes in the shower counting ammonites in its glossy marble tiles, she had headed back downstairs to the first-floor breakfast buffet. She had discovered, then repeated, the pleasures of what the menu termed a "Full English". She had drained three cups of coffee and realised after a tentative nibble that black pudding was not a pudding at all.

At exactly eight-thirty Zoya had exited the hotel and waited outside the entrance. For her first day she wore her favourite black jacket and trousers, tailormade since "short and excessively muscular" was not a sizing niche that any womenswear brand had chosen to occupy (and because she liked the pockets in her trousers big enough to put things in). She had looked around. The day was bright and sunny, and there was no sign of

Robin. She had watched the black cabs dart nervously through the smoky exhausts of red double-decker buses; admiring the dehydrated and entirely unfunctional physiques of the underwear models in the ads on the side of those buses, and trying to read the puzzlingly cheerful and open faces of the men and women strolling past on their way to work. It was an entertaining enough start to the workday, but after fifteen minutes of stationary sightseeing Zoya had begun to wonder what to do next. She didn't have a telephone number for Robin, and the only address she had was on the headed notepaper of her Interpol visa application. At eight-fifty she had asked the doorman to call a taxi.

The chatty driver had delivered her to an imposing, green-tinged glass box on a roundabout. Its sign read Greater Manchester Police. *Greater than what?* she had wondered, at the same time as she had realised there was nothing on the building that mentioned Interpol. She had entered and spoken to the uniformed man at the reception desk. He had looked her up and down with the peculiar English brand of suspicion that she was already growing accustomed to – diffident, unhostile, apologetic – as she had smiled, fighting the urge to introduce herself as Mrs Hardy. After scrutinising her Interpol invitation letter, the man had given her a visitor's pass on a lanyard and directed her to the fourth floor. There she had sat for thirteen minutes in a separate reception area before a pencil-skirted woman with immaculate blond hair that Zoya would have killed for had arrived and guided her to where the Director was waiting in his office.

To recap: *Salam aleykoum*, Anna Karenina, and a cloud of Opium, then she had waited again. Luckily, Zoya was used to it. Long hours of boredom followed by a few minutes of excitement was the detective's universal lot.

Tahiri returned. His suit was more crumpled now.

"Quick, you need to go to the hospital," he said.

*

Zoya thought Robin was one of the few men she had met who looked better out of his clothes than in them. The parts of him that she could see, now that he had been stripped of yesterday's drab brown disguise, were in surprisingly good shape. Admittedly the shape was more marathon runner than weightlifter, but she wouldn't hold that against him. It was, however, unlikely that the professor would be running anytime soon. The skin on his chest and shoulders was covered in dark, swelling bruises and his left arm was strapped in a foam sling over his chest. His face was a mess.

"That looks *minging*," Zoya said with a gesture that covered the various damage he had incurred since she had last seen him. For a moment she was proud of herself. *Minging* was one of the words she had picked up the previous evening from her hotel-room YouTube study of local accents and slang, and within hours she had found a chance to try it out. She thought it meant disgusting or revolting. She hoped she had got it right.

Robin attempted a smile then gave up.

"I dropped you off," he said, "then I drove straight home."

His voice had a familiar wheeze that told Zoya he had either a cracked or broken rib. The thought sent a jolt of acid fury through her gut. This man was her partner after all, even if no one had informed her until this morning. Therefore she was responsible for him, and he was responsible for her.

"There's not much street parking where I live," he continued, "and the nearest spot was a couple of hundred metres from my house. I was almost at the front door when two men attacked me from behind. One had a baseball bat, the other one used his fists. They kept hitting me and asking me questions. That's why I told the office I needed to speak with you."

He was injured, he was in pain. Maybe the doctors had given him morphine, or whatever the English used in cases like this. Zoya unclenched her fists and forced herself to overlook his elliptical storytelling.

"What did they want to know?" she asked, as slowly and gently as she could.

"They just kept on asking the same thing, over and over. 'What's the Ukrainian woman doing here? What does she know? What's the Ukrainian woman doing here? What does she know?'"

CHAPTER 5

Robin's room had pastel-green walls. It was spotlessly clean and smelled of antiseptic. The bed had wheels, grab handles and sidebars, and a motorised back that could be raised into different positions. Next to it there was an overbed table, also on wheels. The furniture was completed by two visitor's chairs – one occupied by Zoya – and a small bedside table. The table bore a vase of artificial flowers, a carafe of water with a glass, and a stack of foil pill blisters. Opposite Zoya's position stood a heart monitor and pole stand for a drip; neither were connected. To the left and right of the bed, the wall had multiple sockers and outlets – electrical, oxygen, medical air – in white, green and yellow. There were two doors (one from the corridor, one to the bathroom), a large window with vertical slat blinds, and a small flatscreen high on the wall opposite the bedhead. Picture on, volume off.

Zoya's eyes flitted and skidded, recording all of this whilst her mind worked at the puzzle. "What's the Ukrainian woman doing here?" seemed an oddly existential question, even if it was one that Zoya had asked of herself on many occasions – usually at the kicking-out stage of her latest vodka-fuelled celebration. The current context, however, was unusual. Although Zoya was used to hostile attention, it didn't usually arrive so fast.

She had flown in less than a day ago and done nothing hugely significant since. She had followed where Robin had led, and had not mentioned her conclusions about the murder to anyone except Robin himself.

She saw two main possibilities:

The simple fact of her arrival was upsetting someone. But who, and why? It didn't make sense for it to be someone on the Ukrainian side, since the week she had waited for her visa to arrive from Kyiv would have been ample time for anyone there to figure out why she was going to England, and to try to stop her if they had wanted to. Therefore it had to be someone here, someone who had just learnt of her arrival. She knew there had been multiple opportunities to spot her. She had crossed a border, so her passport had been registered. She had walked through an airport thronged with hundreds of passers-by and bristling with CCTV cameras. Her details had been recorded at the crime scene. She had checked in at the hotel. Or it could have been none of that. Maybe someone at the Interpol office had said something to someone. Maybe someone didn't like Ukrainians; maybe they didn't like women. All of which was feasible, but none of which explained why anyone would care specifically that *she* was here.

The second possibility was that someone was keeping tabs on Robin's half-arsed investigation or research or whatever you wanted to call it. Either within Interpol or in one of the European police forces he had contacted to gather his files. The Dutch for example, as the main supplier of dead citizenry. Maybe whoever it was hadn't been too worried whilst the queries were coming from an academic with no police experience, operating on his own in the face of his colleagues' obvious scepticism. Maybe they hadn't been so relaxed when they saw him joined by a real-life detective.

Or, more than that, since whoever attacked Robin had asked about "the Ukrainian woman", could it be that there was, bizarrely, coincidentally, a Ukrainian angle to Robin's case that she had unknowingly stumbled into?

Questions with no answers.

She focused back on Robin's face. He had been staring at her with a curious half-smile.

"I'm usually quite good at reading people," he said, "but I'm afraid I failed quite miserably yesterday. It's not exactly that I underestimated you, it was more that my attention was absorbed so completely by the crime scene and my whole Dutch theory that I didn't focus on you at all. But watching you now, I've been remembering a few things. For example, my lecture about statistics in the car. You knew all that already, didn't you?"

Zoya nodded, but didn't say anything.

"And I figure you're a polyglot too," Robin continued. "You started off with some dodgy grammar and a Ukrainian accent that was straight from central casting, but I think you were putting it on. Exaggerating at least. Today you're speaking like a native Mancunian, which frankly is kind of scary. Especially for a southerner like me. So, tell me, Zoya, what other languages do you speak?"

"Apart from Ukrainian, Russian, and English? Well, there's a couple more. But it's not that impressive really, I've just always had this gift. Ever since I was a kid, I've picked up languages and accents like a hyperactive parrot. Plus I have this hobby of trying to find equivalents for different expressions and idioms. Like your 'kicking the bucket', for which we might say 'covered in a copper bowl'."

She thought for a moment, searching for another example.

"Or when in English you say 'the fly in the ointment', and we say 'the spoonful of tar in a barrel of honey'. Things like that. "

Zoya paused. She knew there was no point scaring off the professor with the full list of languages she knew. She was however pleased to have discovered that she was partnered with the rare man who was able to figure out and admit to his own mistakes. She considered a congratulatory kiss on his cheek, until she took another look at the *minging* state of his face. Instead, she pulled Robin's black backpack onto her lap and opened it up. She picked out a file from the front of the bag.

"Enough talk, partner," she said, "let's get to work."

*

When Robin finished explaining the complex multi-factor analysis he had developed to rank the dossiers in order of relative suspiciousness, Zoya's first move was to stack the contents of the backpack on the bed next to Robin's legs and shuffle the files repeatedly. It wasn't that she had a particular reason to think Robin's logic was wrong – but simply that, if she was to apply a fresh set of eyes, she knew it was important to eliminate any preconceptions. For the same reason, although Robin had already studied the files, she rejected his offer to guide her through them. Only after she had spent ten minutes reading each dossier did she start to pose the additional questions that occurred to her.

Although the files had been supplied by different police forces across Europe, their approaches were similar. Each file began with a written report, usually with a short executive summary. The style was universally dry and understated; bets were hedged, unresolved questions highlighted. What came next depended on the situation. There might be a brief doctor's report; sometimes a full autopsy had been performed. Photographs of corpses and locations of death (it was premature to call them crime scenes) were attached. There were statements of varying levels of detail from relatives or friends and colleagues of the deceased, sometimes also from witnesses or neighbours. On occasion, handwritten notes from the investigating detectives had been included. Each file had twenty to thirty pages of information – all of which had been copied and sent through in its original language, then run through a translation program. It was clear that someone had put a lot of effort, and probably a few late nights, into collating the dossiers.

Zoya was quickly sucked in. Her focus was total. She hardly noticed the periodic interruptions: a male nurse who measured Robin's blood pressure and made sure he had taken his pills; a female doctor who checked his charts, shone a torch in his eyes and maybe gave him a pat on the head; the friendly older woman who brought lunch on a tray, or the surly young man who cleared it away; the deliverer – identity and appearance unknown – of the triangular brown-bread sandwiches ordered by Robin, which she bit and swallowed with no more than a passing understanding of what was inside. Meat, chewy.

Five hours later she had finished. The files were reordered into three piles on the bed. Four probables. Four possibles. The rest unlikely.

Zoya stretched and groaned. She stood and picked up her chair, holding it at shoulder level until her muscles protested, before sitting down again with a yawn.

She reopened the first of the "probable" files, flicked through it until she came to one of the photos, then passed the folder to Robin.

"Do you see anything strange?" she asked.

He spent a minute examining the picture: turning it, peering from different angles, thinking. It was of a room in a large modern apartment; bland Scandinavian furniture, empty bookshelves, ceiling-to-floor windows. The space was luxurious but bare, like a short-term rental or a serviced apartment. He saw nothing out of the ordinary. He shook his head.

"The coffee table," Zoya said.

He looked again. Between the leather sofa and the windows. It had a chrome frame and a circular glass top. Wait. There was something. He looked at Zoya. She nodded.

"The shape and size of the tabletop are wrong," she said. "The frame's rectangular, and if you look closely you can just make out a rim inside the frame that's supposed to hold the glass. Which should therefore also be rectangular and slightly smaller than the frame. Instead, the frame now has a circular top resting on it. And if you look at the apartment's dining area – the next photo in the pack – you'll see a very stylish circular dining table on a pedestal leg, which I'm willing to bet is supposed to have a protective glass surface, but now doesn't. And its diameter looks like a match for the glass you see on the coffee table in the previous photo."

"And what does that mean?" Robin asked.

"This guy is marked in the file as a suicide. Supposedly he had financial problems, so to end it all he opened the windows and leapt from the twenty-third floor to his death. My first question is why he went all the way to Valencia, to kill himself. Even if there was an answer to that, I'm still not buying the suicide version. I think there was a struggle and the original glass from the coffee table was shattered. Someone did a good job of cleaning up the mess, but leaving behind a coffee table with no top would at least have raised a question with the police. The bad guys obviously couldn't go out and buy a new top since the body had just hit the pavement, and it would have been too risky to walk out with the table frame. So they did the next best thing and used the glass from the kitchen table. Which was a smart move in the circumstances, but not perfect."

Zoya moved on to the other three files in her probable pile.

"Then there's this one," she said. "Trace amounts of extract from a toxic shrub – gelsemium elegans, also known as 'heart-break grass' – were identified in the stomach of a dead man found in Marseilles. No viable explanation was identified for how he came to ingest it. There was speculation about contaminated tea or the Chinese restaurant he had visited earlier in the day. However, since no unusual circumstances were found in the man's past to suggest he was a murder target, the death was classified by the French police as 'unexplained but not suspicious'."

She took the next file.

"This guy died from a heroin overdose. Easy enough – the syringe was found sticking out of his arm. Portuguese police made enquires via their Dutch colleagues, and several parties who knew the victim confirmed he was a habitual drug user. However, his ex-girlfriend stated that his drug of choice was cocaine, and also that he had an obsessive fear of needles. It's called trypanophobia – it's the same word in Ukrainian as in English. Her account was discounted on the basis that she hadn't seen her ex for nearly two years and that his habits could well have changed, but I'm inclined to believe her. That kind of phobia isn't something you just get over, and even if he moved on to heroin there are other ways to abuse it."

From the last of the four files, Zoya showed Robin two photos. A corpulent man was lying on a steel mortuary table. The skin on his body was scaley and rough, with a closeup of his face showing it to be grossly swollen and discoloured.

"This is from Gibraltar. The doctor's report says the man died after suffering a severe allergic reaction to an unknown substance. The allergic reaction part is true, and I think I know what the substance is. I saw a case like this in Odesa a couple of years back with a guy who had dioxin sprinkled on his food. He was disfigured, but he survived; this guy in Gibraltar wasn't so lucky. And again, a primary reason to downplay the diagnosis seems to have been the fact there was no obvious reason why our victim would have been poisoned. So when the routine tox screens didn't give a result the police didn't take it any further."

"What about the possibles?" Robin asked.

"All apparent accidents," Zoya said. "A car crash, followed by a fire in Belgium. Then a helicopter that hit a pylon coming in to land in Monaco. Another car crash, where blood tests showed the driver was so far over the drinking limit that he shouldn't even have been able to get the key in the ignition. And then one man who supposedly slipped and stumbled off the edge of a cliff when he was trying to take a selfie. For all of them we would need more details and a lot of work to figure out what really happened."

"I remember the crash in Belgium," Robin said with a shudder. "It was one of the first files I looked at, and the only time I tried to speak with any of the relatives. I gave up after that because it was so traumatic. And because I realised that I didn't really know what to ask."

"What was traumatic about it?" Zoya asked.

"Well, first because the crash sounded bad. It was an electric car and you've probably heard how their batteries can burn. It was an inferno apparently. Then I spoke with his mother; a woman in her sixties across the border in the Netherlands. She spoke almost perfect English and she was trying to help, but she couldn't stop crying. It turns out this wasn't the only tragedy in the family. Her husband had gone missing from their home somewhere near Amsterdam, and later the same day the son left. Then the next she heard was when the police called from Belgium. I spoke to her eight or nine days after that, and she said her husband still hadn't been found."

Zoya sighed. She would have fired anyone in her team who had neglected to mention such a major coincidence to her when she had first gone through the information. And even if Robin wasn't a trained detective, common sense should have been enough. She picked out the file and moved it from the "possible" pile to the "probables".

"What do we do now?" Robin asked. "Given that Director Tahiri's favourite line is that Interpol's role is to gather intelligence then coordinate a response. Not to solve specific cases."

"That works for me," Zoya said. "You're on intelligence gathering, and I'll coordinate my response. And who knows if we'll ever solve a specific case ever again. But whilst we have nothing better to do, let's start by gathering intelligence on these five files, plus the sex game guy from yesterday makes six. I need you to find what links them, apart from them all being Dutch of course."

"And what are you going to do?" Robin asked.

Zoya stood and turned towards Robin. She stretched out a hand. He looked puzzled.

"Keys," she said. "I'm going to need to borrow your car."

CHAPTER 6

Even as she exited the hospital, Zoya had known she would end up delaying the inevitable. The truth was that she preferred to walk than drive. At least that was how she liked to put it, since the other version was that driving was one of the few things that truly terrified her. There was just so much responsibility, and from bitter experience she knew that her mind's unpredictable tendency to skip from the tedium of routine activities, like watching the road, to something more challenging – for example right now she was struggling to recall some of the more obscure details of Russian intelligence service wet-work techniques highlighted in a Cambridge post-graduate's recent PhD paper – was conducive neither to her own safety nor that of any driver or pedestrian foolish enough to cross her path. And of course, since she was in England, there was the whole driving-on-the-wrong-side-of-the-road thing to add to the equation.

None of which was enough to halt the pangs of conscience as Zoya stood and waited for her taxi. Almost by accident, but in reality not at all, her fingers closed around Robin's car keys in the hip pocket of her trousers. She cursed softly under her breath. She knew the professor had assumed a series of actions would take place once Zoya left the hospital: he would focus his attention on the research she had asked for; she would tell the taxi driver to take her to the address Robin had given her; she would find his silver VW in its parking spot somewhere nearby; and she would drive from there straight to the crime scene – assumptions that were underlined by the excitement in Robin's eyes and his plea for Zoya to call him immediately if she found anything important. But she hadn't made any promises, she protested. Though, she admitted, she also hadn't contradicted his assumptions.

That was the problem with having a partner: they always needed something from you – and each time you had to figure out if you were able and willing to give it to them. And then you felt guilty when they got themselves beaten up.

Not today. Robin was safe in the hospital; he could wait. Today she would walk through her new hometown and try to figure out for herself what was really going on. Then tomorrow, in the bright and optimistic light of a new day, she would drive.

She told the taxi driver her destination. He dropped her at the hotel, but she didn't go inside. She turned to the right and headed west along Peter Street towards the river.

*

The man waiting in the lobby almost missed her. An ambulance's angry wail dragged his gaze towards the street and there she was: framed by the opening of the hotel's automatic doors, turning away to his left. There was no doubt it was her. Short and wide, untidy black hair, that piercing gaze that seemed to burn everything it touched during its brief scan through the glass. She was older of course than in the latest photos he had of her – she had to be mid-thirties, approaching forty, by now – but still active and energetic judging by her decisive march, which the man thought was good. The forties were the new thirties, and he liked a challenge.

He stood and pocketed the paperback thriller he had been pretending to read. Pulling one of the two caps he had purchased earlier that day low over his forehead, he walked unhurriedly to the exit. When he emerged onto the pavement, she was fifty metres ahead of him. He waited another few seconds in the doorway. He felt relaxed and assured. Urban surveillance wasn't his specialty, but as it was a side-skill that supported his real job he had had plenty of practice over the years. And in any case, today the stakes were low. His instructions had been clear.

"Watch, but stay back. You're on your own so don't take any risks. Better to lose her than to be made. The rest of the team will be on-site in two to three days. Even when they arrive, no intervention is permitted unless the boss is present."

All clear then, at least if he chose to do as he had been told.

He followed.

*

Brewdog and Albert's Schloss. Peaky Blinders opposite Impossible. Dirty Martini and Easy Money. It was a list of bill-boarded temptation that told her she would like this city. The shops had to be somewhere else, since on this street every pavement-level window showcased a bar or a restaurant; seductively lit, brightly painted, expensively decorated. And then there were the people to watch. Zoya had the same impression as in the morning. She saw office workers leaving for home; couples and groups of friends making an early start to the evening; waiters and waitresses displayed behind glass, awaiting their customers; a homeless guy sitting cross-legged on a cardboard carpet in a locked doorway, draped in a dirty sleeping bag. And they kept on smiling, all of them. Some even said hello to her as they passed, without it being a threat or the start of a pickup line. It was disconcerting. Not only did they seem happy, but they also didn't seem to care who knew it.

Zoya reminded herself she wasn't here for enjoyment, and forced her attention to the Dutch. What did she know, really? Pigs, a lot of them. And cows and chickens too, since the Dutch were Europe's biggest exporters of meat. Then there were the tulips, of course, and all those other sundry cut flowers for the lovers and vegetarians of the world. Not to mention Gouda, for people who liked their cheese wrapped in wax and full of holes. And that other place – Volendam, she thought it was called – for people who liked their women wrapped in lacy aprons and ankle-length skirts and . . . and by now Zoya was grinning to herself and thinking that perhaps she had already been infected by the Manchester mood.

As she passed the Opera House, her Netherlands thoughts turned to drama and death and drugs. Not cannabis, despite the coffee shops. That was for the lightweights. Every cop worth a bribe knew that the Netherlands was the place to come for all your synthetic needs: MDMA and all its variants and sub-variants; LSD and GHB; methamphetamines. You didn't even need to make a physical visit – simply access the dark web, scroll through the drop-down menus to make your choice, then transfer payment from your crypto wallet to theirs. Within days any pick-and-mix variety your heart desired would be dispatched in quantities ranging from a Jiffy bag to a shipping container. For wholesale orders you even got to specify colour, shape and logo of the pills to facilitate your onward selling and all-important local brand building.

Where there were drugs there was money. Where there was money there was laundering. Where there were drugs and money laundering there were also violent competition and death. So far, so plausible. Zoya saw just one problem with her theory. Surely, if the dead men were connected to the drug trade, their connections would already have been identified. At least for some of them. More widely, if a whole group of producers or dealers or smugglers had been taken down within a two-month period, that had to have caused some ripples. Yet within the pack of dossiers, Robin had found only one individual with an identified link to the drug trade – the small-scale pusher in Italy – and he hardly fitted the picture of a criminal mastermind.

It didn't add up, not yet, but Zoya thought it was at least an avenue worth following up.

*

She reached the river. It was disappointing. You could tell a lot about a city by how it treated its river, and this one was narrow, sludgy and hemmed in by apartment blocks. She found a noticeboard on the riverbank that told her she was looking at a tributary of the River Mersey, which during the Industrial Revolution had been joined to a network of canals used to transport cargos of coal and wool through the booming nation. The waterways were described poetically as the pulsing arteries of the Industrial Revolution. Two hundred years later, the arteries seemed pretty clogged.

Which reminded her. It had been a few hours since her last meal.

The name of the first eatery she spotted, the Riverside Restaurant, was admirably devoid of creativity. She entered and told the first man who approached her that "mi stomach thinks mi throat's been cut", which, in the local lingo, she thought meant she was hungry and wanted a table for one. It was early, so she received both heartfelt laughter and a place by the windows. She asked for the menu and a sheet of paper so that she could make notes.

Once she had ordered, she called Robin on the number he had given her that morning..

"Did you find anything?" he asked.

"Not really," she replied. "I decided to go tomorrow instead. But I had a question. I don't know much about English football, but what would you say if you noticed a guy walking round town in a red Manchester United cap, who then switched it partway through the evening to a pale-blue cap with a Manchester City logo?"

"I'd say that was completely bizarre," Robin replied. "The guy couldn't be a local. Unless he's got serious psychological problems, I guess."

"That's what I thought," Zoya said. "Which means I've picked up a tail."

When Robin began to burble, she realised that telling him had been a mistake. Especially since there was nothing he could do to help from his hospital bed. The next part was worse, but unavoidable.

"I was thinking," she said, "since at least two of the deaths we're looking at were poisonings, you should be very careful what you eat and drink for the next few weeks."

She paused. She thought she had passed on enough bad news for one call, so she decided not to mention for now her ideas about possible drug connections.

"Goodnight then," she said. "Sleep well."

Her starter had come. It smelt good. She hung up.

*

When she left the restaurant, it was dark and cold. The hotel's parking area was almost empty – apart from the glitter of oil leaks and the two men who slipped out of the shadows ahead of her.

"Hello beautiful," said the one carrying the baseball bat.

Manchester went up another notch in Zoya's estimation. There was no reason, after all, that a car park assault had to be a depressing event. So Zoya did what she knew the men would least expect – she kept on walking towards them.

"Nice to meet you, too," she replied. "And thanks for the warning. I guess it's because you're a little bit ashamed that two big strong lads like you are going up against one woman?"

Ashamed or not, after a sideways glance at his friend, the man with the bat started swinging. Zoya reversed course and watched him as she retreated, assessing, staying just out of his range. He was good. The swings of his bat were fast but controlled, and his body moved well: never overreaching, always keeping his balance. The second man moved off to the right, looking to flank her, and Zoya spotted the glint of metal on his right fist. A knuckleduster. Maybe the odds were more even than she had thought.

Zoya slipped her right hand into her pocket and left it there. She would have only a single chance at surprise, and knew she had to take full advantage.

Not yet.

Not yet.

Now.

As the bat swung right to left in front of her body, she pivoted and pushed off her right foot as she halted her retreat, pulling her weapon free from the sheath sewn down the seam of her trousers. When her fist emerged, it was clasping a cylindrical hardwood handle – slimmer than she would have liked, but all the need for concealment would allow – attached to a stretch of six-millimetre braided steel wire as long as her forearm. Both handle and wire were painted matt black; he wouldn't see them in the dark until it was too late, and she was past him, spinning and turning.

The first strike went low, whipping with all her strength and speed across the outside of his right knee. He screamed as he staggered, as his leg collapsed, as Zoya twisted back the other way. He was now shoulder height for her, her arm level with the stumbling man's head. Next a backhand, aimed at something far off – *strike through the ball, not at it* – and his face just happened to be in the way.

One down, one to go.

The second man was shocked. They had been warned, but of course they had discounted the warning. Their opponent was middle-aged, small and stocky. Their opponent was a woman. They were stronger and younger, they had balls, plus they were fresh from their unopposed victory over the other guy just last night. How hard could it be? Harder than they had thought . . . but the man was no coward. He knew his honour and his future employment were at stake, and apart from anything else he wanted very much to keep this bitch away from his friend, who was lying on the tarmac, whimpering and shaking with pain.

Now Zoya had the advantage of reach, but the second man knew what to expect. At least he thought he did. He pulled himself together and went on the attack. It was soon obvious why he had selected the brass knuckles as his weapon of choice. He was a boxer, and a good one. He jabbed and he punched and Zoya recognised that a single well-placed blow would be enough to put her on her back. She retreated in a wide circle, knowing she would lose her advantage if he got her on the urban equivalent of a boxing ring's ropes – a wall, a fence, the side of a parked car. And as she moved, she never paused the fierce swings of the whip; her blood up already, rejoicing at the wire's shrill swish through the air. The man's guard was strong, fists covering his face when he wasn't striking, forearms covering his body, turning and twisting as fast as she did so that she could never get behind him. But he was taking terrible punishment.

This was nothing like being struck by a padded boxer's glove, however hard the fist inside. Every lash of the steel wire branded his skin with a stripe of raw agony. His forearms were crisscrossed with a lattice of cuts, and his shoulders too. He needed just one of his blows to land, but the woman was never there. She ducked and weaved, and she retreated faster and more confidently than any boxer he had ever fought. They were fighting different battles. He was storming a mobile fortress. She was engaged in a defensive war of attrition, and she was winning.

Until finally, he could take it no more. His lacerated muscles had no more power. His arms fell slack and hung at his sides.

Zoya faced him. She was panting, but could go on as long as it took.

"Who sent you?" she asked as she swayed the whip in front of his face.

"I don't know who he is." The man gulped and wheezed. "He just paid us to take care of you. And the other guy before. A hundred quid each. It seemed like easy money."

Zoya looked around. The first man was still on the ground. The second man wasn't going to be fighting anyone anytime soon. There was nothing more to be done here.

She turned on her heel and walked away.

CHAPTER 7

The next morning, Zoya lay in a dead man's bed and stared up at a crack in the ceiling.

She had slept badly, and when she woke the first thought that had entered her mind was something her mother used to say when she was tired. *Yak vichavlenii limon* – like a squeezed lemon – which was a reasonable description of how she felt, or it would have been if the lemon had been battered with a rolling pin first before it was squeezed. If only she had been smart enough, Zoya had scolded herself, to order a massage from the hotel's spa before she went to bed. Instead, in the morning, she had poured an entire jar of bath salts into a tub of steaming water and basked in its heat until she could take it no longer. Since this had added an extra half hour to her wakeup routine, she had then rushed through a single stacked helping from the breakfast buffet, although she had managed to compensate for the slim pickings by smuggling out two sausage and scrambled egg rolls in a napkin when she left. A few minutes before eight o'clock, she had exited the hotel via the back doors.

Despite the stiff throb of her limbs, she had forced herself to stroll far and circuitously enough to be sure she wasn't being followed. She had hailed a taxi and made a mental note to figure out Interpol's expense reimbursement policy before her newfound taste for the city's black cabs bankrupted her. In the meantime, since she was still moderately solvent, she had exchanged £6.30 for a short drive to Robin's address and a handwritten receipt where the line "total fare paid" had been left empty as a test of her honesty. From outside the house – small, well-kept, unremarkable – Zoya had walked up and down the street until she had located Robin's car under a sad-looking tree a hundred and fifty metres away.

She had pulled the seat forwards, adjusted the mirrors and been relieved to see that the car was an automatic. Once she had figured out the GPS system, it had claimed that the drive would take less than an hour. Zoya had been surprised – it had seemed longer with Robin – but then again it had been raining, plus she knew all about the elastic nature of time. She had made liberal use, Odesa style, of her bumpers – Robin's bumpers – to escape her parking spot, although her attempt at a speedy getaway had been thwarted by the car's disappointing lack of acceleration.

Ten minutes later, when the political debate on Robin's preferred radio station had begun to grate on her nerves, she had twiddled the tuning knob – narrowly avoiding swerving into the car that had foolishly chosen that moment to overtake – until she had found a station that called itself Virgin and was anything but. Between the ads, the DJ had developed a consistent message. "Shut Up and Dance" had been followed by "Wish You Were Mine", then "Promesses" had faded into "Take Me to Church". Entering into the romantic mood, Zoya had sung along with the choruses through her mouthfuls of eggy sausage and had thought the resulting spattered debris would help Robin learn an important lesson – that, statistically speaking, it was always going to be a bad idea to lend your car to a hungry Ukrainian weightlifter.

In the sunshine, Woolton had done a better job of living up to its wealthy suburb reputation. Its collection of grand houses huddled behind low walls whose function was display rather than protection. The owners of the houses – mainly skinny women in jodhpur-style leggings and tight puffer jackets – leapt gracefully into imposingly high cars, whose function was also display rather than protection. There were gravel driveways and long stretches of neatly clipped grass verge; there were a good number of trees and an excess of green plastic wheelie bins. Then a black cloud had appeared, and it had started to rain.

Zoya had left the car directly under a sign that said something about parking. Perhaps it was allowed, perhaps it wasn't; but she was getting wet, and she had assumed Robin would soon be informed one way or the other. At the house, there had been no reply to her urgent knocking. Luckily one of the few items of essential police equipment Zoya had felt confident to pack in her suitcase was her lockpick set. Opening the front door was a simple matter of pressure on a slim titanium tension wrench and energetic use of a serrated rake, then Zoya had plenty of time to work her way through the tumblers of the more sophisticated lock on the upstairs landing. She was in.

She began to search. She upended drawers; she probed the sofa cushions and its base; she sneezed at the dust under the rug. She peered inside the two pairs of shoes, and fumbled through the pockets and lining of the jacket that still hung on its peg. She inspected the screws on the back of the TV, but they showed no signs of having been tampered with. The same with the electric sockets and ventilation gratings. She moved to the next room. There she examined the kitchen cupboards and drawers, including the empty space underneath; inside the washing machine, the dishwasher and the smoke extractor. Oven and microwave too. She dug a fork through packets of cereal and coffee. Then onto the bathroom. She opened its cupboards, and the toilet cistern, and checked the access space under the bathtub. Finally, the bedroom. There was no corpse today. She rifled mattress and bedstand; she flicked through the few clothes in the closet; she dissected the empty suitcase.

It was a small apartment, so it only took twenty minutes to find nothing.

So Zoya stretched out on the bed; dead centre, hands behind her head, under the crack in the ceiling. A couple of hours had passed since she had woken, and her body was finally beginning to loosen up. She was tempted to sleep a little more – the mattress was comfortable, and it didn't worry her that its most recent occupant was dead. She drifted as she pulled herself back to her previous visit and recalled her initial impressions when she had entered the apartment. The lighting had been too bright. The curtains had been drawn. Everything had been clean and tidy, obsessively so. The furniture had been placed perfectly, all parallel lines and exact angles. Even down to the remote control that bisected the corner of the TV stand. *Who did that?*

She stood and went to check. The lights were off, the curtains open. Landlady or police, she didn't know. But the remote was still there, and it still pointed towards the windows. She followed its lead. She probed at the windowsill; it didn't budge. She inspected the skirting board; it was well-crafted and fastened to the wall with a double dose of nails and glue. The floorboards creaked, but they were secure. She ran her fingers around the window frame in case some small object could have been lodged in the gap between frame and wall. Nothing. She was about to give up, then she thought again. The curtains had been drawn, now they were open. She stepped back and took another look. They were thick cloth, which would do a good job of banishing light and cold. Beige was perhaps not the most practical shade, but darker would have been gloomy in such a small room. Nothing out of the ordinary. Zoya stepped forwards and lifted the folds of the material, then moved inside their embrace. Right side then left, looking down and up. And she found what she had been looking for.

*

It was invisible from inside the room. High up, just below the curtain rail, attached to a crease in the cloth with a heavy-duty bulldog clip. An envelope. The dead Dutchman had been tall, and Zoya wasn't, so she carried a chair in from the kitchen. She climbed up, unclipped the envelope, and descended. She took it over to the sofa and shook out the contents. And smiled.

There were two passports. One German, one American, with the same photo and different names.

Inside the US passport there were two pieces of paper. The first was a ticket for passage onboard the Queen Mary 2 liner. Attached was a one-page itinerary, which confirmed access to an Ocean Suite with private sun terrace and set out the dates of the journey: the ship was scheduled to depart Liverpool on 15 March and would call in at Halifax and Boston before arriving in New York ten days later.

Next there were two bundles of banknotes; bright-green one-hundred-euro notes, bright-pinky-red fifty-pound notes. The undamaged bank wrappers on each bundle confirmed that one contained ten thousand euros and the other five thousand pounds.

Finally, there was a single sheet of A4 paper, folded in half. One side had an inkjet-printed photo of a red-painted building that stood on the corner of two streets. It had two main floors with a series of high, narrow windows, and an attic space with smaller windows for the servants. The entrance was on the corner, under a balcony, which in turn was under an onion dome fashioned from the same dark grey metal as the roof. The printed title under the house said "Dusmanic, Serbia". Zoya turned the paper over. On the back, the number forty-six had been written with a thick black marker.

Zoya sat for a while. She decided to leave everything she didn't need. Perhaps whoever eventually found the package would pass it to the police. Perhaps she would even ring in a tip herself, so that her conscience would be clean. But first she used her new mobile to take photos of everything. She replaced the passports and the ticket in the envelope. Zoya stared at the money for a moment. It was tempting, and she knew a cash float was always useful in an investigation. In the end, she reminded herself that she was in boringly honest England, so she compromised by stuffing the bundle of euros back into the envelope and the bundle of pounds into her jacket pocket. The printed paper was the only part she didn't understand. It obviously meant something, but she didn't know what. She took it with her.

Zoya drove the same route in the opposite direction, and this time she was so absorbed in her thoughts that she never noticed the black Ford sedan that had slipped into the traffic behind her and stayed two cars back all the way to Manchester.

CHAPTER 8

Zoya arrived at the hospital in time for lunch. Robin was stretched out on his bed, looking a little more alive than the previous day and poking uneasily at the food on his plastic tray. He had clearly heeded Zoya's warning to be careful what he ate and drank, yet had no idea what that meant in practice. Zoya demonstrated by helping herself to the main course (chicken breast in a lumpy white sauce) and demonstratively not dying. She continued his education by allowing him to assess for himself the potential risks of the stridently coloured jelly that was offered for dessert.

"Director Tahiri dropped in to check up on me," Robin said when they finished eating. "And he left a package for you."

Zoya opened it and discovered her new ID, a security pass for the office, a mobile phone, and a spiral-bound copy of Interpol's eighty-page internal policy manual.

"Everything I need for a long and successful career," she said. "And, just so you know, after we spoke last night, I ran into your two attackers. I convinced them to apologise, and they promised they won't do it again. Then this morning I went back to Woolton to visit the dead man's apartment."

She briefed him on what she had discovered. She showed him the photo of the mysterious red house, but she didn't show him the money. Then she asked what Robin had managed to find out.

"As we agreed," Robin said, "I concentrated on the five probables we have files for. I'll need to look into the Liverpool guy once we have more information. The first thing I saw is that the home address for each of the five was in Amsterdam. You'd expect some of them to live there, since it's the capital and by far the biggest city, but perhaps not all of them. Then, there's their ages. Three were born in 1975, two were born in 1976. So, same place and same age."

Robin paused and stared at Zoya for a moment.

"But you knew all that already," he said.

Zoya nodded, pleased that he was gradually getting the hang of it.

"Sorry. OK, now for what wasn't in the files. Some of this is from simple Google searches; some from accessing the Interpol databases, which have links into everything from local police records to tax filings. I was trying to figure out what these guys did for a living, to see if there were any links. To be honest I didn't really find a connection. There's an ex-soldier from the Dutch special forces and a guy who ran his own travel agency. One man was a surgeon, another used to be a private wealth adviser with one of the big banks, now registered as independent. For one man I found nothing at all: no employment history, not even a social media profile. And the last one, the one with the missing father, he seems to have worked in the family pharmacy business."

"What about where they died?" Zoya asked. "Are you seeing any pattern?"

"At first glance they're about as far apart as they could be, within Europe at least. Marseilles, France; Valencia, Spain; Gibraltar; Lisbon, Portugal; and Liverpool in England. But I was wondering if that was exactly the point. If you have Amsterdam as the starting point, then it's almost like they scattered from there to the furthest points they could find. And each of those towns has a port with good onward connections. For example, the southern coasts of France and Spain give easy access to North Africa. Gibraltar as well. Lisbon is Portugal's main port as well as the capital, and Liverpool is a major ferry and cargo hub. Plus, we already know that our local guy had a ticket from Liverpool on a ship bound for New York."

"So potentially they were running from something," Zoya said, "pausing in different towns or cities whilst they made arrangements to travel somewhere else. Like the guy in Liverpool; his landlady said he rented the apartment just two weeks ago, and his ticket was for a week from now. And that the men had a preference for sea travel rather than flying, probably because there's less security. But if they were trying to run, and they were killed anyway, that means someone was tracking them. And that someone was better at tracking than they were at hiding."

"That's a good example of confirmation bias," Robin said absently.

"How do you mean?"

"Well, we've found a total of six people who we think were potentially trying to escape someone or something. We know they didn't make it. From that you're assuming that someone did a very good job of tracking them. But it could also be that there are a lot more people involved than we know about. Someone caught up with six of them, the rest got away."

Zoya had to admit that it was a good point. Although she didn't think the version of a much larger group of fleeing individuals was particularly likely, it was entirely possible that there was at least one person who had successfully evaded his fate. So far. Which made finding him a high priority.

Or her. Was that confirmation bias too?

"Robin, you started this investigation because your algorithm identified an unusually high incidence of dead Dutch *men*. But what about women? Did you look at that as well? Either dead, or perhaps just missing?"

Robin blushed and confessed he had not.

Another thought occurred to Zoya. About the father who had set up a pharmacy business then passed it on to his son.

"I think you should give that woman another call," she said. "The one with the dead son and the husband who disappeared."

"Her name's Eline Visser," Robin said. "And even if I call her, what am I supposed to ask?"

Zoya gave Robin a disbelieving glare. Obviously, he knew what he needed to ask; he just didn't like the idea of calling her again. She thought she would have to work on thickening Robin's skin if he was going to be any use in the intelligence gathering and response coordinating business. For now, Robin sighed and flicked through the file until he found the Post-it where he had written down Mrs Visser's contact details.

He dialled, putting his phone on speaker mode. After saying who was calling and apologising for the further disturbance, Robin asked whether there was any news about her husband.

Mrs Visser didn't cry this time, though the only sound that emerged through the speaker was scarcely human. It was a wail of pain and protest, devoid of words. Then the phone cut off.

Robin was pale and his hands trembled. Zoya thought it was a sound she had heard far too often in her life. There was no doubt in her mind that Visser's husband was dead, and that his death was somehow connected to that of his son and the other men. And that they needed to meet her.

She stared at the photo on the bed in front of her. Red house. Dusmanic. Serbia. Forty-six. It still meant nothing to her.

She turned to Robin.

"Are you fit enough to travel?"

CHAPTER 9

It took three days to reach Eline Visser's house. Mainly because Robin had summarily rejected Zoya's breezy "we should just leave; we'll ask for approval when we get back" approach. Instead, he had insisted they do everything by the book. They had negotiated sign-off from a clearly sceptical Director Tahiri, who in the end was only swayed by the opportunity to get the troublesome duo out of his immaculate hair for a few days; they had reserved flight tickets and hotel accommodation in full compliance with the relevant travel policies; and, once they knew their arrival details, they had initiated the process of informing local law enforcement agencies and arranging the assignment of a liaison officer from Interpol's office in The Hague. In total, over forty-eight hours of preparation was needed for a simple two-hour flight. At first, Zoya had been disillusioned by the deeply English lack of spontaneity displayed by her partner; but, after she had breathed deeply and eaten heartily, she had forced herself to accept that the slow approach did sometimes have its advantages.

Firstly, both of their bodies had some additional time to recover. By the time they left, the pain from Robin's dislocated shoulder had subsided sufficiently to free his arm from its sling. Which was a definite plus, since Zoya would be expecting him to do his fair share of the fetching and carrying (coffee and snacks, files, maybe even her carry-on bag.) *Nothing too heavy, of course,* she had reminded herself, since his cracked ribs would take a little longer to heal.

Then there was the fact their delayed departure had enabled Zoya to catch her first good look at the man who had continued to follow her. He was medium height and muscular. He had a stubby nose in a round face, under a thatch of sandy blond hair that was sufficiently luxurious to make her think at least some of it had been implanted into his scalp. In addition to periodically changing his caps, he sported an interesting variety of clothes; but he always wore the same shoes – black leather tops, chunky white soles – which attempted to combine smart with sporty, yet failed at both. Zoya was sure she had never seen the man before, though at the same time there was something familiar about him. His ears, maybe, or the way he walked.

Finally, as an added bonus, Interpol's Dutch representative, when he met them at Schiphol Airport, had turned out to be tall and exceptionally handsome, and also displayed the rock-solid gluteal development that only a fellow weightlifter could truly appreciate. His title was Officer First Class, his surname was Scheefnek – which translated as "stiff neck" – and he had a car. All of which, Zoya had accepted, would make their short stay in the Netherlands considerably more enjoyable.

*

And here they were. It was Friday 27 March. They had left the memory of Amsterdam forty minutes to the north and driven on straight roads through wide stretches of flat agricultural land. Raised banks of canals traversed the fields. The sun was out and so was the wind, while the damp in the air and the squabble of seagulls hinted that the sea was somewhere nearby. Disappointingly there were no tulips to be seen, nor windmills for that matter, but there were a few cows dotted around – heavy udders and contented chewing – that stared at the intruders with placid curiosity. And of course, there was the woman's home, which stood on a large plot of land next to a narrow lane. The building was old and looked like it might have been a farmhouse in a previous life. It had white woodlap walls under a steep roof, dark green shutters on the windows and a brick chimney stack. It was well cared for, and a solid looking barn stood off to the side.

Outside the dark gloss of the front door, Zoya glanced at her companions. They made an unlikely trio: a tall, handsome man; a short, muscular woman; a skinny, battered man.

Beauty and the two beasts, she mused as Scheefnek rang the bell, and then thought perhaps she was being unkind to at least one of them.

Whatever they looked like, there was a long silence until he rang again, after which they heard a series of strange sounds from within the house. Shuffle, shuffle tap. Shuffle, shuffle, tap, growing closer. The door opened.

Mrs Visser's clothes were rumpled and smelled of cigarette ash. She carried a polished bamboo cane with a curved handle and a metal tip. Her steel-grey hair hung lank and loose, and her washed-out blue eyes wandered over the features of each of her visitors without understanding or interest. Until, that is, they reached Robin. Her gaze halted and focused, and she examined the bruises covering his face with a sad intensity. She reached out a hand as if she was about to stroke his cheek and muttered something they couldn't hear.

Officer First Class Scheefnek introduced them, and asked if they could come inside. Mrs Visser didn't reply, but when she turned away, she left the door open behind her. They followed her into a large living room with dark wood furniture around the edges and a matching set of chintzy armchairs and sofa at the centre. The curtains were half drawn, shutting out most of the sunlight, and the plants that stood on tables and windowsills were drooping and brown.

"Mrs Visser," Zoya began with a quiet, gentle voice, "we are so sorry for your loss, and for disturbing you at such a difficult time. But we believe the death of your husband and your son are possibly related to a series of other deaths that we are investigating. We hope that you may have some information that may help us."

The woman had propped her cane against one leg. She brushed a hand through her hair as if she was trying to lift it into place. She closed her eyes, and when she opened them again it felt like she had flicked a switch inside. Her voice was dark but calm.

"My husband was sick," she said. "He was no threat to anyone, the doctors said he had only a few months left to live. Then he disappeared. That was the first time you called me," she glanced at Robin, "and no one knew anything. We thought perhaps it was his illness, that he had collapsed somewhere and not been able to call for help. But the police found his body two days ago in a, what is the word for a building where you store things?"

"A warehouse," Zoya suggested.

"Yes, in a warehouse. An old warehouse that was not in use. They said he must have been held for a week at least. They did not want me to look, but I insisted on seeing my Dietrich one last time. It was horrible what they did to him. Like your face," she looked at Robin again, "but all over his body. And much worse."

Zoya hadn't yet received the official report, but she and Robin had spoken by phone with a Dutch police officer who had summarised what had happened. Mrs Visser's summary was an understatement, and Zoya hoped the doctors had managed to spare her the worst of it. Her husband's finger and toenails had been removed. Two fingers and several toes had been crushed with a hammer. There were cigarette burns all over his body, and a series of holes had been drilled in his legs. The eventual cause of death, however, had been simpler. A small-calibre pistol had been pressed against Mr Visser's chest, and a single shot had been fired into his heart.

"All we know at this point about your husband," Zoya continued, "is that he had established a pharmacy business near here, and that your son Jan also worked with him. Do you think there was perhaps something related to his work that might have made him a target?"

"Your information is not entirely accurate, young lady," Mrs Visser replied. "The business came from my side of the family;

it was created by my grandfather, then passed to my father, and then I inherited it. Both my husband and I were involved to some extent, but we had a manager to run each of the stores. And my Jan was hardly involved at all. But maybe that is not the purpose of your question. Of course, I have thought about why these terrible things have happened; and, if it will help you, I will tell you what I know. And also what I don't know. But first, I want to show you something."

On the table at her side lay two thick leather-bound albums, and on top of the albums rested the smaller volume of a Bible with a blue cover and a gold inlaid cross. Visser took the Bible, her hand stroking over the cover, then she picked up the first album, opened it to a page marked with a slip of paper, and passed it to Zoya. A single large photo took up the full page with a date underneath – 24 June 1991.

"My wedding day," she said. "That's me in the wedding dress, with Dietrich at my side. It looks just like a typical wedding unless you know who the people are. You see, everyone in the photo is from my side – my parents, my two sisters, and the rest my family. And my friends. There's no one from Dietrich's side. You see, he moved here from Germany, a little over a year before we married. He told me his parents were dead, and that he had no siblings. I was never sure if that was true, or if something had happened to cause him to lose contact with his family."

"Where was he from in Germany?" Zoya asked.

"From Berlin," Mrs Visser replied. "And yes, before you ask, my Dietrich was an East German, an Ossi as they are called. He moved here almost immediately after the Berlin Wall came down."

Zoya was wondering how to put her next question so that it didn't sound like an accusation, when Robin came to her rescue.

"Did Dietrich tell you why he left Germany?" he asked.

"He was very vague," Mrs Visser replied. "But when I met him, I simply didn't care. I fell in love, and it didn't matter to me where he came from, or what his life was before we met. Over time I thought about it of course, but I never liked to pry. He was a very private man, you see, my Dietrich. Of course, I had all kind of ideas. That maybe he had committed some crime, or there was some scandal he had run away from. But with me he was kind and gentle and honest, and it always seemed that was the most important thing."

"Did he ever say anything about the kind of work he used to do?" Zoya asked. "Before he started working with you in the pharmacy."

"He was a scientist, I know that much; although he never said much about it, not directly at least. But there were things I picked up on sometimes. For example, when one of our customers at the pharmacy told my husband how scared he was that he was supposed to swallow radioactive iodine for the doctors to make images of his thyroid gland, Dietrich spent a whole hour with him, discussing the different isotopes and their dosages until he had convinced the man that it was all totally safe. Or once we were in a restaurant and, quite by chance, we sat next to a group of protestors who were trying to get the nuclear power station in Borssele closed down. He got into such a huge argument with them that we were asked to leave."

"So a possible connection to the nuclear sector," Zoya said, more to herself than to anyone else.

"He had a temper," Mrs Visser said vaguely. "He could be quite tyrannical, you know. But he didn't deserve what happened to him, he really didn't."

They all fell silent for a minute: Mrs Visser lost in her memories, Zoya and her colleagues trying to figure a way through what she had told them. Another thought occurred to Zoya.

"Do you have any photos of Jan you could show us?" she asked.

Mrs Visser smiled sadly and handed over the second album. Zoya soon understood it was entirely dedicated to photos of her son: starting with pictures of him as a baby, then a toddler, and progressing with each page through the years of his life. Zoya forced herself go slowly, although it was really the later years that interested her. The boy entered school; as a teenager he had short hair then long; he had grown taller and filled out. Then she saw a series of class photos from the final few years of school. Zoya focused on the last photo. She counted twenty-six students arranged in three rows, with a few more girls than boys. All were in identical uniforms, their bright faces filled with the sense of launching into a new life. The names of the children were printed, also in three rows, in a strip of white underneath the photo.

"Do you mind if we take this photo?" Zoya asked. "I promise we'll return it."

"Please do," Mrs Visser replied. "I see it in you, detective, that you like puzzles. Maybe you will understand something the local police didn't. They were very sympathetic, but I am not sure they were asking the right questions. And worse than that, when they looked at me, I could see they felt sorry for me. An old woman, half out of her mind with grief. The men, they always underestimate us women, don't you think?"

Zoya thought there was a message there somewhere, a riddle to be solved. Or an answer that was important, if only she could find the right question.

"Was your son married?" she asked.

Mrs Visser stroked her hand over the cover of the Bible again. Her expression was distant. Thoughtful, or maybe regretful.

"No, Jan never married," she said. "Although maybe that's for the best. Given what happened to him."

*

After they left the house, Zoya stood by their car and stared into the distance, the tails of her black coat flapping in the wind.

"I'm not buying it," she said finally. "Go back in there now and she'll be fixing up her hair and watering her poor dead plants. More importantly, I don't understand why she was so precise about some things – about her family business for example – but so vague about everything else."

Zoya turned to Scheefnek. She scanned him head to toe and was pleased to see he wasn't intimidated by her examination. He was a straightforward man; what you saw was what you got – a handsome face with an agreeable slow smile, a great body, and a strong, dependable mind.

"We should go back to your place," she said.

CHAPTER 10

Scheefnek's office was in downtown The Hague, but they took a couple of small detours on the way. Zoya wanted to see the sights, which for her had nothing to do with canals, windmills or fields of bright yellow tulips. First, she wanted to spend a few minutes staring out at the rolling waves of the North Sea. Then she asked to visit the International Criminal Court, since you never knew when the next dictator would need to be brought to justice – and if it was Putin's name that came to mind as she stared at its high glass tower that was no-one's business but her own. Zoya knew the court's processes were slow, bureaucratic and very far from perfect, yet it was still a symbol of something to aspire to. The idea that anyone – irrespective of race, religion, nationality or their position of power – could be held to account. Except the Americans of course, who had a marked preference for imposing justice on others over having it imposed on them.

Next, Scheefnek suggested they stop for lunch. Zoya was pleased she was not the only one who was hungry; and as Robin chipped in to request local cuisine, Scheefnek's answering frown implied that over the years he had entertained more than his fair share of foreign guests with the same stipulation. But then he smiled and took them to an Indonesian restaurant that he claimed, due to the country's centuries-long colonial history, was as traditionally Dutch as *Poffertjes* pancakes. They sat at dark wood tables and washed down generous helpings of nasi goreng with bottles of Belgian beer, whilst Scheefnek entertained them with an exposé of another of the Netherlands' native commercial success stories.

He summarised the two main reasons why a country as small as theirs had become the global hub for the manufacture and export of synthetic drugs. The first, essentially, was that the Dutch didn't care. They placed Ecstasy and its many variants in the same category as cannabis – recreational, only moderately addictive – and didn't much worry if their citizens decided to partake. The only times they had made any serious effort to clamp down on production were in response to other countries' diplomatic pressure. The United States had called the Netherlands a narco-state and withheld signature of the latest trade deal, and for a while the French had flounced around the same idea with a show of Gallic petulance. But attention spans were short, life went on, and production was ramped back up. The other reason was common to all countries – that the bureaucratic process of banning any specific drug had never been able to keep up with the chemical creativity of the producers. As soon as one drug made it onto the narcotics blacklist, its formulation was tweaked just sufficiently to be considered a new, separate drug, and the whole process began again.

None of which meant that the Dutch didn't monitor what was going on. And most importantly, from Zoya's perspective, Scheefnek was certain that there was no indication of any significant recent turbulence in the local drug trade. There was always a background hum of violence, of course – an ongoing trickle of commercial disputes was only to be expected, accompanied by regular beatings and the occasional disappearance or murder – but there had been no coordinated actions, no suggestion of a strategic attempt by any existing group to take over a rival's territory, and no rumours of new competitors trying to muscle into the market. If six men with a connection to the drug trade had been murdered within a short period of time, Scheefnek was certain they would have known about it.

"What about the materials to make the drugs?" Zoya asked. "Where do they come from?"

"It's changed over time," Scheefnek replied. "Now it's mainly China. Russia used to be a big player too, but I heard a couple of factories there have closed down recently. One of them in Saratov maybe?"

He looked at Zoya as if he thought she should know what was happening in Russia. She didn't, at least not about a Saratov chemical plant. She was however aware that there had been a small factory on the outskirts of Odesa that had used to manufacture something she thought was called BMK, which was one of the main ingredients used to produce Ecstasy. And the only reason she knew this was because she had investigated the murder of the man who had owned the plant until it had burnt to the ground. She didn't share the gory details, because something else had occurred to her.

"Damn it," she said. "I forgot the other thing I wanted to ask Mrs Visser. About the photo I found at our first crime scene."

She pulled it from the file and placed it on the table. Each time she looked, she hoped she would see something new. However, nothing. The same red house, the same placename, the same number on the back. Scheefnek examined it too, but had no more idea of its relevance than she did.

They finished up their meal with another local success story: the tale of the plants that had first been stolen three hundred years before from plantations in Yemen. Their eventual transportation, via Amsterdam and Jakarta, to Java, followed by the creation of an entirely new and ruthlessly efficient system to subordinate thousands of land-tied local farmers for their cultivation. In short: the story of traditional Dutch blend coffee; served today with a smile, in delicate white porcelain cups – the bitter legacy sweetened with a well-designed corporate logo and a cube of sugar.

Then Scheefnek paid the cheque, and they all went back to his place.

*

By now Zoya was unsurprised that Interpol was housed in someone else's building – Europol this time, though she wasn't too sure what the difference was. At least Scheefnek had his own office: a bare, glass-walled space that accepted uncomplainingly that its current occupant could be reassigned at a moment's notice.

Zoya took the class photo she had borrowed from Mrs Visser and asked for it to be copied and blown up to A3 size. She placed the enlarged version in the centre of the desk, pleased that the resolution was still sharp. She took the files of their six murdered men, then she flicked through each file until she found the men's photos.

"Another piece of the puzzle," she said. "Let's see who we can identify."

It took them a while. Over twenty years had passed and features had changed, usually for the worse. Wrinkles and frowns had appeared, and bags under eyes. Full heads of hair had thinned and grown bald. Excess weight had gathered under sagging skin. Then there was the small detail that they were comparing the past's living with today's dead. Mortuary shots were never going to be flattering, and these were distorted variously by the impact of poison, of a car crash, and most traumatically by the sudden deceleration inherent in hitting the ground at terminal velocity after a fall from a considerable height.

Even so, they found them all, and ringed the faces one by one with a circle of red marker. Scheefnek took the next step.

"The names are different," he said. "For some of them at least. Three names on the school photo correspond with your files, but three don't."

"Not just a pretty face," Zoya said.

"Before, we had six dead men with no clear connection to each other," Robin summarised excitedly. "Now we know that they went to the same school. They were also probably working together. Not forgetting the father of one of the six, Mrs Visser's husband Dietrich, who was tortured and killed. In addition, we now know that three of the men changed their identity, and we also have the forged passports for the Liverpool victim. We believe the men were running from something, so far unknown. Probably not drugs-related, based on Scheefnek's view of the local drugs business. But probably with some other criminal involvement, since they used fake identities. And since someone wanted them dead."

"All of which," Zoya confirmed, "says we have some homework to do."

CHAPTER 11

Delegation was a difficult skill to master. Not so much the part about telling people what to do: that was easy enough, and Zoya had practised consistently and persistently throughout her childhood (with her schoolfriends; with her brother, who had generally followed instructions; and with her parents, who had resisted as long as they could). The more challenging aspect was achieving the right balance – the knack for telling people what to do without earning their resentment or even their hatred. In this respect, Zoya admitted that she was still a work-in-progress. She felt her latest performance review had summarised her current level of achievement quite fairly, even if she still wasn't sure if her boss's words were intended as a compliment or a criticism.

"Officer Zozulya possesses a burning instinct for delegation," Major Dobroshtan had written. "She delegates fairly to her subordinates, ruthlessly to her peers, and with such subtlety to her superiors that I often find I have completed the assigned task before I even realise what it is that I have been doing for her."

In short, Zoya had been forced to accept that her mastery was not yet complete, and therefore she was always pleased to identify an opportunity for continued self-development. Scheefnek spoke Dutch, of course, and his desktop computer was connected to all the relevant databases. She therefore requested that he take another look into the backgrounds of the six dead men and see if he could find anything that the original files and Robin's research had missed. She thought for a moment about changed names and added an additional question – to understand where an Amsterdam resident would go to get a forged passport. That left Robin; who spoke only English of course, but he had at least brought his laptop with him. Zoya put him to work searching for anything relevant on the town of Dusmanic, the red house, or the number forty-six.

"And what will you be doing?" Robin asked, a little testily she thought.

"I just remembered a friend I haven't spoken to for a while," she replied. "Since you two are busy I'm going to give him a call and catch up."

Robin looked like he was going to say something, but he reconsidered. Zoya smiled sweetly then borrowed some euros from Scheefnek to buy a sandwich from the vending machine in the corridor. Meat, chewy, again. She found an empty conference room so that she wouldn't be disturbing her team's concentration. She dialled her friend's number.

She spoke German to make it easier. They chatted about her new assignment and his recent promotion. Zoya asked after his wife and his two children – one boy, one girl. He asked if she still had a cat, and she said she had left it with her brother. She reminisced about the occasion, a couple of years back, when he had visited Odesa as part of an ongoing investigation. She recalled the day he had spent tucked up in her bed after they had cracked the case, then she reminded him that he had neglected to mention at the time that he was married. And once they had both established that he owed her a very large favour, she asked about the Ministerium für Staatssicherheit, also known as the East German secret police, also known as the dreaded Stasi. She gave him a name, he promised to call back.

*

Two hours later, she reconvened with Robin and Scheefnek in his office. The mood was positive, and it seemed everyone had something to report. Robin began.

"Dusmanic," he said, "is a tiny village with just a couple of hundred inhabitants in the east of Serbia. It's near the Danube River, which forms the border with Romania, and is also on the edge of a national park. There's a well-known cave complex nearby, as well as the Golubac Fortress, also on the river, which dates from the fourteenth century and looks very impressive. The red building in the photo comes up as soon as you type Dusmanic into a search engine. It's there, it's real, but it's not number forty-six on either of the streets it stands on. Nor, in fact, did I find any house with a number forty-six in the village – it looks like all the streets are too small to go up that far. None of which, I know, helps us very much."

He paused to take in the glazed expression in Zoya and Scheefnek's eyes.

"Then I tried looking at it in a different way," he continued. "The photo gives us a specific building. Which, according to Google, used to house a pharmacy. Therefore, I thought that might be intended to point us somehow to the pharmacy business the Visser family runs. Alternatively, maybe the pharmacy part isn't so literal and it's a coded reference to the drug trade. Add in Serbia, and maybe the suggestion is that there's some Serbian group trying to get into the drug trade. Finally I thought a bit outside the box, and wondered if all the rest might be a red herring and Dusmanic might simply be code for something else. An anagram, for example. There are a few possible variants, although I still don't know how relevant they would be."

He pushed forward a sheet of paper where he had rearranged the letters to show the possible anagrams.

DNA Music. Muscadin. Scandium.

It didn't look very promising to Zoya.

She was about to ask Scheefnek what he had discovered, when her phone rang. Excitingly, it was the first call she had received on her new Interpol mobile. She answered warily.

Director Tahiri's voice was loud, excited and a little shocked.

"I need you both back here as soon as possible," he said. "There's only one more direct flight today from Amsterdam, and you and Robin are booked on it. It leaves Schiphol at 16.05, about two hours from now. Get the local guys to arrange a car to the airport – and whatever you do, don't miss the plane."

"What's happening boss?" Zoya asked.

"A massacre, that's what's happening. Twelve dead, multiple gunshot wounds. It's a bloodbath. And current indications are that it's not local. Whoever did it is from somewhere in Europe, which is why we're involved. It's all hands on deck until we figure out what's going on."

"Was there any Dutch involvement?" Robin asked, ever the optimist.

"Forget your damned Dutchmen!" Tahiri snapped. "This is real, and it's happening now. Just get to the airport and get back here."

He rang off.

*

Robin stuffed files and his laptop into his bag as Scheefnek organised a car. He confirmed it would be waiting downstairs in three minutes' time, before riding down with them in the lift.

Zoya didn't like farewells. She never knew what to say.

"It's been fun," she tried, through the open window of the car. He smiled and gave a little wave, and she watched him, perhaps a little too attentively, as he turned and walked away.

And, just for a moment as the car pulled off, Zoya was sad that she had not had the opportunity to share with Scheefnek what her German friend had told her. Until she remembered that a massacre awaited them. Twelve dead and a bloodbath, Tahiri had said.

She leant forward and told the driver to put on the sirens and floor the accelerator.

PART 2

The Hunter

CHAPTER 12

The Hunter had allowed the Lee End gang ample time to settle in. Twenty minutes after the beginning of their ten a.m. meeting, he had given the signal. A plain white van had driven leisurely along the street and splashed through the puddles into the almost empty car park of a single-storey red-brick building. The two guards smoking by the entrance doors had tried to wave the van away. Each had received, in quick succession, two subsonic 9x39mm rounds to the chest.

The gang's weak point had been obvious. The redbrick was a boxing club in an almost abandoned industrial zone on the edge of their territory. There were always at least a few of their heavies on-site; perhaps training for the next fight, probably preening for the next date. Better still, once a week, regular as clockwork, the top men gathered there to count the takings, to discuss any problems, to dip croissants in their coffee for all the Hunter cared, and to do whatever else it was that the overconfident leadership of a big-fish-stinky-pond Manchester street gang did in their weekly meetings. Which meant that on this Friday morning – that of 27 March 2015 – just like every other, they would start early, be done by twelve, then knock off for the weekend.

The site itself wasn't bad from a security perspective. It was set in an area with low footfall. It was surrounded by tall, concrete-slab walls on three sides, with a lower wall to the front. It had small windows set high and steel doors front and rear. With a bit of effort, the building could have been transformed into an impregnable fortress. But there were two problems. First, that if it was a boxing club then it wasn't a fortress. Its clientele, which on any other day of the week ranged from a youth club to the area's yummy-mummy-cardio-boxing contingent, needed easy access and wouldn't have appreciated barbed wire or machine gun posts. The second problem was that – even on a Friday morning, when they were closed to the public and they posted guards – their perimeter was nowhere near wide enough. Especially when their opponents were not the gangbangers from the neighbouring estate, but a squad of experienced and motivated ex-soldiers – including the squad's designated marksman, who had happily spent the night under the stars on the flat roof of a neighbouring garage complex, in the warm embrace of an internally suppressed and virtually silent Russian-made VSS Vintorez sniper rifle.

After his three seconds of shooting practice had brought a permanent end to the guards' morning shift, the sniper stayed on overwatch. Seven men left the van. The corpses were dragged out of sight. Two men moved to the rear of the building, at the same time as four men prepared to breach through the main entrance. The seventh was the Hunter. His men would go first, he would follow, and that was how it should be. His men knew his experience, they knew he was fearless, they also knew he was the boss.

"In four, three, two, one," his voice counted down in their earpieces, and it began.

At the back of the building, flashbangs went through shattered windows and the two men stayed in position to cut down any rats who tried to run. At the front, more flashbangs and a coordinated entry. The four men were up against ten inside, but surprise was only the first part of their advantage. They cleared the changing rooms within seconds, then they advanced into the wide, open space beyond. They spread left and right. They had body armour and overlapping arcs of fire from MP5 submachine guns, and their foe had T-shirts and pistols and few places to hide.

Bullet-riddled bodies soon littered the concrete floor and were finished off with point-blank headshots. A massacre, a bloodbath. But controlled and disciplined, because there was one man the Hunter very much wanted alive.

Once the Lee End gang's boss had been secured in the club's cramped back-office space, the Hunter knelt at his side. The man wheezed and groaned with the pain of the rounds in his legs, but his eyes were defiant. The Hunter didn't bother with recriminations or threats; what was the point? The muscles of his face strained into a painful grimace as he slid the man's mobile phone from his jeans pocket. He unbuttoned the man's shirt. A heavy silver chain draped the man's overdeveloped neck. From the chain was suspended what might have been a standard USB thumb drive but wasn't. The logo on the device was a single word – Ledger – and the Hunter knew it was a top-of-the-range crypto wallet that would link with the mobile he was already holding in the scarred palm of his left hand. If he had the access codes.

"I'm going to need you to unlock these for me," he said.

"Fuck you," the man spat out, much as the Hunter had expected.

He unsheathed his knife and got to work.

*

The Hunter was satisfied with how everything had turned out, even if there had been a few minor bumps in the road. Or rather, come to think of it, there had really been just a single bump – but it had been a pretty bloody major one.

Luckily, the Hunter was a man who believed in learning from his mistakes. A previous challenging experience a couple of years back – Marseilles, early summer 2013; Algerians against the Nigerian underdogs, no clear victor – had convinced him of the necessity to hedge his bets in any corporate dispute. Today, and not for the first time, his belt-and-braces approach had paid off. Four weeks ago, the Hunter had identified that the Lee End gang was the strongest and most profitable of the Manchester gangs. He had entered into negotiations; discussions had been constructive and relatively speedy. As the parties had neared a viable agreement, the Hunter's scout had gathered extensive intelligence on the Lee End gang's competition – the opposing gang that was their target. Key individuals, locations, their routines and their weaknesses, with everything neatly summarised and strategized. However, he had not neglected to carry out exactly the same research on their presumed employer.

At the end of the negotiation process, when the Hunter had walked through the final terms of their contract – verbal, not written – he felt he had been perfectly clear.

"Once you confirm your agreement," he had stated, quiet-voiced over their call in the Telegram messaging app, "there's no going back. No renegotiation, no change in payment terms or in the timing of our project. You pay as agreed, we do the work as agreed, we leave. If you attempt to go back on any element of our contract, we will kill you."

Perhaps, in retrospect, he needed to work more on his tone. He knew his accent when he spoke English was naturally harsh and therefore threatening, but the Hunter had never liked to shout or to swear, and he didn't enjoy adding superfluous gory details to his threats. He considered that the hard work his group had done over the years should speak for itself. They had a reputation; they even had a brand. However, he did concede that violent criminals were not always the smartest of lads. And therefore, going forward, he would need to accept there really was no such thing as laying it on too thick.

In any case, at first these guys had seemed to get the message. The Lee End boss had grunted something that sounded like "too fokking right mate" at the end of the discussion. However, the following day, he had attempted to renegotiate. Worse than that, he had threatened the Hunter and his men. He had yelled that Manchester was his home turf, which gave him the advantage. He had said that the fokking Huntsmen were here now, in his town, and if they didn't follow his fokking rules, then he would be doing the fokking hunting and he knew exactly where to find his fokking prey.

To which there had been only one possible response.

The Lee End gang became the Hunter's new target. The neighbouring clan that had been scheduled for elimination had not only not escaped their fate, they had even benefited from a once-in-a-lifetime, Thursday-evening take-it-or-leave-it offer. A knockdown price, admittedly for a job they hadn't realised the Hunter was furious enough to have done for free.

And at the end of it all, the Hunter had unsheathed his knife and he had continued to hack away at the man who had threatened him long after he had given up all his secrets.

CHAPTER 13

A cauldron of Interpol officers bubbled gently as they waited. Around them, the walls of the meeting room had been plastered with crime scene photos. Corpses and blood-stains, bullet holes and casings. Enough of them that everyone had something to look at. And rows of chairs, with Zoya and Robin – the last arrivals, straight from the airport – at the back.

A woman arrived to stir the pot; Head Chef or Head Witch, all the way up the stairs from the third floor.

"For those of you who don't know me," she said, "my name is Jane Lovell, and I am a Detective Chief Inspector with the North-West Regional Organised Crime Unit. I will be leading the investigation into the events which occurred earlier today."

Zoya examined Lovell and at the same time made a mental note that she needed to figure out how British police ranks worked. For now, she recorded the details – slight, wiry build; blond shoulder-length hair, which Lovell didn't fiddle with when she talked; good skin, with only the lightest touch of makeup; fingernails short and neat and neutrally varnished. And then the important stuff: the confident stance of a woman who didn't take any crap, matched with the calm voice that would say what she needed to but wouldn't shout you down. Plus the watchful expression that combined the fatigue of what the day had already brought with complete alertness for the long night ahead. Zoya thought she would like DCI Lovell even when the time came for them to step on each other's toes.

"First the ground rules," Lovell continued. "I need to be very clear that this is an OCU investigation and that we are requesting Interpol support on one specific aspect of the case, which I will come to in a minute. Before we get to that, a short overview. As many of you are aware, Manchester is home to some of the most active criminal gangs in the UK. They are organised territorially within different areas of the city – as evidenced by the names of the different groups, for example the Braintree Boys or the Pepperhill gang. Or the Lee End gang, which was the target of today's attack. Each gang has responsibility for all criminal activity within its defined area. That primarily means drug dealing, but also includes prostitution, human trafficking and some gunrunning. As you might expect, this regional focus leads to repeated low-level confrontations as members of one gang stray either accidentally or deliberately into another gang's area. Less frequently there have been periodic attempts by one group to take over another group's territory. All initial indications are that this is what we are dealing with now, although the scale and level of violence of today's attack represents a significant escalation compared to anything we have previously seen."

Lovell gestured at the walls of the room to make the point, before continuing.

"However, all of the gangs are local and relatively small. They have little presence outside the Manchester area and none outside the UK. Although they are buyers of non-UK inputs for their business – drugs, women, and guns – they have never attempted to expand abroad, nor are they known to have ongoing links with any non-UK groups. All of which explains why Interpol has not previously been involved."

Lovell gave a dry cough and reached for one of the plastic bottles on the table in front of her. She unscrewed the cap and took a deep gulp of water.

"But this time we're seeing something new," she continued. "Two days ago, a source reported rumours that a suspicious group of foreigners had arrived in town. Nationality unknown, but possibly eastern European; aims unknown; numbering between eight and ten individuals; and suspected to have a military background. My people liaised immediately with Director Tahiri, however the information was not sufficiently specific for either my people or yours to make any headway. That information was followed this morning by an attack that was not just brutal, it was also militarily efficient. Coordinated angles of fire, carefully aimed shots, complete ruthlessness. Two guards and nine known gang leaders were eliminated within minutes. All of which reflects a very different capability from anything any of the gangs have previously demonstrated. The clear implication is that the mystery foreign group was brought in specifically for this attack. Then, as if all of that wasn't enough, we have this."

Behind Lovell was a single whiteboard that displayed an empty face to the room. She turned it to show the other side. A single photo was attached.

"Director Tahiri, would you like to explain?" she said.

Tahiri stood.

"What you see," he said, "is an enlarged image of a calling card left at the scene. The emblem on the card is self-explanatory – the crosshairs of a rifle's sights centred on the silhouette of a man's head. It is significant because this is not the first time this card has been left at a similar crime scene."

He paused for effect.

"Over the past two years," he said, "there have been a number of examples across Europe of inter-gang rivalry which have ended in violent confrontations. At first, we didn't identify a particular link between these attacks. They were sporadic, and they were initially viewed as a natural result of the character of organised crime. There were indications in one case of hired mercenaries being brought in, but at the time that was not seen as particularly remarkable. However, over the same two-year period we began to hear more consistent rumours regarding not just the use of hired guns, but of the existence of a defined group of individuals who made it their business to actively seek out such conflict situations and then to negotiate with one of the two sides to intercede on their behalf. And by "intercede" I mean they made a defined, financially based offer to kill everyone on the other side of the dispute. There were also quite specific indications regarding a rather unusual payment structure, under which the mercenaries set a condition that they would be entitled to all assets they were able to seize from the losing side."

Tahiri gestured at the whiteboard again.

"Now back to this calling card," he said. "Eighteen months ago, we heard a new name for the first time – the Huntsmen. And that's all it was – a name. Beyond the rumours, we had little concrete proof that these people actually existed. And, in some ways, it seemed unbelievable that any group of individuals was able to operate so freely across borders, with no definite sightings, and with no real information emerging on its leadership or nationality or home base. There was even an alternative theory doing the rounds that suggested that during one of many conflicts someone had simply invented these Huntsmen as some kind of criminal urban legend. The theory was that whoever thought it up wanted a convenient excuse to blame a gangland killing on a mysterious external party, and that other groups had simply taken hold of the legend and expanded on it. Then, approximately twelve months ago, we saw this calling card for the first time. It was left on the corpse of a Syrian national who had led a people-trafficking ring operating in northern Europe. He had been tortured, possibly for information, and eight of his men had been executed.

Now, I admit, the calling card still does not give us the level of proof that we are looking for. However, since the people-traffickers incident, we have seen the same card on two more occasions – and this morning of course – and each time with a very similar MO. So, when our analysts put everything together, they do now believe we are looking at a single group that has designed its own unique business proposition. They seek out conflict situations, they exploit them, they loot whatever they can, and they move on."

"And I'm sure the profilers would have something to say," Lovell added, "but these guys seem to have become very open about what they're doing. On one hand that's because they're professional and ruthless, but the whole calling card thing seems quite arrogant to me. If it was advertising for future clients that would be bad enough, but to me it looks like they're sending a message to us – I mean to law enforcement generally – at the same time."

There was silence in the room as everyone absorbed the information. Then a thought occurred to Zoya; which, since she was at the back of the room, she had to call out a little louder than she would have preferred.

"Can you tell us where exactly today's card was found?" she asked.

Lovell glanced around the walls of the room, then walked over to one of the photos.

"It's difficult to make out," she said, pointing at the image. "But this is the charred corpse of Tommy Cartwright, who was the boss of the Lee End gang. We were able to confirm his identity using fingerprints from the three severed digits that were left near his body. He was a rancid and unstable character who absolutely no one will miss, and as you see he received special treatment: preliminary forensics indicating that our Tommy took two rounds to the legs in the initial firefight, then he was dragged into an office space inside the building and secured to a radiator. He was tortured extensively before being doused in petrol, and I'll leave the rest to your imagination. The card was placed in what was left of his mouth."

Lovell moved back to the front of the room.

"And that, ladies and gentlemen, is why we need Interpol's assistance. If this group – the Huntsmen – actually exists, it sounds like they originate from outside the UK, and they operate internationally. They need to be located and stopped before they do any more damage. And preferably, of course, before they leave the country."

Zoya brushed Robin's restraining hand from her arm and stood. She didn't like to be the only person asking questions; but nothing ventured, nothing gained.

"DCI Lovell," she said, "You mentioned that your source passed on some specific information. East Europeans, military background, eight to ten men. Is it possible that the source met one or more of these Huntsmen? And is it possible that he was in some way involved? On the inside, I mean."

Lovell inspected Zoya across the room. Cataloguing her, Zoya thought, just as she had catalogued Lovell a few minutes earlier.

"Those are some of the lines of investigation we are pursuing," Lovell confirmed. "Our source is indeed a low-level member of the Lee End gang; however, he was not present at the scene. And, before you ask, the reason for his absence is that he was the victim of a separate attack several days ago. He can't walk because he has a dislocated kneecap, and he suffered a blow from an unidentified weapon that split his cheek down to the bone and very nearly took an eye out. However, to your other point: it's not clear if he had actual contact with any of the attackers, since as soon as he heard what happened this morning he clammed up and refused to provide any further details. He's terrified out of his mind, which is hardly surprising since the entire leadership of his gang is now dead. We currently have him under police protection, both for his own safety and in the hope that we can eventually calm him down enough to get him talking again."

"Can my partner and I interview him?" Zoya asked, and in the same moment she realised she would need to give some kind of justification for her request.

"You mentioned a possible east European background for zese guys," she improvised, exaggerating her own accent for effect. "If he heard zem talking, maybe ve can figure out vat language zey ver speaking."

Lovell glanced questioningly at Tahiri.

"Lieutenant Zozulya," he said. "From Ukraine."

As if that explained everything. And maybe it did, because Lovell promised to tell her officers to expect Zoya at the source's safehouse at nine o'clock the following morning.

When the meeting ended, Zoya walked the perimeter of the room and examined the crime scene photos one after the other until she reached what was left of Tommy Cartwright. She stood in front of him, ignoring Robin's murmur of horror at her side, and she spent a few minutes thinking about the only other time in her life that she had come across a man who had been attached to a radiator and tortured. Then set on fire.

CHAPTER 14

The man with the round face and the stubby nose who had been following Zoya was used to being yelled at – by drill sergeants on parade grounds, and by arse-covering officers desperate to pin their mission blunders on anyone but the blunderer. Every army did it, and they all expected the same response. Don't move a muscle, stare into the distance and take whatever is thrown at you, then walk away – when dismissed – and don't bear a grudge. But today was different, and only partly because the man thought he had left behind all that break-the-recruits-down-then-build-them-back-up crap. Today, the man was worried. First because he acknowledged that he had messed up. Second because he thought the Hunter was gradually losing touch with reality.

*

The man was known as the Scout. Although the Hunter had never stated it explicitly – he preferred to reserve the option of playing his men off against each other – it was generally accepted that within their organisation the Scout was second among equals. After the boss of course. The reasoning was simple: the bullets sprayed by any one of their soldiers could take or save an individual life; however, only the Scout's reconnaissance expertise and organisational skills could ensure the safety of the entire team. Or kill them all.

The Scout had no false modesty. He was good at his job. He prided himself on being a calm, patient and methodical operator. He also knew he was able to draw on personal experience for every aspect of their missions: target selection, infiltration and surveillance, firefights and sabotage, and – most important of all – extracting himself and his men alive and in one piece. He had been at the sharp end many times. He had survived, and he intended to continue his run of success.

And for nearly three years, their routine had worked well. After the Hunter had identified a potentially interesting and profitable situation, it was the Scout who was despatched to do the groundwork. He researched all sides involved: their leadership, their numbers and weaponry, their financial situation. Their affiliations with other organisations, their influence with local law enforcement, plus any political considerations or government links that could raise the risk profile beyond acceptable levels. He then presented a recommendation to the Hunter – which gang or clan or family they should seek to work with, and which they should seek to eliminate.

Assuming his recommendation was confirmed, which to date it always had been, the Scout was responsible for making initial contact, and he was the only individual the client would ever meet in person. The Hunter believed some degree of face-to-face contact was important, primarily because it gave a trusted member of his team an opportunity to gauge the intent of their client, but he was entirely paranoid about his own face ever being seen. Which, given his history, the Scout could understand. Therefore, whenever the Hunter conducted negotiations himself, his communication was online and securely encrypted. The Hunter had suffered once, he would not let it happen again.

Next, once the shape of their deal began to emerge, came the vital skills of infiltration and exfiltration. Getting the men in unseen. Getting them out alive. Which, since they were not in a warzone, didn't mean choppers or parachute drops. Not usually at least. It meant false identities and travel documents; transportation that circumvented security checks wherever possible. Sea travel was a favourite, since ports generally had less security than airports and there were infinite possibilities for beach or river drop-offs. Separate provision had to be made for bringing in weapons or sourcing them locally. And, last but not least, they needed accommodation where a team of between five and fifteen men could be housed and concealed, and which could be defended if concealment didn't work. With all elements of the plan stress-tested and reinforced with backups, fail-safes and cutouts.

In short, the Scout possessed an impressive skillset. To all of which, if there had ever been a written job description, might have been added a last-line catch-all: the candidate will perform other tasks as requested by management. For example: when requested, kill a man in Liverpool if you happen to be nearby, and make it look like an accident. Or: following the boss's explicit instructions, tail the Ukrainian detective and attempt to discover what she's up to.

And this last one was the reason for the Hunter's fury.

*

"Tell me again, you halfwit!" he yelled across the oak rectory table. "I dare you to tell me again!"

Their temporary base was an abandoned chapel forty miles north of Manchester, within the perimeter of the picturesquely named Bowland Forest. It was easy to guard, secure and secluded, and the fallback was the thousands of acres of dense woodland directly behind them. It was an ideal location, identified and provisioned in advance by the Scout – though much good that would do him. As always in life: achievement would be taken for granted, failure would not be tolerated.

In the boxing club, the Hunter's men had gathered evidence of identification for all the men they had killed. Since they were in the UK there was no requirement to carry a passport or an identity card, but they found a sufficient variety of driving licenses, credit cards, football season passes and library cards to form a list. They had accounted for all the gang's leaders, however the list was still one man short. The missing man wasn't one of the Lee End bigwigs – in fact he was no more than a runner or a messenger. The only reason he had made it onto the Hunter's radar was that he had been responsible for delivering several of his messages to the Scout. It was bad enough that the man had seen the Scout's face on more than one occasion, but the threat didn't stop there. The Scout of course knew everyone else in the team. If he was ever captured, he could bring down all of them.

Therefore, after the assault, the Scout had been despatched to the man's house. He had walked the length of the street and discovered a two-man armed police protection team standing guard. He had known immediately that he would have to tell the Hunter that part; the only question was what to do about the rest. Whether to bluff and suggest that the man's absence had been a coincidence – that he had survived because he had slept in, or because he had food poisoning or the flu, or anything else that came to mind – or to come clean.

And it wasn't a question of principle. The Scout had left those behind a long time ago. The problem was that the Hunter had an uncanny ability to divine the truth, and an ironclad rule to kill without hesitation anyone he caught lying to him. So, the Scout after thinking it through had told him everything.

Now he stood to attention, fists clenched at his sides, eyes staring into the distance somewhere over the Hunter's head.

"He was one of the two men I hired to rough up the professor who's working for Interpol," he said.

"And?"

"And then I paid them to attack the Ukrainian woman."

"And why the fuck did you do that?"

The Scout had already said it once, so he already knew how ridiculous his reason sounded.

"I wanted to see if she was as good as you said, boss."

"And tell me again, what exactly were your fucking conclusions?"

The Scout had watched from the shadows as the woman had circled the car park; as she had retreated under perfect control; as she had used a steel-wire tactical whip to demolish two strong and overconfident men, then walked away as if nothing had happened. His conclusions had been that the woman was pretty damned impressive. Also, although he couldn't be sure, he had thought that she had probably spotted him.

He lowered his eyes to the Hunter's face. It was hardly surprising that the man was losing it. The scars had begun seeping again – he had to be in agony – and then there would be the psychological impact of looking at *that* every day in the mirror. Even so, the biggest rule, the unbreakable rule, of any operation like theirs, was simple. Don't let it get personal. And the Hunter's obsession with the Ukrainian woman seemed undeniably personal to him.

None of which he said. None of which, since the Hunter's hand still rested on the butt of his pistol, he would even think of saying unless his boss ever managed to calm the F down.

CHAPTER 15

On Saturday morning, Zoya was listening to Okean Elzy's "Embrace Me" through her EarPods as she walked from the hotel along empty streets towards the address she had been passed by one of DCI Lovell's officers. The lead singer's voice was hoarse but liquid, and its familiar warmth flowed deep in her heart. For a moment Zoya was homesick, then she began to sing.

Until she reached the corner of the street, where Robin was waiting for her as agreed under the partial shelter of a bare-branched tree. She stopped to say good morning.

It was twelve minutes to nine. They were early, which for Zoya was a rare occurrence since experience had shown her it was often a useful tactic to keep suspects and superiors waiting. However, there were exceptions. Like today. DCI Lovell had passed on a strict warning that Zoya was not to begin her interview before the arrival of the assigned officer from the Organised Crime Unit. Which had seemed fair enough, although when Zoya had heard the instruction she had felt it left some room for interpretation. She had discussed her doubts with Robin to gain his native speaker's perspective. What exactly, she had mused in his direction, did "begin her interview" mean? It seemed to her that, strictly speaking, the interview would only begin when she asked her first question. And that a friendly greeting could surely not be considered part of the interview.

With the same logic, a friendly greeting might be accompanied by a friendly threat, and that too could happen before the interview actually began. At first Robin had tended towards a narrow reading based on what he thought Lovell's intention had been. Fortunately, Zoya's pointedly long silence had given her partner sufficient opportunity to broaden his approach. All of which explained why today she had made her exception and arrived, with Robin in tow, seven minutes ahead of the meeting's scheduled start time.

Which was when, shortly before his nine a.m. shift change, the firearms officer posted by the front door saw a short, wide woman in a black coat, with no umbrella and drenched by the morning's unremitting rain, striding through one of the more dangerous gang-infested areas of Manchester and singing like she was on a school outing. Accompanying her was a slight man with a slight limp and a guilty expression, who didn't seem to know the words to whatever the woman's song was. Luckily, the policeman had been warned more or less what to expect.

Zoya and Robin presented their Interpol IDs, and the officer signed them in. They entered a small living room where a miserable-looking man in shorts and a hoody reclined on a long, charcoal-grey sofa, one leg stretched out and bandaged, opposite a very large flatscreen TV. Zoya left the empty armchair for Robin and bounced herself down onto the sofa at the man's side. She was pleased to see him flinch when he recognised her.

"Hello beautiful," she said and ignored his groan of pain as she pressed a hand solicitously onto his leg.

"I'm sure you understand," she continued, "that the local guys are itching to find a reason to arrest you. Because as soon as they do, you lose any leverage you currently think you have. And that's exactly what will happen if my partner and I decide to describe how you, together with your boxer friend, assaulted first my partner outside his home, and then two days ago attacked me in the car park of the Riverside Restaurant. A car park that, I noticed, had at least one security camera that will back up my account."

She examined the man's face as she spoke and took no pleasure in the damage she had done. The ugly, crusted slash stretched from the back of his neck, under his ear and across his left cheek, and ended just short of his eye. The edges of the deepest part of the cut had been stitched together, and the whole left side of his face was a swollen yellow-green-purple bruise. But then Zoya looked across at Robin; and, for the first time since they had met, she saw real anger in his usually mild-mannered eyes as he stared at the man. And when she remembered Robin's face after the attack, and his cracked ribs, she realised she did feel some pleasure after all.

"What do you want from me?" the man asked.

"Not much. I just want that when the detective arrives you answer all our questions fully and truthfully."

The man didn't reply. He looked at Zoya, he looked at Robin. He nodded and shifted his leg on the sofa, then turned to stare out of the window.

"Perfect," Zoya said. "Now I'm going to make some coffee. Would you like a cup?"

*

When Lovell's man entered the house punctually at nine a.m., he found Zoya and Robin in the kitchen, stirring instant coffee granules into five mugs of steaming water. He introduced himself as Detective Constable Johnson with a look of wide-eyed innocence that suggested his boss's expectations of the meeting were low enough to have despatched her most junior officer.

"For the suspect, for the three of us, and for the officer outside," Zoya said, gesturing at the cups as she examined the new arrival. Jesus, he was young. Or perhaps she was old. In any case: ginger hair, freckled skin, and a skinny-fit, navy-blue suit that left too little to the imagination.

"Now that you're here, let's begin the interview," Robin said brightly.

They carried in two chairs from the kitchen and placed them opposite the sofa. Everyone sat and they sipped genteelly at their coffee.

*

The source's name turned out to be Mickey. In any other circumstances he would have talked up his importance, his credentials and his status in the Lee End hierarchy. Today, his interest was to appear as insignificant a cog as possible: an impression that, Zoya thought, he achieved with remarkably little effort. A few times he had dealt, Mickey admitted, but most of the time all he had done was deliver messages and perform whatever errands Tommy – the boss – asked him to. When Zoya raised an eyebrow, he added that Tommy had told him he was still on probation, and he would get his big opportunity sooner or later. Which, given that he had joined the gang nearly two years back, Zoya figured to mean that somewhere along the way he had been consigned to the too-dumb-to-do-anything-else box.

One day, about four weeks before, Tommy had told Mickey to meet with a man who called himself the Scout. Mickey said Tommy had talked up Mickey's role as go-between, but the more likely interpretation seemed to be that Mickey had served as an expendable cut-out until Tommy had figured out what it was that the Scout wanted, and who he represented. Once Tommy had felt secure enough to invite the Scout to his office, Mickey had also been present – no doubt invisible and forgotten in the background – during several of the calls with the Scout's boss.

"Can you describe this man, the Scout?" Zoya asked.

At her side Johnson sighed mournfully, knowing that DCI Lovell had gone through the same line of questioning and received no meaningful answers.

"Blond hair, a lot of it," Mickey replied. "Round face, quite tanned, small nose. Blue eyes, very cold like. Medium height and a tattoo of a cross on the back of his hand and he talked with a foreign accent. Like."

Johnson started. Then he fumbled through his pockets for his notebook and pen. It was time to take notes.

"Did you ever hear him talking in a different language, or did you just hear the accent?" Zoya asked.

"Yeah, I heard them talking a couple of times on the calls. The Scout guy was in the room, his boss was on the other end of the line. Well, not really a line as such. They were using the Telegram app on their mobiles. You know the one I mean? Anyway, the Scout's boss was, like, giving him instructions in this foreign language. He sounded right bossy, like he was angry all the time."

"OK, that's good," Zoya said. "Then I'm going to try a few languages. You tell us if you hear something that sounds familiar."

She started from home then cycled anticlockwise through the main Eastern Europe countries. The same phrase each time – "Hands up or I'll kill you" – in Ukrainian, Russian, Polish and Serbian. No one cared about Belarussian, but Robin mumbled "Bulgarian" from his armchair and Zoya gave him a grateful smile since she had forgotten the first time round. Each time Mickey's face twisted with effort, but nothing seemed familiar. Having covered the Slavs, she moved onto the rest. Turkish just in case, then the strange anomalies that were Albanian and Hungarian. She counted her blessings that she didn't need to struggle with the Baltics, because at that moment Mickey yelped with delayed-reaction excitement.

"The last one," he said. "That word you just said. *Vras.* They kept on using it. *Vras, vras, vras.* I'm sure."

Zoya took Johnson's notepad and pen from his hands. She covered the page so that Mickey couldn't see it, as if it was a big secret, and wrote: "Vras. To Kill. Albanian". She showed Robin, then Johnson.

"How about names?" she asked. "You met a guy who called himself the Scout. Did you ever hear a real name for him, or nicknames or real names for anyone else on the line?"

"Just the one," Mickey replied. "My boss Tommy asked what name he should use for the guy he was talking to. The guy said to call him the Hunter."

It was at this point that Johnson decided he should also contribute to the meeting. Which he did by blundering straight into a line of questioning Zoya had wanted to leave to the end.

"There's one thing that isn't making sense, Mickey," he said. "If your boss was negotiating with these Albanian characters – Scout and Hunter – how come it was the Lee End gang that ended up as the victim?"

Mickey stared around him with a sudden expression of terror as if he had only just remembered the massacre that had happened the previous day. Then he uttered every criminal's favourite TV-serial line.

"That's all I'm saying. If you want the rest of what I know, I need a deal."

Zoya sat back and glared in frustration at Johnson. He was young and inexperienced; he had plunged in, reached the main event far too fast, and his rushed approach had left Zoya way short of satisfied. Still, it wasn't all bad. They had made some progress. Zoya had been able to leverage Mickey and friend's gratuitous car park attack into some useful information: that the assault team were Albanians, probably; that two of them had nicknames, Scout and Hunter, which seemed childish to Zoya; and what was all that shit with the calling card? And why did it feel like there was a message in there for her that she didn't quite understand? Anyway, at least the police now had a moderately accurate description of the Scout, and Zoya had a perfect one, since the features of the man who had been tailing her were impressed like a watermark in her mind. Plus, she realised, there was a potential trap to be set, although she knew that Lovell wouldn't like her idea. And Robin would positively hate it.

So, it was just as well, Zoya thought, that she still had another bargaining chip or two to play.

CHAPTER 16

The Hunter wasn't sure if it was the painkillers wearing off or the coke kicking in. Whatever it was, his skin was crawling with ants and burning with tiny flames – a million fire ants with their claws and their ugly, burning, biting jaws, crawling across his face, chewing at his flesh – and he wanted to scream, and he wanted to smash them away, even when he knew there was nothing there. And what was that shit with his hair? Like he was moulting, the strands and tufts bunched every morning in the teeth of his comb. Or was it all in his mind? Was he imagining all this crazy, weird, whacked-out shit? It was the coke, it had to be. Delusions, illusions – whatever the hell the difference was. He knew he should stop, and at the same time he reached for more. His mouth was dry with his need; the white powder was glossed and slick, mixed with the sweat on his fingertips, as he reached up to smear it over his gums.

"Boss?"

A voice from far away.

"Boss?"

The Scout, sticking his nose in like he always did. But no, he was unfair. The Scout was his friend, his brother-in-arms from the killing fields where it had all started to go wrong. His friend was worried about him, that was all. And, being honest for once, he had every reason to be.

The Hunter knew he had to pull himself together. It was natural enough to want to celebrate after their win, but the coke had been a mistake. Especially coming so soon after his interrogation of the Lee End gang's boss, and with the stench of petrol still fresh in his nostrils. Torture always gave him a high, and his nerves were on edge, that was all it was. Which meant he needed a downer, not an upper. The Hunter let his hand fall back.

"Brother, sit with me," he said. "I know you've always got a bottle of something good stashed away. Let's drink, let's talk."

Painkillers, coke and whiskey; it was a godawful mix, but still he welcomed the warm burn of the first gulp, then with each sip he let the harsh tangle of his thoughts slip and drift away.

The setting was gothic: a small side-room with a view of the altar; for enrobing, disrobing – whatever it was that priests did before and after. A stained-glass window coloured the moonlight. Panelled walls and heavy oak furniture were carved with the wings of cheerful cherubs and hung with the crossbeams of crucifixion. Since space was limited, the Hunter was sharing the room with the Scout, their camping mattresses and sleeping bags rolled up on the floor whilst the rest of the men lined the nave. Eighteenth-century, the Scout had said, it had been a private chapel for the hunting estate down the road. The manor house had burned down decades before – a freak accident, a lightning strike or perhaps an insurance claim – then the chapel had been abandoned by the faithless. He talked too much, the Scout, and he still thought that senseless history could give meaning to the senseless present. This present, their present, where a derelict chapel sheltered a group of mercenaries on the run.

There, he had said it. Mercenaries. That's how low he had been brought, because everything else he had tried had failed. First his home on the outskirts of Kosovo had been shelled by the Serbian army. Then worse horrors had arrived when the Serb police entered the destroyed village. The executions, the rapes, the beatings and abuse. The terrible things they did, the terrible things he had been forced to watch. The surviving villagers had trekked through the nights and slept during the days as they struggled towards the Albanian border. It had taken a week and they had lost more on the way. When the remnants of his family had reached safety, he had returned to fight. It was then that he became the Hunter; when he had begun to chase down and execute the men who had destroyed everything he had loved. And in the end, he had let himself become no better than they were. There was no court, and no evidence to present. His rule was that it was better to kill than to let a suspect go free. The Hunter knew there was nothing noble in what he did; that he had transformed himself into a starving, wounded wolf that howled with pain in the night; one that emerged from the forest to chew on the bones of the guilty and the innocent alike, then skulked away into the dark and the snow. Sated, until the next time.

The war had ended. The Hunter had at least had the strength to know that this revenge would be never-ending and all-consuming if he let it control him. He had fought against his instinct, his need. He had ideas, he had made plans, he had wanted to build something. Something criminal, to be sure – what other option was there? – but something that would at least be better than what had gone before. There had been disappointments along the way, there had been failures, but finally the Hunter had found something that seemed to work. That had worked until the day when . . .

Enough. It had worked, and then it hadn't. That was the nature of life, and the Hunter had forced himself to accept that he had to reinvent himself. Yet again. And, this time round, he had decided not to plunge himself into the next bright idea that came along. He would take a more reasoned and considered approach. He had begun, as every good businessman should, by researching the market. And he had come to a singular conclusion. His study of organised crime operations around the world had highlighted for him the one simple weakness that he believed had been the undoing of every mafia and crime gang in history.

Every gang, every family, every time: they all had always begun their life in a specific town or region, with a specific geographic focus; and, even when they expanded, they remained wedded to their starting point. Therefore, since they were essentially immobile, they were forced to expend huge resources not on the productive growth of their business, but simply to ensure the security of their local base, and therefore their own survival. At the same time, the more successful they were, the more attractive a target they became, both for law enforcement and for other gangs. Out of necessity, their teams of heavies grew into private armies. Their envelopes of cash to the local cops swelled to suitcases for regional and national politicians. To the Hunter, it was clear that the net result was always going to be a guarantee of diminishing returns, whether those returns were measured purely financially or in the eventual captivity or death of the gang's leaders and men. In short, he had found the concept unoriginal and essentially self-defeating.

Research completed, the Hunter had decided he would no longer accept the fallback position that was meek and uninspiring imitation, or even allow himself to believe that it could ever be enough simply to implement an inherently doomed concept better than it had previously been implemented. His ambition was different. He would become a disrupter. His business would require low capital investment yet ensure a sky-high return, and over time he would create a platform with multiple opportunities for profitable spin-offs. Instead of seeking to rival the established crime families, he would exploit the weakness he had identified. And the genius part of it all was the payment structure.

In addition to a fixed fee, negotiated in advance, his terms included the right to strip the vanquished enemy of any and all property they possessed. In another age it would have been called looting; in today's cut-throat business world he saw himself as taking the logic of asset-stripping to its natural extreme. It was corporate raiding with a juicy, tangy citrus twist. Private equity firms, after all, did much the same. They took over a business, they secured every valuable asset they could find, they hacked staff costs to the bone, then they moved on to the next target. The Hunter would simply reverse the process. His first step would be to axe the troublesome workers – or shoot, or bomb, or whatever was most convenient – and only then would he follow up by seizing everything the losing side had worked so hard to accumulate (cash, crypto, bullion and drugs being his preference, but the Hunter really wasn't choosy).

The concept had already proved its viability. The profit and loss account from each of the first two years of operations was astronomically in the black. There was no shortage of clients, and they found their way to him entirely by word-of-mouth, with no advertising required. In fact, the Hunter's challenge was exactly the opposite – he and his men had far more work than they could handle. Which had been a clear indicator that it was time for stage two of his plan.

First there was franchising. The Huntsmen brand had a high level of recognition in its market niche, which gave him an ideal opportunity to leverage the model he had created. The Hunter had already recruited a second team and they were currently doing a reasonable job on their first special project, even if the Hunter thought their leader might eventually need to be replaced. That didn't worry him too much – there was no rush, after all; they would take baby steps before they began to run – but the end picture was clear. The Hunter would control a pool of trained and quality-controlled teams operating under an umbrella structure; their results would be guaranteed to the client; their revenues apportioned, to ensure a generous share of the profit from each operation flowed up through the organisation in return for the right to use his concept, his brand and his logistical support.

Then there was diversification. Here the Hunter's long-term concept was to evolve into a one-stop shop capable of supplying all his criminal clients' needs. He already had a deal in the works that would add the first entirely new service line to the core offering. Admittedly it had been a bumpy ride so far, throwing up pretty much all the difficulties highlighted during his extensive reading of the corporate acquisition case studies (valuation gaps, a business owner whose expectations needed to be managed, a number of team members who had proved resistant to joining a different cultural environment – at which point even the Hunter had to smile at how he was dressing it up). The simple truth for any business he elected to take over, current or future, was that either they accepted his offer or someone died. That was the advantage he had – his ability to combine a keen understanding of business theory with the backstop of extreme violence.

It was a combination that meant the possibilities were endless.

If only she didn't screw it all up again. And then the ants were crawling on his face again, and he slapped at himself with a rough palm to brush away what wasn't there.

"Boss, should we give the men the good news?"

The Scout once more, trying to distract him. And succeeding, more or less. The Hunter drained the last finger of whiskey from his steel mess cup. He stood and pulled himself straight. He holstered his sidearm and he became the only thing that always kept him grounded and sane. The visionary, the leader of his men.

He walked into the nave, lit by storm lanterns, where he stood tall and proud.

"Brothers, we did well yesterday," he said. "First and most importantly, there were no deaths and no injuries on our side. Soon we will all return to our families. Which isn't to say that everything went smoothly. There was that little last-minute change of plans when the Lee End fuckers forgot who they were dealing with."

An appreciative rumble of laughter.

"But as you know, this wasn't the first occasion a client has proved less than reliable, and we were prepared. Thanks to the Scout's excellent reconnaissance, we were able to negotiate in short order with the competition. We secured a flat fee for our services to eliminate the Lee End gang, with the added agreement that we would help ourselves as usual to whatever we found in the process. So that fee was our starting point – four hundred thousand British pounds."

He looked around at seven hungry men and let them stew for a moment. He knew as well as they did that, divided between them, four hundred thousand would have been slim pickings. He held up the device he had taken from around the neck of the Lee End boss.

"And now, welcome to the new digital word. This tiny piece of plastic and metal holds a sizeable stack of Bitcoin and Ethereum – which I had heard of – and something called Tether, which is a new one for me. All in all, it's worth just over two million US, and since I was able to persuade dear Mr Tommy fucking Cartwright to reveal his passcodes, we have full and untraceable access. Then, in addition to the crypto, we also liberated a stash of fifteen kilograms of high-grade coke from the boxing club. To avoid the hassle of transporting it out of the country I've reached an agreement to sell it on to our new Manchester client with a twenty percent discount off street value. That will bring in an additional million US, give or take. And finally, there's the smaller stuff – cash, watches and jewellery – that we took from the dead men. Probably close to a hundred thousand there as well – not huge, but it will help to cover our expenses."

"You're killing us boss," one of the men called out. "What's the split look like?"

"With a two-times share for me," the Hunter continued, "and a one-and-a-half-times-share for the Scout – everything transparent and accounted for as always – each of you will receive approximately three hundred thousand dollars. I'll be able to confirm the exact amount in a few days. Not bad, I think you will agree, for a morning's work."

Applause and cheers under the vaulted ceiling, and the Hunter bowed his thanks. Next it was the Scout's turn.

"All the money in the world is no use to us," he said, "if we're stuck in a ruined church in the middle of a forest. So now I'll take you through the exfil plans. As always, we will avoid moving everyone at the same time, plus we have a small additional task here. I will be asking for three volunteers to remain here with me and the boss for the next ten days and earn themselves a nice little bonus in the process. The other four men leave tomorrow, heading east."

The Hunter zoned out as the Scout explained details he already knew. Then his phone rang. He walked back into the side room to take the call. It was good news. Scout Two, recruited six months ago and still desperate to earn his spurs, had made a breakthrough.

"I have a new job," he said; in English, since he was the first non-Albanian the Hunter had allowed onto the team. "I'll be heading to the region tomorrow or the day after. With time for initial recce, I expect we'll be able to commence negotiations within three days."

"Do it carefully," the Hunter said. "This last job has presented some client-related challenges. I want the next one to be smoother."

He rang off.

It had been the Hunter's decision to recruit a second scout – the first small step in his long-term plan – since it was clear that the time needed for reconnaissance had become a bottleneck in their system. This way they could always be working on the next deal, and the assault team could keep moving from one target to the next. The Scout – he really hated being called Scout One – had been against it. Just as he had been against the calling card idea. He hadn't understood that they needed to consolidate their branding position. He had said they had a good thing going, that they had achieved a solid reputation whilst keeping a low profile. He had said they shouldn't put everything at risk. The Hunter had overruled him, but he hadn't appreciated the challenge.

And yes, he knew that one of the possible side effects of his ongoing coke habit was paranoia. But he couldn't help thinking that Scout One – his friend, his brother-in-arms – was preparing to make a run at the top dog position.

Paranoid or not, the Hunter dipped his finger back into the powder and this time he didn't even try to stop himself. The wave hit him an instant later; the buzz, the glow, flooding through his body. His hands swept over his head, his nails scratched at his scalp, and when the Hunter lowered his arms his hands were trembling and his fingers were tangled with long black strands of hair.

CHAPTER 17

"I'm sorry about Crimea," DCI Lovell said, referring to Russia's annexation of Ukraine's territory in February 2014, just over a year prior.

They were Lovell's first words after they had taken their places at a corner table under a well-used wall-mounted dartboard, and for a moment Zoya wanted to hug the detective. Instead, she tunnelled her gaze into the laminated menu and concentrated on the bacon, sausage and egg butty that was on offer for £3.50 on toast or a brioche bun with Heinz red or HP brown sauce. Once she had everything back under control, Zoya looked up; and if her eyes were a little moist, Lovell didn't seem to notice.

"That was impressive work this morning," Lovell continued. "I got a very confused account from young Detective Constable Johnson, so I'm interested to hear how you managed to get under Mickey's skin so fast."

Then the waitress arrived. Lovell ordered the same B.S.E butty that Zoya had been contemplating – toast and brown sauce – and Zoya knew this was a woman she didn't want even to try to deceive. She confessed. She told Lovell about the man who had been following her, motives unknown. She described the attack in the car park, motives also unknown, and apologised humbly for not having reported the incident earlier. Lovell grinned.

"Nice one," she said. "And it's good that you told me, since I already knew. Maybe you were looking to build trust with me, but I suspect you also thought I would already have figured it out. Johnson said you arrived ten minutes before he did. Mickey wanted to cut his little deal, so one of my conditions was that he tell me how you got him to talk. Now that we both know we're not stupid, let's eat. And I'm afraid we'll need to be fast, since I have to get back to work."

They were two hundred metres from the office in a pub on a busy road, which looked like an ordinary house to which extra satellite dishes had been added and a one-storey brick extension tacked to the front. When Zoya had suggested they speak, Lovell had mentioned she hadn't had time for breakfast and said it was a choice between the New Crown Inn and the Delightful Garden Chinese Restaurant, and she didn't have anything against Chinese food but thought MSG was better for dinner than for lunch. Zoya had realised that Lovell was already thinking one step ahead and had decided she would prefer to consider whatever idea Zoya was planning to put to her out of the hearing of her OCU colleagues. Zoya also thought it was just as well she had an ace hidden up her sleeve.

Then the food came and Zoya discovered a new love in her life. Tangy; layers of tomato with a bite of spice and vinegar and a lick of molasses. The wondrous tamarind-inspired creation that was HP Sauce.

"I'll be taking some of this back home to Odesa with me," she said, brandishing the tall, square-sided bottle.

So they talked about Ukraine whilst they ate. Which didn't take long. Lovell was slim, but she had no problem packing her food away; and Zoya wasn't, but she had decided this wasn't the best time to order seconds.

"What else did you get out of Mickey?" Zoya asked.

"A few useful things," Lovell replied. "First, his account of the negotiations. He said the Hunter kept dressing it up pretty like – Mickey's words, not mine – with all kinds of corporate terminology, which his boss Tommy kept laughing about. Not hugely significant, but maybe it gives an idea of the Hunter's psychology. He kills and he tortures but he wants to see himself as something more. In the same vein, the Hunter said that if Tommy had any doubts about how good his team was, he should look into a couple of the jobs they did over the last few years. He mentioned the one your director talked about, with the Syrian people traffickers, and also a job in Sweden eight months ago involving two rival biker gangs. Which I've checked on, and it did actually happen, with a similar MO, so that's a good admission of involvement to have on record."

"Or it could just be an attempt to claim credit," Zoya pointed out.

"Or that," Lovell agreed. "Then back to DC Johnson's rather premature question about how the Lee End gang started out as the client and ended up as the target. There were only two possibilities really: either Tommy and the Hunter weren't able to make a deal, or they made a deal and Tommy went back on it. Mickey confirmed it was the latter. He said Tommy started drinking, then he started snorting coke, then he started mouthing off at the Hunter. Threatened him and tried to renegotiate. Trying to prove to his men how big his balls were. Which obviously backfired spectacularly."

"So simple revenge by the Hunter for this Tommy guy insulting and betraying him; or, as an alternative, or a bonus maybe, the Hunter could have made a last-minute agreement with the people they were originally supposed to take out."

"And we've spoken with them," Lovell said. "The Braintree Boys, from the estates to the north of Lee End. They're smaller, but faster-growing. Jamaican roots. They of course deny any knowledge of the Hunter and his merry men, although their boss didn't even try to hide his glee that their main rival had been exterminated. In any case, for now we have nothing concrete to tie them to the Hunter."

"Do you know if the original negotiations included any discussion about the Lee End guys providing practical support for the job? Weapons, transport, a safehouse, anything like that?"

Lovell nodded approvingly.

"Yeah, I had the same thought," she said. "But it seems not. The Scout arrived on the scene before Tommy Cartwright even knew about the group's existence. The Hunter and the rest of the men came later, but there seems to have been no discussion about supplying weapons or transport, nor about helping them with their escape."

"So equally they wouldn't have asked for anything from these Braintree guys," Zoya said. "Especially if a Braintree agreement was made at short notice. Which means they arrange their own logistics, and I have to think they'd be too careful to make a sudden break for the border with a ten-man team. But I assume you've alerted all airports and ports anyway?"

Zoya realised it was a potentially insulting question. Luckily Lovell didn't take offense.

"First thing we did," she confirmed. "The alert we issued was complicated by the lack of descriptions, but even so I tend to agree with you. The UK's borders are a little less porous than moving from one country to another within mainland Europe, and if they have any sense they'll be cautious and take their time. And I agree they certainly won't want to move as one big group. My bet is that they're holed up somewhere relatively close for now, hoping for our attention to die down, but I could be wrong. And even if I'm right, frankly we have no idea where they could be. The van they used in the attack was found abandoned nearby, in Lee End territory, and of course the gang makes sure there's no working CCTV anywhere near them. And there are no witnesses; at least, none who are willing to talk. Therefore, we have no idea what vehicles they transferred to, and no way of tracking them."

"Then either we hope someone stumbles across a group of suspicious men at a safehouse somewhere and calls it in, or—"

"Or," Lovell interrupted, "you finally get round to telling me what's on your mind."

Zoya smiled. Then her eyes flashed, and she became deadly serious as she set out her idea.

"The Scout is their weak link," she said. "He knows Mickey can identify him, which wouldn't have been a problem if

Mickey had been in the boxing club on Friday, serving tea or whatever they have him doing. Therefore, we can assume the Hunters now have some level of interest in taking Mickey out, although admittedly that will be balanced by the desire to leave the country as fast as possible. But what they don't know is that I've also seen the Scout; that I spotted him tailing me a few days back. Which, since I have Interpol's resources behind me, means I can chase the Scout across Europe, not just here in the UK. I'm thinking that has to make me more of a threat than Mickey, in their eyes at least. So, how about we get Mickey to tell them what I know? We can dress it up as Mickey trying to cut a deal – his safety in return for telling them how they can get to me. There's no guarantee of course, but at least it's a chance to bring them out of hiding. Instead of us chasing them, we bring them to us."

Lovell decided their discussion was worth dessert. She ordered something called a jam roly-poly, served with something Zoya had heard of but never tried – custard. Zoya asked for two helpings of chocolate cake. And custard too. And coffee, of course. Both Lovell and Zoya checked their phones as they waited. Lovell had a text from her boss asking for an update, and she fired off a quick response. Zoya had a text from Robin, saying he had some new information he wanted to discuss. She was about to reply, honestly she was, but the incoming twin plates of cake distracted her attention. And then Lovell was talking.

"My guess," she said, "was that you were going to suggest Mickey as bait. Which I had mixed feelings about. I know he's a gang member, and there's the whole thing with him attacking you. And the other Interpol guy before that. Even so, I feel kind of sorry for him; he's a toerag who's clearly way out of his depth. But you're actually suggesting yourself as bait."

"Mhmm," Zoya replied through a mouthful of layered chocolate whilst she wondered what a toerag was. "We can keep Mickey out of it completely. Physically, I mean. They used Telegram to speak before, so we just do the same. Mickey doesn't need to go anywhere near them."

"The first possibility," Lovell said, "and quite a likely one, is that they don't take the bait. That would be the conservative course of action – they stay holed up wherever they are until they try to leave the country. In which case your idea doesn't achieve anything, but it doesn't lose anything either. In any case, we're not going to stop searching for them. Maybe we find them, maybe we don't. But even if they do come after you, if they have any sense they wouldn't involve the Scout since we know what he looks like. In fact, if they're smart, they'd just send their sniper. They'd put him somewhere on a rooftop and shoot you down when you're leaving the hotel in the morning, or when you arrive at the office, or when you go on your next walkabout around town. There are a lot of possibilities, and we're not the Secret Service – we don't have the manpower to guard against all of them."

"It's a risk," Zoya agreed. "But I don't think that's how it will go down. From what I see, this Hunter guy takes things very personally. Look at what he did to Tommy. Even if he needed information, he could just have put a bullet in his head when he was done. But the Hunter took his time torturing him, and then, when the guy was still alive, he set fire to him. I think he enjoyed it, or at least it satisfied some deep psychological need. To me that doesn't sound like a man who'd send a sniper to do anything that was remotely personal for him."

"I agree, but I'm not sure that makes it any better," Lovell said. "If you're right, then instead of a nice, calm sniper, you'd have a highly skilled psychopath after you with petrol and a match. And we have no idea what he looks like."

Since Zoya had finished the second portion of her dessert, she felt it was time to come clean. She told Lovell what she had seen before, just over three years back.

That there had been another man, chained to another radiator. Three fingers had been severed from his right hand, although admittedly in their case the digits had never been found. The man's body had been sliced and stabbed by multiple knife wounds, each carefully sited to cause pain but not death – wounds just like the initial forensics report had identified in the corpse of Tommy Cartwright. Then the man, when he had to have been close to death, had been burned alive.

Then Zoya told Lovell that she didn't have a name for their suspect. But she did have a photo.

CHAPTER 18

When they returned to town, the Scout's role was limited to driver, which he accepted but didn't like. He pulled his cap low over his face and got on with the job. He had at least been able to give the rest of the team a few starters for their reconnaissance. The woman's hotel, including her room number; the location of the Interpol office within the Greater Manchester Police building; the name and address of Professor Robin Rutherford and the registration number of his car; and the pages of the Scout's own neatly noted observations on Zoya's daily routine, although the Scout admitted his information was incomplete and subject to change.

The Scout's other contribution was the serviced apartment he had leased when he first arrived in town. He had registered with a fake French ID card and paid with a shell company's untraceable corporate card. There were still twenty days left to run on his two-month lease. It was in a purpose-built block on a bustling street on the outskirts of the city centre, and with multiple new guests moving in and out every day they would not stand out. It also had PIN code access from the street instead of a reception desk, to keep the owner's costs down. It was a risk, like everything else in life, but as far as they knew none of their faces were known to the police except for the Scout's.

The Hunter thought the risk level was acceptable, so they set up shop, told the Scout to stay out of sight, and set to work.

On the first day, the sniper was tasked with investigating sites for possible overwatch or assassination. He headed first to the Interpol office and excluded it immediately. The heavy police presence was an obvious challenge, but it wasn't the biggest issue. Worse was that the building stood on raised ground, next to a bare grass roundabout then a busy main road with no parking. Beyond the main road there was a wide stretch of two-storey houses, all of which stood on land that was lower than the target building. There was simply nowhere he could take a shot from.

He returned to the city centre. Directly opposite the Edwardian Hotel, on the other side of Peter Street, stood a multistorey car park. He walked the floors – bottom to top, then back down again – discovering that from the top three storeys he would have a good downward angle of fire, not too steep, with perfect visibility of the hotel's main entrance. He imagined backing a van up to the low exterior wall and firing from inside the vehicle. He thought everything was perfectly feasible, yet there were two problems. First, that the Scout had reported that, when he was watching her, the woman had used both front and rear entrances of the hotel – the car park giving coverage only of the front of the building. The second concern was that, even if the woman used the front entrance, the sniper would have at best a few seconds to identify her and take his shot. Still, he reported, it was a possible location, especially if he had the luxury of a spotter to tell him when the woman was about to enter his field of view.

On day two, the sniper was sent off with a different brief: to prepare for a scenario in which they had an opportunity to direct the woman to a specific location. He walked the town and identified two preferred sites. The first was a riverside pub with an open veranda overlooking the water, and with a thick tree line on the opposite bank where he could put his nest. The second was the city's touristic quay area, where pedestrian walkways circled each of the water basins and where he identified multiple oversight spots on the roofs of the surrounding buildings.

The sniper worked patiently and diligently, each evening reporting his progress. The Hunter appeared satisfied with his reports, but gave no indication of a decision or even a preference. The sniper accepted this calmly; as a natural part of his profession, in which long hours of preparation occasionally brought a result but more often didn't. Yet, as a watchful man, he was concerned by the other thing he had observed. That the Hunter had changed. He had always been temperamental, but not like this. The mood swings, the feverishly darting eyes, the staccato bursts of speech followed by long minutes of silence. They were the exact opposite of the sniper's nature, they scared him, and he told himself that once he had finished this job, he would look for a new employer.

*

The Hunter also set off each morning. He went alone and gave no indication of where he was going or what he was doing. It was on the second evening, when he was sitting in the apartment with the Scout and a reheated chicken tikka masala curry from an overpriced supermarket down the street, that a call – no name visible – came through the Telegram app on his mobile. He put the phone on speaker mode, no video, and took the call.

It was Mickey, the feeble-minded Lee Ender. His voice pleaded. He said everyone was after him. The Braintree Boys were mopping up the last of the Lee End gang, and he knew he was a target; the police were telling him they would arrest him if he didn't agree to testify about the Scout and the Hunter; and, if he went to jail, that too was a guaranteed death sentence. Mickey said all he wanted was to run – maybe down south to London, maybe to leave the country – but in either case he had no money. He claimed to have information for the Hunter and asked for a modest payment in return. Twenty big ones would do the job, he said. Or ten, he said, as he bargained himself down. The Hunter thought for a moment. He gave one short instruction and made a promise he didn't know yet if he would keep.

"Fifty-fifty," the Scout said when the call ended. "Either he's just stupid, or he's stupid and someone's using him."

The Hunter thought he didn't need the Scout to tell him the obvious.

An hour later, he wandered into the living room and announced that he was sick of sharing an apartment with three other guys and their takeaways and their dodgy hygiene. His men sniffed at unwashed clothes and armpits and accepted the criticism. After a few minutes, the Hunter apologised for the last part and said, "Guys, it was nothing personal", and his men knew something was wrong because sorry was not a word they had ever heard emerge from their boss's mouth.

Then the Hunter told them he had found somewhere else to stay, but he didn't say where. He said he had an idea on how to deal with the woman, but he didn't tell them what it was. He told them he would call when if he needed support, but he didn't say when. Then he left.

CHAPTER 19

On the day after Zoya's lunch with Lovell, nothing happened. Which was pretty much as Zoya had expected. They had agreed that Lovell would need time to mount her surveillance operation, and that Mickey should call only once she was ready. There was of course no reason for the Hunter to expect an offer of help from Mickey or anyone else, and therefore there was no reason for Zoya to suppose that he would be sitting and waiting for the weather from the sea, as Ukrainians liked to say. Or twiddling his thumbs, as the English put it.

If the Hunter had in fact decided to stick around to tie off the loose ends that Mickey or Zoya represented, he would probably already have started his search. However, Zoya didn't think the threat was imminent. First it would take time for the Hunter's men to locate their targets. Then, the one thing that Zoya was already sure about was that the Hunter was a man who wouldn't rush into an attack. His endgame might involve either subtlety or overwhelming violence, but in either case he would plan conservatively, he would consider all contingencies, and he would make very certain he had a secure exit route.

Therefore, for now, Zoya reassured herself, she was safe. Relatively speaking. Which didn't explain her overflowing sensation that *he* was out there somewhere. Watching, waiting.

Hunting. She knew neither the feeling nor the words made any sense. Of course, he, or they, were out there *somewhere* – by definition, since they existed. But his somewhere could be just round the corner – armed with a radiator, some cable ties and a very sharp knife – or it could be back in Albania or wherever the hell else the Huntsmen called home. Or, after the exertion of hundreds of rounds fired into almost defenceless flesh, followed by the Hunter's stimulating torture and barbecue session, the team could have jetted off to sun themselves on a tropical beach thousands of kilometres away. Zoya knew all this, but it didn't help. She still couldn't shake the tingle between her shoulders.

So, she swore loudly and repeatedly – *pizdets, pizdets, pizdets* – shrugged her tingling shoulders, and then got back to work.

*

First, Zoya contacted her boss, strictly speaking her ex-boss, in Odesa and asked for the relevant files to be scanned and emailed. Major Dobroshtan had grumbled, complaining that it was Sunday, and he was at his dacha, but he had promised to put someone on it.

A few hours later she was ready for a sit-down with DCI Lovell and Director Tahiri. Everyone would be working weekends until the case was solved.

"I was brought in," Zoya said "after the Fire Department tackled a blaze at a factory in Odesa's main port. The firemen already suspected arson, then they discovered this."

Zoya handed over the photos.

"The first similarity, strangely enough, is that the victim was attached to a radiator. Maybe that isn't particularly significant, but it was actually the first thing that caught my attention. Then of course there's the use of fire on both cases, although there was one big difference. Here in Manchester, just the victim himself was set on fire, whereas in Odesa the whole factory was burnt down, with the man inside."

"But he was also alive when the fire started?" Tahiri asked.

"He was. Forensics showed the victim had significant smoke inhalation and also trauma to his arms and legs from thrashing around when the fire reached him. But even when you put those two things together, the radiator and the fire aren't conclusive on their own – they were just enough to get me thinking. After all, I'm sure we could find numerous cases over the years of people being interrogated and set on fire – I understand it's a party favourite with Mexican drug cartels, for example – and for that to work the victim would have to be restrained somehow. However, when I looked at the forensics report for the Lee End guy, it struck me that the knife wounds followed a similar pattern to something I had seen before. And now that I had a chance to re-read our Odesa ME's report, I can tell you that the pattern's not just similar, it's virtually identical."

She laid down the two forensics reports side by side.

"Ours is in Ukrainian, but you can see the wounds marked on the body diagram, and you'll have to take my word for the rest. First, the two reports reflect an almost identical conclusion on the size and type of knife used. A straight-edged blade, approximately twenty centimetres long and five centimetres wide. With that weapon, multiple stab wounds were inflicted in both cases, with almost identical placement. There was a total of eighteen in our Odesa victim, nineteen here in Manchester, and I would say it takes considerable skill and discipline to stab someone that many times without killing them. Especially when more than half of the wounds were to the torso. Then we shouldn't forget the fingers – the same three digits on the same hand were severed in both cases. It's an interesting combination: complete and horrific violence, but inflicted very carefully. It's like the killer's following a blueprint he has in his head; and we can't tell, but I'd bet he even follows a defined sequence."

"It's not a hundred percent, but it's certainly persuasive," Lovell said. "Let's assume for now it's the same person. What can you tell us about the background of your Odesa case? Why was this specific factory targeted for example, and the guy inside? Do you see any similarities there?"

"To be honest, not so much. Which doesn't change my conclusion that it's the same killer, but I have to admit that the situation and motivation were very different. The first thing is that there was only one victim in Odesa. He was the owner of the factory, and he was abducted from his home in the middle of the night by either three or four men, then transported to the factory. His wife and two children were tied up but not harmed. The wife saw the abductors, but they wore gloves and masks, and she wasn't able to add anything useful. Apart from the owner no one else was targeted, and there was no collateral damage. That's quite a different set of facts from the boxing club attack. Moving on to the factory itself – it was a family business, medium size with about sixty employees. It manufactured all kinds of industrial chemicals and solvents, for use both in Ukraine and for export. At first it looked quite innocent, but once we focused on the details we understood they had a definite specialisation. When you put it all together, it was clear they were shipping a complete shopping list of all the input chemicals needed to produce synthetic drugs. All the recipient would have to do would be to mix everything in the right proportions, press it into pills, and package and ship the finished product."

"And what was the motive to take the factory out?" Lovell asked.

"We never got a definitive answer, just lots of theories. Maybe it was a competitor, or maybe someone just didn't like what they were doing. Perhaps the owner owed someone money, or he paid off the wrong guys for protection. We even thought about a real estate angle, because the factory was in a prime location in the port. Like I said, we never got to the bottom of it – and that's also different from here, where we were able to identify a clear business arrangement, which was mixed in with revenge later on."

"And your photo of the suspected perpetrator?" Lovell said. "That was an interesting story?"

"That's for sure," Zoya replied with a smile. "We'd pretty much given up on identification since there were no witnesses and the computers that stored the factory CCTV coverage were fried in the fire. Then we found the factory's safe – a big, old-fashioned floor unit – which we opened to see if cash or documents had been taken. There was no cash, but we did find something completely different. The wife told us later that four people had access to the safe: the owner and the wife, since it was their business, plus the factory's chief accountant and their lawyer. The problem was that money had been going missing; small amounts, but regularly. The owner knew it wasn't him and he trusted his wife, or at least he said he did, but he had no way of telling which of the other two was stealing. Or if someone else had got the combination somehow. So, he had decided to install a miniature camera – battery powered and motion sensitive – at the back of the safe."

"Beautiful," Tahiri exclaimed. "And instead of catching a thief, it caught a killer?"

"It did. The killer must have got the combination from the owner. He opened the safe, he bent down and reached inside to take the cash, and the camera filmed him. Full face, good definition. Luckily, he closed the safe door behind him, and the safe was sufficiently heat resistant to protect the camera. We had his picture, but we never found a name. Admittedly we were concentrating on locals, by which I mean Ukrainians and Russians; we didn't have anything back then that suggested an Albanian or other foreign connection. We had a local alert out for him for over a year, with no results. After that I persuaded my boss to put out an Interpol red notice just in case, but we never got any hits."

Lovell had already seen the photo; Zoya passed it to Tahiri. The image wasn't perfect, mainly because the man's face was backlit as he stared into the dark of the safe, but it was good enough. He was around forty years old; his hair was blond and short-cropped; his skin was wrinkled and tanned from an outdoors life; he had light coloured eyes – maybe blue, maybe grey – and over the right eye you could make out the darker blotch of a mole or a birthmark. His lips were thin, with a slight twist up to the right. He could have been handsome if he didn't look so angry.

"We already distributed it," Lovell confirmed. "And the facial recognition systems we use are pretty sophisticated. If this is our guy, and if he appears either back in town, or at any border checkpoint, there's a good chance we'll pick him up."

*

Robin was waiting for Zoya in the corridor outside Tahiri's office. He seemed to be having difficulty standing still, which Zoya interpreted as a sign of either excitement or a delayed need to use the bathroom. Next came a sudden flash of guilt, since it was only when she saw him that Zoya realised she had forgotten to reply to Robin's message the previous day. For that matter, she had hardly even thought about his Dutchmen since her return to England. Zoya knew Robin deserved better, but then again she also knew how rarely people – criminals or detectives – got what they deserved.

"Sorry, I know you have other things going on," he said with a nervous smile. "But I have a couple of things for you."

"Go for it," she said.

"The first thing is about Dusmanic. We never got round to discussing my idea about anagrams, but I looked into it anyway. If you remember, one of the variants I found was the word Scandium. At first that didn't look particularly relevant. Scandium's one of the so-called rare-earth elements, which in this case sounds more exciting than it actually is. As far as I can tell, it's not particularly valuable and the total volumes produced are far too small to be worth killing over. Also, it's mined in various locations, including by the way in Ukraine, so even if someone had found some revolutionary new use for it, it's not like they could monopolise production. Despite all that, it's the only thing I've found for which the number forty-six – from the back of the photo – has any relevance. Put those two together and you get Scandium-46, which apparently is far more interesting since it's . . . drum roll . . . an artificially produced radioactive isotope."

"That sounds like it could be relevant," Zoya said. "But then you get into the obvious questions. What's Scandium-46 used for, and why would our dead Dutchmen be interested in it? With radioactivity, are you thinking weapons, dirty bombs, something like that?"

"I don't know yet," Robin replied. "The only thing I found so far is that it's used as a tracer in the oil industry. When oil companies pump their oil, they can introduce small amounts of this Scandium-46 if they suspect there's a leak in the pipeline. I guess the radiation's easier to track than the oil itself. But since I'm not an expert, or even a scientist, my thought was that we'd need to find someone who is. So that they can tell us what else, if anything, you can do with it."

"Then I guess you remembered Dietrich – Mrs Visser's husband?"

"Exactly. Not that he can tell us anything himself, of course. Just because of the coincidence. Mrs Visser mentioned that her husband had a particular interest in nuclear science, and one of our dead men, if I'm right, has left behind a clue pointing at a radioactive isotope. It has to be worth following up."

Zoya thought for a moment. It was like watching a rope being braided: gazing down with satisfaction at a completed tight-woven section, then tracing her eyes along the individual strands of hemp as they were dragged in from the unseen distance. In that far-off headspace, something occurred to her.

"Did the husband's autopsy report come through?" she asked.

Robin nodded proudly and brandished the buff envelope he had been holding. They walked through the office until they found an empty meeting room. He laid out the contents of the envelope on the polished wood of the table.

"I got it yesterday," he said, "it's in Dutch of course, but I got Scheefnek to take me through it."

Zoya was already skimming the pages. Mrs Visser's husband had been extensively tortured, as they had already heard from their previous phone call with the Dutch policeman. *But wait.* She looked enquiringly at Robin.

"It's strange, don't you think?" he said. "Finger and toenails torn out, fingers and toes crushed. As we were expecting. But the report says the cigarette burns and the holes in his legs were post-mortem. Why would someone want to do that?"

"It is strange," Zoya confirmed. "There was a pimp I arrested once in one of the bars by the Odesa Port who liked to punish his younger workers with a cigarette. He was lucky I had just made detective, if it had been a few years later I would have given him a taste of his own medicine. But only when he was alive. What would have been the point of burning him if he was already dead?"

Zoya shuddered as she imagined the twin smells of ash and burning flesh. She read on.

"He had pancreatic cancer," she said. "That's one of the fastest-acting types. It's not specific in the report, but he probably didn't have a lot of time left. So Mrs Visser was telling the truth. About that at least."

"About the truth," Robin said, "I know I'm not a detective, but doesn't she seem strange to you? Mrs Visser, I mean. For example, on one hand she said she didn't know anything about her son's business or his friends. But she just happened to have the albums on her table, which enabled us to link everyone together."

Intelligent men would always be her weakness, Zoya thought, especially the shy ones. Especially the one shy one who was so shy and so intelligent that he didn't even notice the sudden hot stab of Zoya's eyes.

"Never believe the words," she said. "Only the facts. About the husband, for example. He was tortured and he had cancer – everything else is open to interpretation. Especially when part of his torture wasn't torture at all. Which means we need to speak with Scheefnek."

There was a moment's confusion when they realised that neither of them had his telephone number. Robin ran to his desk then returned. Zoya dialled.

"Officer First Class Stiff Neck," she said.

"Lieutenant Cuckoo," he replied, and for a second Zoya felt absurdly pleased that he had bothered to look up what her surname meant.

"Today's our lucky day," Zoya continued. "No one's died, not yet at least, so we had a minute to give you a call. I know you already discussed Mr Visser's autopsy report, but Robin has also found out something new."

Whilst Robin explained about Scandium-46, Zoya let her mind drift back to the meeting with Mrs Visser. After they had departed the grieving widow's home, Zoya had stored up everything that might be relevant – her impressions, her doubts, her questions – and left it all to stew and simmer over a low internal flame. Add water and stir periodically so the mix doesn't stick to the pan, season for taste. *So much food*, she thought, *and so little time*, switching back into the conversation just as Robin finished his explanation.

"What do you need from me?" Scheefnek asked.

"A few things," Zoya replied. "Number one is that when we were there, I forgot to show Mrs Visser the photo from our Liverpool crime scene. The one with the red house. I want you to visit her again and see if anything there means anything to her. Try her first without any extra clues. Just show her the house, the village name and that it's in Serbia. And the number forty-six. If that doesn't work, then try with Robin's idea that it could be a reference to Scandium-46. See if that's something her husband ever mentioned."

"So far, so good," Scheefnek said. "And what else?"

"Two more things," Zoya said. "The first one's the barn next to her house. I didn't pay it much attention when we were there – other than thinking that her house might have been a farmhouse once, so owning a barn would make sense. But an old farmhouse would have an old barn. It would probably have fallen into disrepair, or it would at least be showing its age. But their barn was freshly painted; there were no gaps in the walls; it had a nice, solid roof. Now I'm wondering if they used it for something we should know about. Particularly her scientist husband."

"I don't have enough to get a warrant," Scheefnek commented.

"You'll just have to be charming," Zoya replied. "Ask her nicely, and if she says yes, see if you can find anything at all that's relevant. About Scandium-46 or any other radioactive stuff, or anything that might just link to the other dead men. And if she says no, that will at least tell us she's got something to hide."

"Got it. Anything else?"

"One more thing," Zoya said. "I've been remembering how Mrs Visser was holding onto her Bible when we spoke with her. I thought grief at first; some kind of religious consolation maybe, I don't know. But I also remember having this strange impression when she stroked the cover of the Bible after I asked whether her son was married. It could mean different things. Maybe the son was doing something a religious mother wouldn't approve of, maybe he was gay, or maybe she just doesn't like people living out of wedlock. Alternatively, I had a thought that she might be trying to protect someone, and then there was that strange comment she added about underestimating women. Anyway, I want you to see if you can understand if there was something behind all that. More specifically, she already told us her son wasn't married, but we didn't ask about a fiancée or a girlfriend. Or a boyfriend. I don't know what it is, but I have a feeling there's something we're missing."

Scheefnek laughed and said that Zoya's wish was his command. She liked the sound of that, although she liked it a little less when he told her he wouldn't be able to visit Mrs Visser until the following day. Or maybe the day after that.

They ended the call and Zoya stared at Robin until it happened – unpredictably, out of her control: the moment when her thoughts had taken her as far as she could go with the Dutchmen and a switch clicked inside. And then Robin's face faded and was replaced by the Hunter's, growing clearer and harsher until all she could see was his fierce expression, his pale eyes, the birthmark over his right eye.

"Nineteen stab wounds," she said. "Each one carefully placed. And I know he's still here, Robin. He's somewhere nearby, and soon he'll have to make his move. I can feel it."

CHAPTER 20

On the afternoon of the second day – Monday 30 March – Lovell confirmed they were ready. Zoya and Lovell sat with Mickey and took him through his lines; multiple times, role-playing, imagining the possible responses and questions until they were satisfied that he had at least a reasonable chance of not screwing it up.

Then he made the call. Zoya listened fiercely, hoping to dredge out more insight into the Hunter's psychology from his tone and his words, but he hardly spoke. Silent as a fish, as the saying went. Mickey ran through the script they had agreed and told the Hunter what he wanted from him. Finally, he told the Hunter what he had to offer in exchange.

"The Interpol woman saw your guy," he said. "The Scout, I mean. When he was tailing her. She knows what he looks like, but that's not all. She's threatening to make other stuff up as well. She says she'll spread it through the Interpol network that they've got faces for both of you. I mean for the Scout and for you as well Mr Hunter. She says it'll kill your business if your clients hear that all the facial recognition systems everywhere in Europe have searches out for the guys they might be looking to hire. Then she said something about Albania, that you're from there, and that's where she'll concentrate her search. I'm telling you, she's a crazy bitch, it's like she's obsessed. It's not me you should be worried about, it's her."

He paused for breath and waited for his Oscar. *Not bad,* Zoya thought. He'd rambled a bit, but that was good. And she even preferred the *crazy bitch* to his previous *hello beautiful.* But the Hunter still hadn't replied, so Zoya nodded to Mickey to continue.

"Well, I can tell you how to get her. The police just told me there's going to be a meeting at the safe house. Me, the police inspector, and the Ukrainian woman. They said they've cleared my deal and they're going to bring the papers for me to sign. What exactly I'm supposed to say in return for them not arresting me. There's protection of course, at the house, but it's just two guys. One out front, one at the back. No one inside. Nothing you can't handle."

"Send me the address and time," was all the Hunter said. "If it checks out, I'll make sure you get the money."

*

It was Tuesday. Lovell thought her team had done a superb job. The safe house was one they had used before. She had selected it from within a list of similar properties because it was regarded as mid-range in terms of its relative level of security. It was good enough to be believable, but not a fortress where the Hunter would take one look and decide he had no realistic chance of attack. It was a bungalow on a quiet cul-de-sac that backed onto an area of communal allotments. They had two snipers hiding amongst the lettuces, with verified overlapping angles of fire. In addition to the team inside the bungalow, they had arranged to occupy the next-door property for the day and inserted a second armed response team. The existing CCTV coverage of the area had been augmented with additional hidden cameras, and best of all they had two specialist officers armed with the latest drone technology sweeping the skies above the streets.

And even though Lovell knew and had approved every detail of their surveillance, she spotted no sign of any of it as she and Zoya approached the property in a gleaming black Land Rover. Which was one additional precaution: the car borrowed from Lovell's boss with the logic that it gave better cover for one of the weak spots the tactical team had identified – the short walk from the pavement up the bungalow's driveway to its front door. Added to that were Kevlar vests for both women, since they had agreed that there was no point taking stupid risks.

Lovell parked. Protected and vested, they walked into the bungalow. No one got shot. They sat inside behind drawn curtains and waited.

All team members had been issued with descriptions and artist's drawings of the Hunter and the Scout. They saw no one matching the descriptions. Twenty minutes in, one of the drone operators reported a white van that had made two circles of the surrounding block of streets before approaching the cul-de-sac. It drove towards the bungalow as the office team tapped away to verify the registration number. Registered to a freelance plumber, they reported, at the same time as it stopped four doors away. The driver carried a bag of tools; the door of the house was opened by an elderly woman who seemed to be expecting him. Then it was quiet again.

They waited. They talked about makeup or fashion or whatever it was that men thought women talked about when they were left to their own devices. An hour passed. Any longer wouldn't have seemed realistic, given what Mickey had told the Hunter about the purpose of the meeting. They left the bungalow and walked back towards the car. By now their wariness was mixed with a disconcerting hope that they would actually be shot at. They weren't.

*

"Drop me off at the Riverside Restaurant," Zoya told the police driver. "I need some fresh air before I go back to the hotel."

She sat for five minutes on a bench next to the water and called Robin. She briefed him that there was nothing to brief him about and she asked him what kind of music he liked. When he told her he liked jazz, Zoya was disappointed but not entirely surprised, so she moved swiftly on.

"Did you manage to find a nuclear physicist we can speak with?" she asked.

Robin confirmed that he had contacted someone and was waiting for a reply.

"Were you able to find out where Mr Visser is buried?" she continued.

"Still working on it," Robin replied.

Zoya didn't know what else to ask. She rang off and followed the same route towards the centre that she had taken on her first day, back along Peter Street. Past the Opera House, past bars and restaurants that she still hadn't visited. It was almost five; the air was cooling, but there was no rain today. And by now Zoya's mind had flitted far away, imagining her favourite walk in Odesa – along Primorsky Boulevard towards the cranes of the port. She was ambling the length of the shaded alley that threaded through the trees, that danced with thickets of red carnations, that soaked her in the smell of the sea off to her left. There was laughter and singing in the air, the sounds of her town. Perhaps she was picking some guy up if the mood took her, or taking a turn at the open-air weightlifting area on the beach if it didn't. She was home.

Which was why she didn't spot the man until it was far too late.

He was thirty metres ahead of her, leaning against the trunk of an elm tree. His face was in shadow, and she couldn't make out his features. He wore a black baseball cap – it wasn't Manchester United, and it wasn't Manchester City – and she wasn't sure about the rest of his clothes. But there was something familiar about him: his height and build, his posture too. And then she saw the shoes. Chunky white soles and black leather uppers, at which point Zoya had to force herself not to make any sudden stupid moves. She needed to know if the Scout was on his own, but she couldn't be obvious about it. She caught at reflections in the hotel windows and saw nothing unusual. She let her gaze wander up towards the sky, seemingly admiring the shifting clouds and the threatening rooftops. But she had no time to figure it out, and she sure as hell wasn't going to turn and run. She kept going.

The Scout hadn't been imagining walks in Odesa or anywhere else. He was fully focused. After two days stuck in the apartment, he had been a little surprised when the Hunter had finally given him this task. But he was determined not to mess it up. He had been in place for over an hour, and he had spotted Zoya a hundred metres out. He had no doubt it was her. He had spoken softly into his sleeve and, on the other side of the street, on the fourth floor of the multistorey, the sniper had opened the back doors of his van and readied the tripod of his rifle on the concrete parapet in front of him.

"Fifteen metres," the Scout said.

"Boss?" the sniper asked.

"Take the shot," the Hunter confirmed.

Zoya was almost at the hotel doors. She turned towards the entrance, but she kept her gaze on the Scout. His eyes met hers. He knew she had seen him, and a slight smile lifted the corners of his mouth.

And Zoya watched as, ten metres ahead of her, the Scout's head exploded.

PART 3

The Detective

CHAPTER 21

The hotel gym was empty, which was a relief. A necessity, really, given her mood. Zoya loaded ninety kilos on the bar – a long way from her personal best, but it would do for now. With her feet at shoulder width, and her hands as wide as they would go, she squatted, hips below knees. She adjusted her grip, then unleashed the tight-wound coil of her body as she exploded back and up, swinging the bar up above her, rising, then sinking back into the squat. A second's pause, holding the weight steady and balanced. Then a last effort, powering up vertically this time, arms and bar a proud triangle over her head.

She held it.

She let it drop.

She stared furiously at the mirrored walls, where a squat woman in sweaty, mismatched lycra puffed and strained.

"How could you have been so stupid?" Zoya yelled at the woman. "The worst your tiny-ass brain could imagine was that the Hunter wouldn't take the bait. Well, it turns out that wasn't even close to the worst. So how come you're only figuring it out now when it's too bloody late?!"

Squat. Power up. Hold it. Let it drop. Damn it was loud.

"He sent you a fucking message," she shouted. "He's smarter than you are, Zoya. And he's more ruthless. It was too risky for him to try to take out both you and Mickey, and killing one without the other would have achieved nothing. You left him absolutely no choice – that's what he's telling you. That this one's on you."

Squat. Power up. Hold it. Let it drop. Damn it was loud – but at least that was one thing that wasn't her fault.

"And if he figured it out, then why the hell didn't you, Zoya? That it didn't matter if someone could describe the Scout's face if the Scout was dead. No man, no problem: even Joseph fucking Stalin knew that much!"

Squat. Power up. Hold it. Let it drop. And who the hell doesn't put padding on a weights-room floor?

"What were you thinking?" Her voice was quieter this time; dazed and a little desperate. "Why would you decide to rush forward and try to save a man who had just been shot in the head? The next bullet should have been for you, but that's not what he wanted. I don't know why, but he wants you to suffer, Zoya."

Squat. Power up. Hold it. Let it drop. Dripping with sweat and grunting with the effort.

And Zoya had no strength left to shout or to speak as the memories flooded in. The ambulance had arrived, chased by Lovell with her team. Lovell hadn't screamed or shouted; worst of all she hadn't even had the decency to snap at Zoya that she was a dangerous and incompetent bitch. So why had Zoya fallen silent now, when she was the only person left to break the news of this goddamn undeniable truth to herself?

Squat. Power up. Hold it. Let it drop. It was a relief how loud it was.

Then Robin had called her, when she was standing there on the pavement next to a dead man. And how could he have such terrible timing? He had started talking about his Dutchmen again, and she had lost it and she had sworn *pizdets, pizdets, pizdets* and she had yelled into the phone that right now she didn't give a damn if every single Dutchman in the world dropped dead right in front of her; and now she would have to apologise to him too.

Squat. Power up. Hold it. Let it drop. And it was nowhere near loud enough as she screwed her eyes tight to banish the reckless and foolish woman in the mirror.

"There's one thing I still don't understand," she muttered. "Mickey told the Hunter that I've seen his face too. So what's the real reason he didn't he shoot me when he had the chance? Didn't he believe Mickey? Or doesn't he care?"

Squat. Power up. And this time Zoya couldn't hold it and the bar fell to the floor and she collapsed beside it; her legs twitching, the muscles of her back burning and protesting, and a spark of painful, beautiful bright clarity that lit up her mind.

Hold it Zoya. Then let it drop.

*

But she still had some pride left, and Zoya was back in the office the next morning at nine a.m. sharp. The hotel concierge had smiled at her as she was leaving, warning her that it was April Fools' Day and she should expect pranks and mischief. Zoya had thought that Odesa's equivalent – the annual *Humo-*

rina festival – would be kicking off; but that here, today, no one would have time for jokes.

Inside, the first thing Zoya did was to walk down a floor to Lovell's office. The two women looked at each other and perhaps they thought the same thing. Neither of them, after all, had foreseen the Hunter's move. Lovell's face seemed calm, and Zoya wondered about the Detective Chief Inspector's equivalent of her own stress-relieving weightlifting routine. Cold Chablis perhaps, or rosé, but she looked too healthy. Yoga then, but that would be too sedate; or pounding out long circuits of a park somewhere, alone in the dark and the rain. Or perhaps Lovell was one of the few who managed to juggle the life of a senior police officer with some semblance of a normal relationship, a family even. Two kids and a dog. Then the soft rim of skin under Lovell's right eye began to tick and twitch, and when Lovell saw that Zoya had noticed, she smiled with her newly chapped lips.

"We've got a lead," she said. "From Mickey of all people."

It turned out that one of Mickey's old schoolmates was a member of the Braintree Boys; a low-level runner, who from the sound of it had been no more successful than Mickey himself. But that was irrelevant. What mattered was that he and Mickey had stayed in touch over the years despite a formal ban on contact between the rival gangs. And he had called Mickey late the previous evening. Crowing, like he had got one over on Mickey. Laughing, because a deal was about to go down for the Braintrees to buy the Lee End coke stash at a huge discount – and what did Mickey think of that?

And it turned out that what Mickey thought was that this tidbit of information should earn him a finder's fee from his favourite police lady, as he called her. Even if he hadn't actually found anything because his mate didn't know when or where the buy was supposed to happen.

"I've agreed surveillance on all known Braintree people," Lovell said. "Maybe we'll get lucky."

"Was that the good news?" Zoya asked.

"I'm afraid so. The bad news is we have nothing on the shooter. We know they had a sniper in the boxing club assault, so he's the obvious candidate. But this was a short-range shot with a stationary target, so it could probably have been anyone in their team – or the Hunter himself. Whoever it was, they used a van in the car park across the street and left it there, though we found absolutely nothing of any forensic value. The van was reported stolen yesterday, it had been wiped down with bleach, and the shooter took the spent brass with him. He also fired a frangible round that exploded in the victim's head, so we had nothing for ballistics to analyse there either. And we're thinking he, or they, left the car park via one of the pedestrian exits, since there are cameras next to the exit barriers and in the street outside that would have caught at least one face if they used another vehicle."

"We lost them," Zoya said, struggling to make her statement sound like a question.

"For now. Our short-term hope is the coke deal, because other than that they have no reason to stay in town. If that doesn't give us anything, then the border checks are our last line of defence. Unless you have any other thoughts?"

Zoya shook her head. For now, she had nothing further to add.

*

After Lovell, Zoya couldn't avoid it any longer. She went to see Robin.

"Listen, I'm so sorry, Zoya," he said before she had the chance to speak. "I only found out afterwards what had happened. I had no idea."

Zoya had no wish to get into a competitive apology session, so she forgave him instead. She pulled a chair into his cubicle and faced him in the cramped space between the partitions.

"You were about to tell me something," she said. "When you called."

"That's right. I didn't find out where Mr Visser's buried yet, but there's something else. I don't know how important it is, but I got an email from Belgium. It turns out that when a case is flagged by Interpol then any status updates get sent through to us automatically."

"Belgium – that's where Mrs Visser's son died? The car crash and fire?"

"Exactly," Robin continued. "The car was a Tesla, and apparently the company like to do their own investigation when there's a crash, especially if one of their vehicles catches fire. This one took a while, mainly because they had to wait for the car to be released by the police, but the company's engineer has finally issued his report. His conclusion was that that the fire was started deliberately, after the crash. And the status update that came through was because the Belgian police have decided to take another look at the whole file."

"It'll be good to have it confirmed one way or the other," Zoya said, "but I'm not sure what it adds, even if the police team confirm in the end that it was a murder."

"Well, there's one other thing," Robin said. "The officer I spoke with said the body in the car was too badly burned for a visual identification, or even to use dental records. Which they weren't too worried about when they were calling it an accident; and because they thought their assumptions were pretty safe since the son had disappeared and he was the registered owner of the car. Plus they had spoken with Mrs Visser, and she had confirmed that her son had been driving the car when he left her house the day before the crash. But since there's now a doubt about the cause of the fire, the police want to see if there's any other way they can confirm the victim's identity."

"They might get a DNA sample if they're lucky," Zoya surmised. "But they might not be. I read that those big lithium batteries burn hot enough to incinerate even genetic material. It's definitely an interesting angle though."

Zoya leant forward, elbows on Robin's desk. Her violent bout of exercise had taken the edge off her fury, but aftershocks of anger still pulsed inside. Worst of all, she didn't know what to do next. She stared into Robin's face and felt something spark inside. She told herself that seducing him in her wonderfully luxurious hotel room would be a stupid idea. That right now, she needed a friend more than she needed a lover. Which left only one alternative.

"Let's go drinking this evening," she said. "You and me."

Robin met Zoya's gaze. He knew he wouldn't last long in a drinking session with her. He also knew that Zoya's invitation was as close to an apology as he would ever get from her. All of which was fine with him.

CHAPTER 22

"I did warn you," Robin said as he paused in the living-room doorway on his way to the kitchen, "Guinness really is an acquired taste."

"I know," Zoya mumbled. "And you even told me it was Irish, not English. You called it Ireland's revenge, and then I told you about my dream from my flight on the way over to England."

On the plane, Zoya had dreamt that she had wandered with Sherlock Holmes through the thick fog blanketing the Thames. And that the following morning, in a brick townhouse, a black-suited butler with handlebar a handlebar moustache had served her cold porridge followed by breakfast kippers, which she had washed down with a pint of Guinness. The series of imagined scenes had been filtered and reduced when she woke. She was pretty sure she wasn't going to meet Sherlock Holmes after all, and she knew the Thames was a long way from Manchester. When it came to the food, porridge – cold or warm, with sugar and butter added in the Ukrainian manner – was hardly an unknown quantity in Zoya's life, as it had been the cheapest staple throughout many years of childhood breakfasts. Kippers, too, since she thought the English variety was unlikely to differ substantially from the many variants of canned sardines and sprats that had been a repeated and much-resented last-week-before-payday mealtime offering from her mother.

Which had left just one remaining viable ambition. So, the previous night Zoya had determinedly ignored Robin's warnings and, in the bar, she had done Guinness. Or, more accurately, Guinness had done her.

Now she winced and forced herself to swallow her mouth's hoppy ale aftertaste.

And then none of it mattered, because she had a word – no, two words – written on the palm of her left hand.

Almost as soon as Zoya had become aware that *in vino* there is indeed *veritas* (which in her case was at the tender age of fifteen), she had also understood that discovering the truth was no help at all if you couldn't remember it when you sobered up. After a sequence of frustrating fumbles, Zoya had always made sure to carry a pen with her whenever she went to a bar, and she had scribbled her drink-fuelled revelations on any suitable or unsuitable surface she found nearby. Napkins, bills or credit card slips were favourites; but, failing that, any tabletop or scrap of clothing or exposed area of flesh would do. The only problem that remained in the morning was interpretation (to which, sometimes, were added the complicating confusion of sweat or other bodily fluids).

The two words were smeared on her skin. She peered closer.

Off to her right an electric grinding sound began, followed by the welcome smell of coffee. Then Robin reappeared, wearing a thick dressing gown with a disorienting paisley swirl design and carrying a steaming mug in each hand. Zoya pushed out her palm towards him. Robin stopped, thinking that was what she was signalling. Then he was confused as she waved him on. Then he adjusted his spectacles on his nose, understanding what she was showing him.

"No face," he read on her hand. "What does it mean?"

"It means we need to go back to see the grieving widow and mother," Zoya said.

*

This time the logistical arrangements were faster. Zoya claimed that the travel approval they had previously received should surely still cover this trip, since last time round they had been forced to leave before their investigations were complete. They decided to fly economy, just in case Zoya was wrong and they ended up having to pay for their own tickets, and they found there were places available on the same morning flight they had taken before. The following day, Zoya called Scheefnek on the way to Manchester Airport and he confirmed he obviously had nothing better to do than meet them at Schiphol arrivals. They flew, they arrived, and he was waiting for them. He was as handsome as last time, his glutes were still rock-solid, and he still had a car. It was like they had never left.

"Good timing," he said through a mouthful of *Hagelslag*, "I had already agreed with Mrs Visser that I would come round today. We can go straight there."

"How did she sound?" Zoya asked.

"Calmer, I would say. But not happy. Wary more than anything."

"That's a good sign," Zoya replied.

They drove south, on the same roads through the same fields and in much the same weather – hesitant sunshine and cold wind from the sea. Then the seagulls appeared and the full-udder cows. No tulips yet.

Everything changed when Zoya stabbed a finger against the brass doorbell.

Instead of a slow shuffle-shuffle-tap, this time they heard a continuous and energetic tap-tap-tap on the stone flags of the corridor. The door opened vigorously. No slippers today for Mrs Visser; instead she wore patent leather mid-height heels, and her cane was clenched like a weapon in her bony hand. She was dressed for battle – long-sleeved beige silk shirt, dark-green knee-length skirt – and scented to ward off evil spirits. She wore a string of pearls, her hair was clean and tightly curled, and her eyes were direct and firm. She also seemed taller. Pity hadn't been enough to spare the grieving widow a further inquisition, and now Visser would attempt to face them down on different terms.

"Come on in," she said a little too cheerfully. "Can I offer you a drink?"

Coffee, tea and a glass of water were requested and served in the living room, where the three guests sat in a neat row on the long sofa. The curtains were wide open today, and the plants had been watered and waxed. The photo albums had been removed from the low table by Visser's armchair, but the blue-bound Bible remained on-guard and had been supplemented by an empty glass tumbler and a square-sided bottle containing a dark amber liquid. *Protect us from our sins, and lead us into temptation,* Zoya thought. Since the vaguely familiar label on the bottle said it contained something called Echter Aromatique, Zoya decided to divert from the script she had suggested a few days ago to Scheefnek. Attack, after all, was the best form of attack.

She took their files from Robin's case and extracted the enlarged version of the classroom photo they had borrowed during their previous visit. She passed it to Visser.

"Please take a close look at the faces we have circled," she said.

Visser looked attentively at the photo, then she looked at Zoya and nodded. Her expression was unreadable.

"Would it surprise you to know," Zoya continued, "that each of those six individuals, your son and five other boys from his class – they would have been grown men now, of course – have died recently in unusual circumstances?"

Visser rubbed at the side of her face, then fumbled a hand towards the curved handle of her cane.

"I am sorry detective," she replied slowly, "but why do you suppose I would know what happened to my Jan's old friends? I truly wish I could be of more help, but I admit to having become a bit of a hermit since my accident." She paused and lifted the cane in confirmation. "Now I find I am quite content to live out here in the middle of the fields, so much so that I rarely even find a reason to venture into town."

Obfuscation, and answering a question with another question, Zoya thought. *Always useful tactics.*

Zoya then selected the files for each of the men. She would have liked to lay them out in a row in front of Visser, but there wasn't enough space. Instead, she stacked them in a neat pile on her knees. For a moment, she considered showing Visser the photos of the men's corpses, but she decided that open hostilities could wait for another day. Instead, she flicked through details she knew by heart as she read out – sonorously, slowly – the original and the assumed names of the five men, and the date, place and cause of each man's death. Adding, of course, the sixth – Visser's son. This time Visser's hand moved towards the table at her side, and Zoya waited to see if she would seek the comfort of her Bible or the bottle of Aromatique. Visser's hand hovered for a moment, then she took the bottle. She poured herself a stiff two-finger measure and began to sip. Zoya continued.

"Mrs Visser, we believe that the death of these men is not just unusual, nor is it coincidental. We suspect that some or all of them were murdered. We also believe it is possible that these men worked together with your son and that the nature of this work was possibly a factor or indeed a direct cause of their deaths. Therefore, I need to ask you Mrs Visser: are you aware if Jan worked with these men?"

Visser shook her head, but Zoya sensed a crack in her defences.

"Or perhaps it was your husband," Zoya continued. "Did Dietrich work with either your son or the other men?"

Visser attempted to camouflage her reaction with another sip – more like a gulp – but this time Zoya was sure. The woman had flinched.

Scheefnek had noticed it too. He attempted a flanking manoeuvre.

"Mrs Visser," he said, "you mentioned last time we were here that neither your husband nor your son were significantly involved in the family pharmacy business. Then may I ask what exactly was it that they did? For work, I mean?"

"Consulting," Visser replied reluctantly. "My Jan was a security consultant, he worked with alarm systems and computer security and things like that. He tried to explain it to me, but the technical details were too complicated for an old woman like me to understand. And I suppose it's possible that he worked with my husband on some of project or other, but I don't know exactly."

Zoya had to smile at that one. *Too complicated for an old woman like me.* Who did she think she was kidding?

"And might that work have involved any of the other men we've mentioned?" Zoya asked. "One of them used to be a soldier for example, and another was a doctor. Before they were killed."

"Detective, don't you think I already answered that? I had no reason to know the profession of my son's friends, nor was I involved in Jan's business affairs. But, speaking simply from common sense – I find it hard to imagine that there was much need for a doctor in Jan's work. Or for a soldier, for that matter."

It was time to set a trap. A simple yes or no question.

"Did your son or your husband ever do any work in your barn?"

"The barn?"

As if she had forgotten she had one.

"The barn," Zoya confirmed.

And it didn't even matter what the answer was. If it was yes, Zoya would ask whether Visser would mind if they took a look inside. If it was no, she would ask exactly the same thing. The best part was that, after evading all the previous questions, Visser had made it virtually impossible for herself to refuse such a straightforward request.

Robin scented blood and added to the pile-on. He showed Visser the picture of the red house. He took her through their questions. Dusmanic, Serbia; the house with an onion dome over the entrance, which used to be a pharmacy. The number forty-six. Nothing. But when he asked about Scandium-46, Visser paled, and this time it was the Bible that she reached for.

"You told us before that your son wasn't married Mrs Visser," Zoya said. "But did Jan have any other long-term relationships? A girlfriend or a boyfriend, a fiancée maybe?"

Mrs Visser seemed relieved at the change of subject. Was it safer ground? It turned out that her son had indeed been involved with a lady friend, as Mrs Visser called her. That they had talked about marriage, but they had decided it wasn't the modern thing to do. Unless maybe they decided they wanted children at some point. Zoya wondered if that was the son's version or her mother's, and why Mrs Visser hadn't mentioned any of this before. She tagged it as something to come back to later.

"Why don't we take a quick look in the barn then?" she said. "Then there'll be at least one question that we can cross off our list for today. And maybe we'll even be able to throw a little light for you on some of those technical details of your son's work."

*

Mrs Visser had given them a single heavy brass key, but she didn't accompany them outside.

Scheefnek, Robin and Zoya paused in front of the barn. It had a pair of heavy wood-beam doors on rollers that would have been used for access by tractors and other agricultural equipment. A standard-sized hinged door, set into the beams, looked like a more recent addition.

"You think she's hiding something, don't you?" Robin asked.

Zoya looked across at Scheefnek. Since that was a rough approximation of what they thought, they both nodded in reply. Zoya reflected on the hundreds of hours of lies and prevarications she had sat through since she became a homicide detective and, for a moment, she envied Robin's childlike mix of insight and naivety.

Then she inserted the key, turned it in the well-oiled lock, and opened the door.

CHAPTER 23

The sound of sirens heralded the arrival of the police team, summoned by Scheefnek from The Hague. An hour and a half had passed. Once the cars had rolled up, Zoya, Robin and Scheefnek left the barn and went back inside the house. They were still shocked by what they had seen. In the living room, Mrs Visser still sat where she had sat before – with the same straight-backed poise, as if nothing had changed, and with only the ebbing level of the amber liquor in its bottle to record the slow passage of time.

Since Robin had discovered the lead, Zoya had volunteered him to begin the questioning.

"I noticed your reaction before," he said. "You knew about the Scandium-46, didn't you Mrs Visser?"

Mrs Visser nodded and stared down at the floor. A show of contrition, Zoya thought. Or of doubt: as if she was pretending that she hadn't already decided exactly what she was going to say.

"I'm sorry," she began. "It's just that I didn't want you to get the wrong idea. But you're right. Dietrich was obsessed with his Scandium. He was a scientist, as I told you before, and he told me he had worked with it before he came here. When he still lived in Germany, I mean. Of course, I can guess what you're thinking, and I promise you there was nothing bad or dangerous about what he was doing. He was simply trying to figure out better ways to track radioactive materials, at least that was what he told me. He explained how important it was, for safety reasons, to be able to distinguish between different isotopes at as great a distance as possible. He was proud of what he was doing. He said it would be revolutionary if he was able to get it right."

"Why did he use Scandium-46 specifically?" Robin asked.

"That I don't really know, young man. He had mentioned the name a few times, which is why I reacted when you mentioned it earlier. I don't know anything about its properties, but I did understand that it is quite cheap and easy to obtain. Compared with other radioactive isotopes at least. And Dietrich said it has a short half-life, which I understand to mean that it is also quite safe to store and to use. Although even so I never let him take it out of the barn."

"You know what your husband did," Zoya said. "You also know his real name, don't you Mrs Visser?"

She didn't reply.

"After our last conversation I was curious about your husband's past life," Zoya continued. "About why he had no contact with his family or his past friends. So, I spoke with a colleague in Germany. He mentioned that in the months after the fall of the Berlin Wall, hundreds of thousands of people left the country. Naturally, there were all kinds of people looking for a better life, and that certainly included a large number of scientists who knew they could do the same work but earn much more elsewhere. Your husband could have been one of them, but that wouldn't explain the lack of family connections or the fact that he didn't work here, at least in any paid capacity, as a scientist. Then my colleague mentioned another category of people who left: the Stasi agents and informers, who were terrified they would face reprisals once their identities became public knowledge; and when all the sordid details emerged of who spied on their fellow countrymen; of who the jailors were, and who the torturers were. He also told me that the Netherlands was a popular choice because they had a long history of looking the other way. And because the language is fairly similar of course."

Mrs Visser stared down at the floor. Silence.

"I gave my colleague a description of your husband and the photos we had on file. Also, his age and his current name in case it was an alias that had previously been used. The Germans have a reputation for their recordkeeping, so I'm sure they'll find him eventually. But if you tell us his real name it will not only make our search much faster. It will also, I believe, be a significant step in helping us to understand who tortured and killed your husband and what happened to your son and his friends. You do want that, don't you Mrs Visser?"

When she looked up, Mrs Visser had tears running down her cheeks.

"His name was Harald Bergmann," she said, then she rushed out of the room.

And for the first time since she had met Mrs Visser, Zoya believed that the woman's emotion was entirely real.

*

"Kiss & Ride!" was the instruction on the sign, yet they were doing neither. They had waited a day to receive the police team's preliminary thoughts on the contents of the barn. Now, on the following morning, the three Interpol officers rested in a leather-upholstered car, weighed down by their long days of international crime detection. Not for long though, since the only real choice offered by the drop-off zone outside Schiphol Airport departures was between a free ten-minute wait or a hundred-euro fine. With nine of the ten minutes left, Zoya swivelled and stretched out across the back seats, head cradled in her hands. Scheefnek and Robin were up front. They talked.

"That was something else," Robin said. "The barn I mean."

And it certainly had been. There had been nothing remotely agricultural about the interior of the barn. Five metres in from the front wall, an entirely separate structure had been constructed out of wood and glass. Its single door was locked and Zoya had used her lockpicks. Inside they had discovered a cross between a laboratory and an engineering workshop, and even if they didn't know what exactly all the different equipment did, there had been one common and excessively obvious theme. It was spelled out in huge red letters on the walls. Periodic tables were pinned up and feverishly circled. Flowcharts of the mining and production process led to helix diagrams of its elegant chemical formula. The whole place was a shrine to one man's favourite radioactive isotope. Scandium-46.

"But I still don't understand what else it was," Scheefnek said. "The police team couldn't give us much we didn't already know. They've identified the right scientists to bring in, and hopefully they'll be able to tell us what exactly he was up to. Because right now, it doesn't seem to make a lot of sense. This guy – an ex-Stasi agent according to your version – labouring away all on his own, or maybe with his son I guess, in a barn in the middle of nowhere. Doing something unknown with his infamous Scandium-46. We had thought about dirty bombs as a possibility, but from what I understand the whole point is that you need to use some form of conventional explosive to scatter the radioactive stuff. But we found no trace of explosives; nothing that looked like a delivery system or a timer, not even any suspicious wiring. And I know Mrs Visser called her husband obsessive, but just think about how much all that stuff must have cost. It looks more like plain crazy to me."

"That's one question," Zoya said. "And I have another. Or a series of questions. About Mrs Visser. She was never straightforward or truthful, right from the beginning. But at the same time, she gave us a lot of information she didn't need to. The photos of her son and his friends for example – as Robin pointed out. That was what enabled us to make our first firm link between the six men. We'd probably have got there eventually, but why did she volunteer it? Or the wedding snaps, and that strange discussion about her husband leaving his family behind. It was only because of what she said that I called my German friend. Then there's the barn of course. I didn't make it easy for her, but she could still have refused to let us in. Alternatively, her husband's death was weeks ago. She's had plenty of time to remove anything interesting if she wanted to, or she could just have burnt the whole thing down."

"Any theories?" Scheefnek asked.

"I don't know exactly," Zoya replied. "The problem is that her tearful exit got her out of any more questions. I'm not sure if that was deliberate or not, but there's still plenty to think about. In the meantime, we have this."

From the deep pocket of her coat Zoya extracted a blue-bound book.

"You took her Bible?" Robin asked.

"I know that eternal punishment awaits, but I couldn't resist. When we were about to leave, you two perfect gentlemen went off to check if Mrs Visser was OK. I'm no gentleman, and it was a spur-of-the-moment thing. And now I have another idea about why she kept holding onto it. Look what I found inside."

She handed over a piece of paper. It was a photo of a woman. She was in her early thirties, with black hair and blue eyes. The photographer had captured a serious, watchful expression, but the pattern of wrinkles around the woman's eyes suggested that she spent more time laughing than frowning. She looked smart, she looked interesting.

"See if you can find out who she is," Zoya said to Scheefnek as she and Robin exited the car with one minute to spare.

*

They caught their plane, they flew north. They were tired, and another night out on the town would have been pushing it. They took separate taxis from the airport.

In her room, Zoya showered and wrapped herself in the hotel's thick white bathrobe. Then she walked to the closet and extracted the second souvenir of the trip from the other pocket of her coat. She wondered what to do with it.

It was from inside the barn. There had been a long table placed against one of the walls. On the table had been set out a row of what they recognised as Geiger counters. They were arranged neatly, as if for an exhibition or a shop display. The first one was chunky and heavy. When Zoya picked it up, she had seen a date on the case and the markings that showed it had been manufactured in East Germany in 1985. Moving left to right, each of the counters looked progressively more modern and sophisticated. Zoya had taken the last one on the right. She hadn't been sure why: she had no idea what she would do with it now she had it, and she had even been slightly surprised that airport security had let it through without comment. But here it was.

She switched it on. The needle on the display jumped then began to flicker furiously. Zoya pointed it at different areas around the room. In some directions it was calm and indifferent. In others not so much. She ran it over the bed, the armchair, she went into the bathroom. The same thing. It seemed to believe there were multiple radiation hotspots in her hotel room. She ran it over herself. Nothing. She even went out into the corridor – nothing to the left, flickering needle to the right. It didn't make sense, so Zoya switched it off. So much for Dietrich the wonder scientist – now she would need to find someone to show it to; someone who knew what they were doing, and could figure out why the damned thing didn't work.

Then Zoya towelled her hair and recalled a view of Mrs Visser's slumped spine as she had run crying from the room.

And yes, it was true that for the first time since she had met her, Zoya had believed the woman's emotion was entirely real. But right now, Zoya was sure of something else. That Visser's emotion wasn't grief, or pain. It was guilt.

CHAPTER 24

Lovell was clearly a positive, glass-half-full kind of person. As opposed to Zoya, whose belief was that if fifty percent of your drink remained in the glass, it simply meant that you had some more drinking to do. In any case, two days later, the half-full news came from Grimsby, which Lovell explained was a fishing port on England's North Sea coast a couple of hours drive east of Manchester.

"There's a fisheries inspector who visits," she said, "to make sure the trawlers, the few that are left, don't exceed their fishing quotas. He relies heavily on the fishermen's own declarations of course, but he also does random spot checks of the catches. To help him, since he can't be on watch round the clock, the docks are equipped with cameras to monitor boats berthing and unloading. So, when the harbour master mentioned that a Danish-registered vessel had made an unscheduled stop in the port then left the same night, the inspector decided he should take a look at the footage. He didn't find anything relevant to fishing, but he did spot four men who didn't look anything like fishermen boarding the trawler in the middle of the night, shortly before it set out to sea. Luckily, the harbour master had read our alert, and he forwarded everything to us."

Lovell pushed over a selection of stills. There wasn't a huge amount to see. The trawler looked like a standard fishing boat: mid-sized, blue hull, cluttered with nets and gear. The men had climbed aboard then straightaway they had gone below, out of sight. The night-time resolution wasn't strong enough to make out faces, but it was true that no one would confuse these arrivals with fishermen. They wore leather jackets and jeans rather than oilies, they were all of a similar age and build, and each man carried a single black roll bag. The impression was of a well-matched team of heavies or a squad of soldiers. But it was the last photo in Lovell's pack that left no room for doubt. When one of the four men had swung his bag down from his shoulder, the movement had lifted his jacket above his belt. Where, clearly silhouetted against a pale coloured shirt, they could see the dark butt of his handgun.

"Only four," Zoya said.

"Exactly. And they were long gone before this information reached us. Into international waters, and the boat's AIS transponder has gone dark. But only four is good. It works with our theory that it would be too risky for the whole crew to try to leave at the same time. And the silver lining about the four escaping is that we've discovered the gang's exit route without them knowing."

"You're hoping the others will try to go out the same way?"

"Exactly. We keep the alert current at all our other border crossings of course, but we'll also add real-time surveillance in Grimsby. We'll put people in the port itself for the next few days, and we'll see if we can get a Coastguard vessel standing off at sea."

Zoya thought it made sense, but that Lovell's silver lining came with its own issues. In this case, the accompanying black storm cloud was the overview of life on a large island fringed with thousands of miles of jagged coastline. There was no guarantee that Grimsby would be repeated. The killers could use one of the hundreds of ports or marinas around the country to board either a fishing or a pleasure boat. Or, even worse, a RIB could be launched from pretty much any secluded beach. All they could do was hope.

*

Lovell's Grimsby silver lining was followed by a series of half-empty updates.

Director Tahiri had called her in. He had been surprised, he grimaced, to discover that Zoya had made a second trip to the Netherlands without seeking his approval. He had told her that might be how things were done back home in Ukraine, but it wasn't how things were done here. Zoya hadn't exactly or even approximately apologised, instead she had promised she would make time to review the staff manual Tahiri had passed on to her at the hospital. She had, however, neglected to mention that life was short, and that her reading list only ever seemed to get longer. Tahiri had stared at her for a moment with an expression that said he knew exactly what she was doing. Then, since he had been sensible enough not to pursue such a tedious topic, she had rewarded him with a briefing on what they had discovered at Visser's home. And then Tahiri had made a suggestion, which Zoya had thought was actually quite sensible and that she had promised to follow up.

Next Robin had confirmed that he had finally received an email reply from the nuclear physicist he had contacted a few days before at the University of Manchester. They had agreed a meeting time for the following morning.

Then Zoya had called Scheefnek. He had seemed surprised at the call, although he should have known better by now. He had only had a day, he said; and no, he hadn't yet uncovered the identity of the woman who had been hidden between the pages of Mrs Visser's Bible.

Finally, Zoya had called her German ex-colleague, ex-one-day-lover, maybe-friend. She had given him Visser's husband's real name – Harald Bergmann – spelling it out just in case. He had promised to look into it. Five minutes later she had remembered Tahiri's comment and called her maybe-friend back to add another question. This time his reply had been impatient at best, and he had ended the call without adding any further promises. Friendship had retreated, Zoya had thought, but maybe she would make it up to him one day.

Since she now found herself at a loose end, Zoya had purchased another sandwich from the vending machine. And as she was eating (meat, chewy, again), Detective Constable Johnson – still ginger, still premature, still too much on display – had rushed in.

*

She followed him down the stairs but refused to run. The sign on the door said Situation Room, which seemed a strange name for a room. Inside, a wide arch of screens covered the walls, operated reverently by a team of hushed and very serious uniformed police officers. It was the unit's own private NASA mission control, without the rockets.

Since Lovell was otherwise occupied, Johnson explained what was going on.

"The guvnor thought you would want to watch. We've been tracking the Braintree guys. One of them picked up two bags from the left luggage lockers at Manchester Piccadilly about five minutes ago. We have reason to believe he's taken possession of the drugs from the Lee End haul."

Lovell was watching intently as the screens tracked a black taxi driving steadily through light afternoon traffic, whilst her team continually switched from one street camera to the next to keep it in sight. At the same time, she was arguing animatedly on her mobile.

Zoya tuned in. The argument – she assumed it was with Lovell's boss – was about the best place to intercept the taxi. Lovell insisted it was too risky to allow the taxi into Braintree Boys territory. It seemed that whoever she was talking to wanted to wait, presumably in the hope that they could nab both the courier and whoever he passed the bags to. Based on what she had heard about the Braintree Boys' fondness for violence, Zoya thought Lovell was right. She was also clearly used to getting her own way.

As soon as Lovell finished the call, she started giving her orders.

"Alpha and Bravo units, this is DCI Lovell. You are cleared to intercept. The target is a black taxi heading east on Ashton

New Road, now approaching The Etihad. It is imperative you stop the target before it reaches the Braintree turn-off. Use of firearms is authorised, but caution is advised, and I remind all teams that the taxi driver is a civilian. How do you copy, Alpha and Bravo?"

Zoya heard no reply, and then she understood that everyone else in the room was wearing headphones. It didn't matter; she could see perfectly well what was happening on the screens. One showed a street map format, with the target a slowly moving red dot being tracked by the two fast-approaching green dots that were the Alpha and Bravo teams. The next screen showed a view of the same area from the cameras of a helicopter hovering overhead. The gap was narrowing fast, and less than a minute later the latest in the sequence of street cameras caught the taxi at the exact moment it was overtaken by one of the pursuit cars. Within seconds the intercept was over. The taxi was boxed in, and it slammed to a halt. Four armed police officers circled it and shouted their orders. A few seconds after, the passenger struggled out of the taxi, his movements complicated by the order to keep his hands above his head. He folded himself down and lay prone on the tarmac as a policeman cuffed his hands behind his back.

"Show me what's in the bags," Lovell instructed.

One of the officers holstered his weapon and entered the taxi. He pulled out two black roll bags. He unzipped one, took a look inside, then held the bag up at shoulder height in the direction of the helicopter. He had a wide grin on his face. And the energy in the Situation Room changed immediately as the intense focus of Lovell's entire team was transformed into a round of back-slapping and applause.

Thirty minutes later, when Lovell had completed whatever other celebratory things she needed to do, Zoya found Robin and the two of them joined the Inspector back in her office.

"It was a joint win," Lovell said. "We only knew to put the Braintree runners under surveillance because you were able to get Mickey talking. So, thank you for that. As a result, we've seized fifteen kilos of cocaine in the two bags, which means plenty of credit to share around – and that's a big deal for my team, especially given all the negatives of the last few days. We also have a Braintree foot-soldier in custody, so it's possible we'll be able to sweat something useful out of him."

Zoya smiled humbly as she thought they should really be thanking the Scout's stupidity for having Robin and then her followed and attacked. Although she did recognise that the ability not to interfere whilst the bad guys messed up was one of her strong points.

"Then there's this," Lovell continued. "I'll show it all, but I think the main point of interest is the drop-off guy."

The video was black-and-white, high-quality, with the date and time conveniently displayed. It showed that, at 13.05, a man had entered the left-luggage area and entered a four-digit code into the keypad on the door of one of the lockers. He had then taken out two identical roll bags and walked away; casually, with no thought that soon he would be face-down on the ground with his hands handcuffed behind his spine. Next, Lovell scrolled back and showed another clip from just under ninety minutes earlier. This time they watched as a different man walked across the concourse carrying the same two bags and stowed them in the locker.

Lovell passed over printouts of a series of images of the drop-off man. They were from various angles, from four or five different cameras, with each one zoomed as close as the pixels would allow. Despite the baseball cap on his head, there were two shots that had managed to capture an almost complete image of the man's features: one where he was glancing up as if he was scanning the walls for cameras, the other with him looking off to the side.

"It's not the Hunter. At least, he's nothing like the photo we have," Robin said.

"No, it's someone new. And from the way he's behaving, I would say he's no expert in either surveillance or counter-surveillance. But at least it's another face from their team to add to the list."

"I've been thinking it through since we spoke this morning," Zoya said. "Only four men left on the boat, so based on what we know about the assault team it's likely four or five are still somewhere nearby. Which has to include the sniper, since he shot the Scout after the boat had already left. It's also highly probable that the Hunter would have stayed on to lead his team, as the decision on who to eliminate – Mickey and me, or the Scout – would have been far too important for his operation, and for him personally to trust to anyone else.

If I'm right, that means the two highest-value guys – the boss and the shooter – are still here. Therefore, on one hand our priority doesn't change. We do everything we can to capture them before they cross the border; maybe in this Grimsby place, maybe somewhere else. However, I was also thinking through what happens if we miss them. And I have an idea for a possible consolation prize."

Zoya paused, gathering her thoughts, then she continued.

"I think we have an opportunity to cause a huge amount of disruption to their future operations. The more pressure we put on them, the more likely they are to do something stupid, and the more likely it becomes that we catch them next time round. Which we do by making sure anyone who's remotely important in the criminal world hears about all the different ways these guys screwed up this operation.

First, there's the fact that they killed off the people who were supposed to be their client. I know the reality was a little different, but we can spin it as the Hunter being unreliable or outright treacherous. Then they allowed one of their key men to be spotted by at least two witnesses, after which they assassinated him smack in the centre of a busy city. Again, that gives a picture of disloyalty and not caring about the mess they leave behind. And what just happened adds an extra pile of steaming dung to their pigsty. They sold-on a load of looted coke, but because of their carelessness it got intercepted, with the buyer losing his money and one of his men in the process."

"I love it," Lovell said. "I can get my team spreading the information through their contacts with the European equivalents of our Organised Crime Unit. You do the same with Interpol. We all rely on informers, snitches, sources – and it'll be easy enough for them to get the message out. After a few weeks of that, the Hunter's business is going to collapse."

And it was only when they had left Lovell's office that Robin introduced the treacherous seeds of caution.

"Are you sure this is a good idea?" he asked. "We know the Hunter decided just two days ago to kill his friend simply because you – and Mickey of course – had seen his face. What's his reaction going to be when we attempt to trash his whole business?"

Zoya frowned as a big black storm cloud of doubt passed overhead. And this cloud's only silver lining – since Lovell had immediately begun to pass the orders to her team – was that Zoya knew it was already too late to back down.

CHAPTER 25

As he drove, Robin was thinking how much his life had changed since Zoya had appeared on the scene. He had seen his first murder victim in the flesh, and learnt the importance of neat knots and ligature width in the practice of erotic asphyxiation. He had reviewed multiple crime scene files, and even begun to imagine he was getting the hang of what to look for. He had visited Holland without seeing a single tulip, clog or van Gogh painting. He had learnt his two first Ukrainian swearwords – if you counted the one Zoya had muttered repeatedly as she was falling asleep on his couch. And, set against these wondrous experiences, the few minor inconveniences he had endured had even acquired their own peculiar charm. He had been attacked; he had survived. He had come to anticipate poison in every bite of every meal; he had survived. He had even gone partying with a Ukrainian; he had survived. So what did it matter in the overall scheme of things that the interior of his car was spattered in yellow flecks that he recognised as egg, and other randomly coloured flecks that he didn't recognise at all? All in all, it had been a good week.

At his side, Zoya was simply happy that Robin had stopped wearing brown. Today's suit was conservative and slick with over-ironing, but navy was a small step in the right direction;

and, if Zoya survived long enough, she thought she might even be able to convince him to buy some new shoes. This thought reminded her of her mother, who had been of that bizarre you-can-always-judge-a-man-by-the-shoes-he-wears persuasion, but then again it was always easier to work on others than on yourself. Then Zoya transitioned to that other thing her mother used to say – about the value of clean underwear – and rather more sensibly in her daughter's opinion. Which in turn forced Zoya to confront, mentally at least, a vital practical detail in her glamorous globe-trotting, crime-fighting life.

"Do you have a washing machine?" she asked Robin.

He looked confused, but he nodded.

"That's good," Zoya said. "Because I'm getting to the point where my only other choices are hotel-bathroom-sink handwashing or city centre underwear shopping. Neither of which sound very enjoyable. And you know how to cook, right?"

Robin confirmed that he also knew how to cook, at which point Zoya's review of his domestic arrangements ended. The redbrick spires of the University of Manchester had arrived, and Einstein awaited.

*

A lookalike, not the real Einstein. With the hair, but without the moustache. And he was charming too. He said he was delighted to be able to help both Interpol and a fellow U of M professor in one fell swoop, as he put it. He apologised for the delay in his reply to Robin's meeting request, which he admitted had been caused by the requirement to inform the security people – which Zoya assumed to mean MI5 rather than the overweight uniform at the end of the corridor – about any potential nuclear-related issue. When he learned Zoya's nationality, his face briefly contorted with concern, presumably because he thought this was information he should perhaps also have mentioned to the powers-that-be. Then he grinned, confessed to his love of Ukrainian borscht, and offered them a tour of his laboratory. His name was Professor Paul Mulligan and, Robin whispered, he was a legend in his field.

The tour mainly involved a careful inspection of thick-walled machines, inside of which invisible but very powerful reactions were induced and, hopefully, controlled. In other words, there would never be much to see unless something had gone terribly wrong. But since Professor Mulligan had shown them his, Zoya decided to show him hers. Which, after a few minutes of experimental probing, had got the professor all hot under his floppy collar.

"It's the best I've ever seen," he said. "The sensitivity is off the charts. I have to know, my dear Zoya, how exactly did you come to have such a superb example?"

Zoya blushed at his praise and then she confessed.

"To be honest I only tried to use it once," she said, "and it had me flickering all over the place. I wasn't even sure it was working." Then she added, in case it helped: "It's from a barn in the Netherlands".

To Zoya's surprise, it turned out that the Geiger counter she had brought with her not only worked, but it was also highly sophisticated and extremely accurate. Its directional capabilities were outstanding, and Mulligan said its range was almost unprecedented in a self-contained handheld device. Which, naturally, raised a number of questions in Zoya's mind, which she filed for later consideration.

After which, Professor Mulligan admitted to a consuming passion for Geiger counters. He said that in no small part this was due to the coincidence that it was right there, in the University of Manchester's research laboratories, that the counter's underlying detection principle had been identified more than a hundred years prior. Mulligan explained how the Geiger-Müller tube functioned, and the differences in the inert gases used to fill it. He talked at length about the Townsend discharge effect, how it could be amplified, and the importance of getting the right voltage selection.

He went on to comment that the holy grail – and no one knew if it was even possible – was to develop a Geiger counter that could be tuned to detect only a specific radioactive isotope; to a particular wavelength, he tried to explain, although he conceded that talking about wavelengths in relation to radioactivity was not strictly accurate. He was already moving on when Zoya interrupted.

"Why, Professor Mulligan," she asked, "is the ability to tune to a specific isotope regarded as the holy grail?"

Mulligan grinned and ran a hand through his wispy Einstein hair. He said he wanted to be sure that Zoya and Robin understood that he would need to report the details of their discussion up the line. Zoya agreed that they had been appropriately warned. Then he began to tell them stories about spies.

*

Mulligan began by leaning forwards and whispering "Polonium-210" in Zoya's ear. He said it was a Russian specialty, and shot her a glance of apology. He hinted that he had been consulted on a case only last year, quite dreadful, where the poor man had taken six weeks to die and there had been absolutely nothing the doctors could do about it apart from watch him grow weaker and weaker as they dripped water from a sponge into his mouth and his organs had failed one after the other. He had been a banker, of all things. An exile apparently, not a spy; and their assumption had been that he had been misspending someone else's money, since that was what bankers tended to do.

Then Mulligan cheered up and moved on. He said that fortunately, knock on wood, he didn't think poisoning was what they were looking at in this case. Because of the Geiger counter, he said. Zoya mentioned that they had discovered a possible East German connection and Mulligan confirmed that made sense. The Stasi, he continued, had spent a lot of time scattering radioactive stuff all over the place. They had seemed to enjoy it. Not to kill, mind you, just for tracking and surveillance – they had used low-intensity radioactive isotopes. Robin interrupted to ask if Scandium-46 would fit the bill, and Mulligan confirmed it would be just perfect.

"There were different things they did," the professor continued. "Sometimes, for example, they would sprinkle the floor of an entire room with radioactive dust. It would be where they knew some clandestine meeting was taking place, but they didn't know who was going to be there. Or, even if they did know and they just wanted to follow everyone after the meeting ended. The spies or dissidents or whoever they were would come into the room, they would walk around, and of course the soles of their shoes would get coated in the dust. Which meant that wherever they went for the next few days, the Stasi could track them."

"That sounds dangerous," Robin said. "Did they ever get it wrong and end up poisoning someone they were just trying to follow?"

"People are often very worried about radioactivity," Mulligan said, "and understandably so. But for it to be dangerous you really need one of two things. Either a single high dose – which might come from a deliberate poisoning of an individual, or if you're thinking about wider effects then a bomb or a meltdown like at Chernobyl," this last one he accompanied with another apologetic glance at Zoya. "Or you would need repeated smaller doses over a long period of time. The dust on the soles of the shoes trick doesn't really qualify. Although the other stuff they did was potentially more dangerous, mainly due to the possibility of human error."

"What other stuff would that be?" Zoya asked.

"Well, what I just described – the dust on the floor – was a tactic that would have worked reasonably well for a group of people. A scatter-gun approach, if you like. But they needed a more refined approach if they wanted to follow just one person. They could introduce the isotope into someone's food, or they could access an apartment or a hotel room and use an aerosol to spray it on their clothes. Injection was even a possibility, although I understand that was quite rare due to the difficulty of achieving it without the target noticing. And in those types of cases I have heard of mistakes being made. It really depended on the training of the individual agents, and you know how it is once us scientists are taken out of the loop. There was a funny story, coincidentally from our East German friends, which involved one of their agents who was supposed to enter a suspected French spy's hotel room and administer a single spray of Scandium-46 on his overcoat and a second on his jacket. Instead of which, better safe than sorry, he sprayed everything, including the poor man's underpants. Multiple times. The target would have glowed in the dark for weeks after that. Until he died of course."

Zoya wanted to ask which was the funny part – that the glowing dead man had radioactive underpants, or that he was French – but Mulligan had already moved on.

"Which brings us back to the Geiger counters," he said. "Powdering and spraying are the easy parts. True success really depends on your ability to track the target. The first devices they used were big, bulky things, typical Soviet Bloc industrial production. I think I've got some photos around here somewhere. They had to be carried in a heavy shoulder bag, which would have made them conspicuous, and more importantly they had poor battery life and a pretty unsatisfactory range – with a maximum, at least a reliable maximum, of twenty to thirty metres. Plus, they were very bad at distinguishing between different types of radiation, so any background noise could really mess everything up. Anyway, that type of device was the starting point; then things got incrementally better and better over the years, until we arrive at something like the one you brought in today."

"Which you said is very sensitive, good range and so on. But what level of improvement are we talking about? Does that mean a hundred metres, or a thousand? Or more perhaps?"

Mulligan took a moment to consider his answer. Then his phone rang. He took the call. He listened and he flushed red, and his eyes flickered over Zoya and Robin. He put down the phone.

"I'm sorry," he said. "I can't tell you any more right now. And I'm going to need to keep hold of the Geiger counter if that's OK with you. Our friends," he pointed at the phone, "are even more interested than you are to understand its capabilities."

They all stood. The meeting was over. It had been a lot to take in, but at least Zoya now had a reasonable understanding of what Mrs Visser's husband had been up to.

*

When they arrived back at the office, Zoya decided to call Germany. Nervously, because of the recent appearance of Big Brother in her life. But, she thought, what was the worst that could happen? Exile to Odesa, after all, sounded like a perfectly acceptable option right now.

So she called, explaining what she had discovered and adding her own conclusions on the likely role that Mrs Visser's husband – real name Harald Bergmann – would have had within the Stasi. Her maybe-friend seemed less than overjoyed to hear that Zoya already knew pretty much everything that he had spent the last few days investigating – at great personal cost, he pointed out, in terms of egos massaged, favours provided, and debts cancelled. To which Zoya replied that he should stop sulking and he should instead consider just how encouraging it was that they had both reached the same point using their very different methods, especially since hers had involved neither massaging nor providing nor cancelling.

She asked if he had found out anything about her second question. He answered that he might have been able to if he hadn't wasted all his time finding answers she already knew. And then he thought for a moment, and he laughed – with the same rumbling laugh that had been the reason she had taken him into her bed – and said that, in any case, Zoya had just done the easy part. The real question, he said, was not what Bergmann-Visser was doing, but who he was doing it to. Zoya knew this was true. But she also thought it was a rather cruel thing to say, considering the long and tortuous route that had brought her this far.

But who believed in all those romantic myths of post-sex friendship between men and women anyway? Not her, not today. So Zoya said she hoped he would have an answer when she called again tomorrow. The she asked him, rather cruelly, to pass on her regards to his wife, and that was the end of their conversation.

CHAPTER 26

After lunch Zoya called Scheefnek. He said, with only a hint of sarcasm, that he had been eagerly anticipating her call. She proceeded to brief him on all matters radioactive; except for the unexpected involvement of the spooks, since she didn't want to spook him.

"And I have news for you too," Scheefnek replied. "We did a reverse image search on the photo from the Bible. I know who she is."

"Are you going to tell me?" Zoya asked.

"Her name's Anna Vries," he replied. "She's an artist who works from a studio in Amsterdam, and she specialises in woodblock printing. She has her own site, so you can look her up after we finish talking. The problem is, I haven't been able to reach her. There's no answer on any of the phone numbers I've found, and she seems to have gone silent. She was active on social media until about a month ago, mainly posting on Instagram with stuff relating to her art, then everything stopped. On the other hand, no-one's filed a missing person report in her name, and we don't have any unidentified female deaths over the last month that could answer her description. In the Netherlands at least; I haven't checked other countries yet."

"And you're planning to drive up to Amsterdam?" Zoya asked. Or suggested.

"Tomorrow," he replied, then Zoya heard someone in the background calling Scheefnek's name.

"Sorry, got to go," he said.

Zoya found Anna Vries's site easily enough. She had always admired woodcut printing, ever since she had visited a travelling Hokusai exhibition as it passed through Kyiv. There was *The Great Wave,* of course, but Zoya had preferred his intricate and intimate scenes of everyday rural life. This hardly made her an expert, but her unexpert opinion was that Vries's work was very cool. She was clearly a fan of cityscapes, mostly of Amsterdam, yet she had entirely avoided the typical tourist views of tall, skinny houses on the canals. Instead, there was a long, flat skyline under an almost entirely black sky; a canalboat listing over to the side as a crane attempted to rescue it from a watery grave; a twilight view – spectral blues and oranges – of the port. The work was incredibly detailed: each one must have taken hundreds of hours to create. But, more importantly, the images were warm and human.

And Zoya liked that the work had pride of place on the site. The information about Vries herself was limited, and hidden on the last page. A single photo showed her smiling into the camera, and there was a short biography. She lived in Amsterdam and had been inspired by her father, who had run a printing and engraving business. Outside of her artwork she loved reading and travel. She had a cat.

Zoya followed the link to her Instagram account. It was similar: welcoming enough, but professional rather than personal. There were a lot of pictures of her various works, plus a few more photos of Vries – each of which showed her busily creating in her studio. There were no family or friends on display, no photos of pets or what she had eaten for dinner, and no pouting selfies. And, as Scheefnek had said, there had been no updates to her account during the last four weeks.

Zoya scrolled back to the top of the page and started again. She focused on the photos of Vries at work. Zoya tapped, she enlarged, she inspected the details. The paint-stained apron. The shelves and the workbench behind Vries, cluttered with pots of ink and paint, with brushes and chisels and pre-sized forms of hardwood. Then she cursed and she called Scheefnek back.

"It's urgent," she said. "You have to get to her before anyone else does."

*

At first Scheefnek had protested – he had thought Zoya was being unreasonable and overly demanding – then she had explained. And although he still thought she was being unreasonable and overly demanding, he also knew that she was right. He stayed an hour for a meeting that he couldn't avoid, but as soon as it ended he had left the office and driven to Amsterdam.

Which was something he usually tried hard to avoid. Too many tourists, too much litter, too little parking – and don't even mention the red-light district, with its swarms of stag-night Brits attracted like flies to you know what. Even on a day like today – a wet Wednesday afternoon – he would bet they would still be there: ogling through windows, playing who dares wins; tonight and every other night's prize an unpleasant but hopefully curable disease to take home to the family.

Then he had cheered up. He had entered the address of Anna Vries's studio into his GPS and zoomed in for a closer view of the street map. It turned out that his destination was on the southern circumference of the Singelgracht – the outermost of the network of canals that formed the loops and whorls of the fat thumbprint smudge that was Amsterdam's historic centre. If he was lucky, Scheefnek thought, he would see nothing at all of what everyone else came to the city so desperate to experience.

An hour later, he arrived. It was nearly five. He even found parking on the canal bank on the opposite side of the street. Within minutes he understood why Vries was based here. He walked past a redbrick building called *de Ateliers*, which he had read in some lifestyle guide was a trendy centre for experimental art. The smaller next-door building was a mix of craftspeople and internet startups. Then he found the address he was looking for three buildings down. It was four floors, brick-built again, with high, narrow windows and a sharp peaked roof. He went inside. Vries's name was over a glass door on the second floor, with two of her prints showcased in the adjacent window. But that was as good as it got. The door was locked. Scheefnek rang the bell, then he rapped with his knuckles. Nothing. He peered inside and saw a stack of mail on the floor. There was no one home.

The next-door space buzzed with the distinctive hum of a tattoo gun. A pierced teenager smiled welcomingly until he showed her his ID. She said she was new, and she had never met Anna Vries. A voice called out from behind a bamboo partition and asked for a couple of minutes so that he could finish up with his client. When the man emerged, he peeled blue latex gloves off long thin fingers covered in white metal rings and ran them over Scheefnek's credentials as if he was reading braille. He reported that everyone in the building loved Anna, and that they had all been worried when she had popped round to the neighbouring businesses to tell them she had family issues to deal with and wouldn't be around for a few weeks. About a month back, he said. And no, she hadn't contacted him since, he said.

Through the door on the other side of Vries's studio, a young woman in a dusty apron and safety glasses took a pause from tapping with her flat-blade chisel at a block of marble and said the same thing in exactly the same words.

Scheefnek didn't believe either of them.

He walked back down the stairs and stood outside the building, wondering what to do next. He had Vries's home address on a scrap of paper in his pocket. It was the obvious next stop, even though he had to admit that it didn't make a lot of sense that Vries would shut up shop, abandon the studio and the work that she gave every appearance of loving, just to hang out a few kilometres away in an apartment whose address anyone reasonably competent could find in ten minutes flat. Scheefnek thought that if she had any sense she would be long gone – buying a one-way ticket to a deserted tropical island, packing a bikini and going to ground. Then again all of this had begun with six men who had tried to run, not forgetting that one of them was her boyfriend, and look where it had got them.

At the same time, he knew he didn't really have a choice. He couldn't just ignore Vries's home, however excessively obvious it seemed. And at least it was nearby.

Scheefnek walked east along the canal. He turned south onto Van Woustraat and kept going for five hundred metres until the woman with the sultry voice who lived in his phone told him to turn right. And there it was: a long, industrial-looking block that looped around a small, wooded area. He passed an Indonesian restaurant and the Hotel Victorie and found the entrance to Vries's staircase. The brass panel of doorbells had her name at the top, and he buzzed just in case. There was no answer.

He waited. Ten minutes later the door opened and an old woman with a small dog exited. Scheefnek flashed her his most dazzling smile and slipped through the door. There was an ornate metal-cage lift that he ignored, choosing to walk the stairs instead. He was looking for apartment eight, according to the address he had. This he found on the last floor, six storeys up, thinking he should have taken the lift after all.

He rang and knocked. Nothing. He grinned when he caught himself thinking *What would Zoya do*? The woman had got inside his head, and he didn't even know her, not really. It was a good question, though – even if it was rather irrelevant, since Scheefnek knew exactly what she would do; though he had neither the equipment nor the skills to do it (no lock picks, and no training in their use).

But one characteristic he shared with Zoya was that he didn't like to give up. He looked around. Would Vries have left a key somewhere perhaps? He tried the obvious places: lifting the doormat, running his fingers over the top of the doorjamb. There were three plants on the windowsill by the door. He lifted each one, even digging his fingers into the soil. He found nothing. Or maybe he had found something. The plants were healthy and green, the soil was moist. Vries's apartment was the only one on the floor, but someone had been here. Someone had watered the plants.

A last thought occurred to him. Something he had read about. He lifted the flap of the apartment door's letterbox, peering through and seeing only the dark of the unlit room beyond. He groped with his fingertips, and in the right corner he felt something – a screwhead, and attached to it a thread. He caught hold of the thread and pulled gently, keeping going until the object it was tied to appeared in his fingers. A key.

*

He unlocked the door and went inside. He could tell immediately there was no one home. The air was still and musty and the silence was total. He walked through the rooms just in case: the living room and separate kitchen; two bedrooms, each with their own bathroom. The apartment had high ceilings and generous proportions, and Scheefnek wondered how a woodblock artist could afford a place like this. He checked the fridge, which was almost empty, what little it contained being long past its expiry date. But the plants inside the apartment had been watered too.

He opened closets in the main bedroom. The first was lined with dresses and skirts and blouses, with a smaller section off to one side reserved for a man's shirts and trousers. The second had coats and jackets and a surprisingly large selection of denim dungarees. Both closets were reasonably full. There were some empty hangers, but maybe she always kept it like that; and Scheefnek had no way of knowing what, if anything, Vries had taken with her.

Behind a stack of shoeboxes, he found a safe. Interesting, but not particularly unusual. And safe-cracking was no more one of Scheefnek's skills than lock picking. He walked back into the living room and looked through drawers, then inspected the bookshelves. On the top shelf, he found something that shouldn't have been there. Almost invisible, poking out from between two paperbacks, was the round black lens of a micro-camera. He pulled out the two books, followed the cable clenched between them and found the small plastic box that contained the camera's transmission device. Then he put everything back just the way it had been.

What would Zoya do?

She would eat, that much was for sure.

Scheefnek remembered the restaurant he had seen nearby. Indonesian, which reminded him of Zoya and Robin's visit; and he also happened to be hungry, which was a good enough reason in itself. In a bowl on the kitchen counter he found a spare set of keys, and he thought it was likely that one of the set would open the street door. He walked back down the stairs. At the restaurant he ordered nasi goreng and beer, just as he had when he had eaten with Zoya and Robin, and thought through what he had seen. It was possible that Vries had rigged the apartment with cameras herself, as a general precaution against burglars or as specific current precaution to detect whoever was going around killing her boyfriend's friends. Or more likely, he thought, whoever had killed those friends was also looking for Vries and had rigged the apartment in case she returned.

In either case, Scheefnek knew that Zoya's first instinct would be the same as his. She would attempt to provoke a reaction, and then she would deal with the inevitable fallout. He thought it was a good instinct and that simple plans were the best.

He finished his meal and walked back to the apartment, letting himself in again. He closed the door behind him and wedged a chair under its handle, before washing his face and helping himself to an unopened toothbrush from one of the bathroom cabinets to clean his teeth. He thought Zoya would have taken a shower, but that was one step too far for him. He also thought she would have slept in one of the woman's bedrooms, but that was two steps too far for him.

Instead, he stretched out on the sofa in the living room. He allowed his gaze to drift towards the bookshelf. He yawned, and wondered if someone would come for him. He closed his eyes and pretended to sleep.

*

Less than a kilometre away a small man sat in a small room and watched his screens. He wondered who the big man on the sofa was, and he cursed. The watcher had been promised backup, but he knew he couldn't afford to wait. He set himself a deadline. If support didn't arrive by the morning, he would have no choice. He would have to take Anna Vries on his own.

CHAPTER 27

In the dull light of an overcast day, Scheefnek thought it had not been such a great plan after all. Partly because of the ache in his back from twisting and turning on a sofa that was far too short for him. Also, because when he had woken in the early hours to the drum of rainfall on the tin windowsills, he had been filled with the realisation that he had just set himself up against the kind of people whose hobby seemed to be travelling Europe and assassinating anyone they took a dislike to. Especially since he was unarmed, and let's all chorus together: "Interpol officers don't carry guns, since their role is to gather intelligence then coordinate a response". Which was the worst part of his job. It was a stupid rule, but that's how it was.

Those were the partial reasons, but the main one was that nothing had happened. He had waited, he had slept, it was morning.

Vries had a fancy coffee machine, and it took Scheefnek a while to figure out how to use it. There was no milk, so he added sugar. He drank two cups, then he cleaned his teeth. He resisted the temptation to say goodbye to the camera, locked the apartment door behind him, and went out into the rain in search of breakfast.

*

He called Zoya and told her what he had found, and what he hadn't. She said she was pleased he was taking the initiative. She commented that provoked reactions were strange things. That you sometimes waited hours or even days for one, then, when you had almost given up, two came along at once. Scheefnek understood this to mean she was warning him to be careful.

He decided to try the neighbours. Inside, after all, was better than out on a day like this. He knocked on doors and discovered it was a friendly building. Most of the doors opened and the apartment owners were happy to chat. They all knew Anna Vries, and they all shared a general opinion that she was charming and helpful. But no one had seen her for weeks; and no, she hadn't said where she was going or when she would be back.

Scheefnek returned to her workplace. The tattoo parlour was open, and he heard the pounding of metal on stone from the sculptor's studio. He thought there was no point trying either of them again, so he walked into the other workshops and studios on her floor then strolled the floors of the building and spoke to as many people as he could. The businesses he found were similar: artists, metalworkers, jewellery designers, an architect, a dance studio. And everyone he talked with said one of two things. They either didn't know Anna Vries. Or they did, but they didn't know where she was.

By the end of the morning, he had reached two conclusions. First, that someone was watching Vries's apartment. And second, that all the people he had spoken to today had seemed sincere and truthful, whereas the only two he had spoken to yesterday did not. The tattoo man and the sculptor woman, who were Vries's closest neighbours, had told him the same thing in exactly the same words. He had believed neither of them.

It was a long shot, but Scheefnek decided he would follow them, one or both, when they left the building.

He looked at his watch. It was 12.36. He found a tree opposite the entrance, whose branches sheltered a small circle of pale pavement from the drizzle. He waited.

*

Lunchtime was busy, as throngs of people left to eat before returning to the building. The tenants, the owners, their customers. He saw nothing out of the ordinary. The afternoon was quieter. A few people arrived; a few people left. The rain didn't stop, it just got heavier. Shortly after 1700, a slow trickle began of people setting off for home. He noticed that the pierced teenager who worked in the tattoo place was one of them. By 1800 the trickle had dried up. Neither the tattoo artist nor the sculptor had left. Scheefnek realised that despite watching for much of the day, he hadn't thought to check if there was another exit from the building. He went back inside. All he found was the sign that pointed down the corridor to a fire exit. At the end of the corridor another sign warned that the door was alarmed. Scheefnek remembered similar signs and similar alarmed doors on the other floors. He hadn't heard an alarm and, in any case, why would the two people he was interested in both choose today to leave via a fire escape instead of using the main door?

He waited some more.

At 1900 he walked up to the second floor. His clothes were dripping wet and his nose blocked, and he was just happy to be out of the cold. Which didn't change the fact that the doors to both the tattoo parlour and the sculptor's studio were closed and locked. He began to explore.

He went up floor by floor and walked the corridors. Most of the businesses were closed for the night. He walked down again. Around him the building was quiet and calm, with zero hint of trouble. Scheefnek saw only one other person, a man – short, wearing a puffer jacket, with dark hair, strong cologne and a scar on the back of his right hand – who gave him an indifferent smile as they passed on the stairs. And then he was back down at street level without having met anyone else.

He stood outside and tried to figure out if he had missed something. Was there some other explanation as to why tattoo man and sculptor woman hadn't left the building, yet were nowhere to be seen inside? And why did he care? Why, when it came down to it, had he spent seven hours waiting for them, freezing his butt off, when he had absolutely no reason, other than the belief that there was something they weren't saying, to connect them with Anna Vries?

Then the rain stopped, and images of hands suddenly pulled fresh and sharp into Scheefnek's mind, and he turned and sprinted up the stairs.

*

As Scheefnek climbed, he remembered the tattoo artist's right hand from the previous day. It had been crusted in white metal rings of all shapes and sizes. But his left hand had just the one, on its fourth finger: a wedding ring with a difference – a small skull pressed flat against the wide white band. And the sculptor had been wearing exactly the same ring.

As Scheefnek climbed, he saw the scar on the right hand of the small man who had passed him on the staircase. It was round and raised and puckered with spokes of paler tissue. It was unmistakeable. It was a bullet wound.

He had reached the third floor. He panted, and his eyes and ears strained as he walked the length of the corridor. Nothing but closed doors and silence. His mind cursed as he searched desperately for something, anything, he could use as a weapon – even as he remembered that his designated role was to gather intelligence then coordinate a response. He paused, took a series of deep breaths, and did what he was supposed to. He called the local police and coordinated their response. Then he did what he wasn't supposed to – he kept going up the stairs.

On the fourth floor, a bronze figure stood on a plinth on the landing. It was somewhere between African tribal and Giacometti. It was a stretched man, striding forwards. Maybe it was art, maybe it was valuable – but it was definitely a heavy piece of metal. Scheefnek shed his wet coat onto the ground and strained as he picked up the sculpture. He hefted it to find a balance point, and in the same instant he heard a crash off to his right. Something falling – a chair, or a table – then a scream split the air and Scheefnek ran.

He reached the last door – wooden, ajar – as another scream came from inside; more like a howl this time, pain and anger intertwined. Scheefnek smashed a shoulder into the door, losing his balance and stumbling forwards. The room was long and narrow, equipped as an apartment not a workshop. It was crowded. Four people were already inside, and Scheefnek made five. All were frozen for an instant by his arrival, and he had to act fast or they would all die.

The tattoo man lay on the floor by the window. The sculptor, his wife, crouched at his side. There was blood, lots of it, and both of them were clutching at the man's right leg as Scheefnek swivelled to the side.

Puffer jacket man's back had been to him, but he was already turning. His arms were held high, stretched out in a double-handed grip on the gun he had been pointing at the second woman. Her face had been hidden from Scheefnek by the gunman's body, though now it was revealed. Anna Vries, no doubt about it, and Scheefnek's eyes refocused, finding the black barrel of the Glock that was already aimed straight at him. Scheefnek did exactly what Zoya would have done: launching himself through the air, spearing the bronze statue towards the man's masked face, as Anna Vries screamed and the man's gun boomed.

CHAPTER 28

Zoya was thinking about watermelons – fresh-picked from the black earth fields of Kherson; the hollow knock of your knuckles on the heavy, ripe gourd; the sweet, crisp flesh when you split it open – as she walked to the Interpol office the next morning. She said *dzien dobry* to the security guard on the front desk (since she had discovered he was Polish) and set off up the stairs to the Interpol floor. She found it was strangely deserted, and it was only when she switched on her computer that Zoya realised that, after a week that had passed fast and then slow, the weekend had come round again. Her screen told her it was Saturday 11 April.

Zoya wondered what the protocol was. Back home she'd have had no hesitation in phoning colleagues at the weekend – and in the middle of the night for that matter, which in part explained why she had been passed over for promotion to captain two years running. But here? In the land of excess apologies, friendly compromises and the strange new concept that was work-life balance? And besides, it wasn't even nine o'clock yet. She decided on her own friendly compromise – which was to wait another hour and then start balancing everyone's work and their life, whether they liked it or not.

She browsed the staff manual that Tahiri had so kindly passed to her; starting with the section on expense reports, which was clearly the most urgent given her current financial situation. She skimmed the guidance and found the appropriate form. She was about to begin compiling her report when she realised that she had left all her receipts back at the hotel. The thought of her hotel room reminded her about its radiation hotspots, and the puzzling fact that Professor Mulligan had claimed the Geiger counter was working perfectly.

Zoya found no good theory to link the two contradictory concepts, and by then it was already nine-thirty. She flicked through a sheaf of Interpol red notices, admiring particularly those submitted by the Russians – whose common theme seemed to be that they wanted to arrest everyone who didn't love the President, wherever they happened to be. Next she drank a cup of coffee and ate a chocolate bar, for the simple reason that the vending machine was out of meaty, chewy sandwiches.

It wasn't yet ten o'clock, but Zoya had nothing else to do. She began to call.

She started with Robin, got an engaged tone, and wondered who else he had in his life. She called her German. He didn't answer, and she knew who else he had in his life – he was probably at the park with his wife and the two children that she also hadn't been told about at the time, although she admitted to herself that she hadn't actually asked. She called Scheefnek, and by now she was already getting a little annoyed. So what if it was Saturday? Why the hell was everyone ignoring her?

A few minutes later Zoya was pleased when Scheefnek called her back, until that is she saw his face on the screen. He explained what had happened, and then she was suddenly furious.

"What the hell were you thinking?!" Zoya yelled, and Scheefnek smiled weakly from under the crepe bandages that were swaddled around his head. He could of course have told her the truth – that he had been thinking at the time that he should do what he thought Zoya would do – but right now, even to him, it sounded like an overly complicated explanation and a poor justification for his unforgiveable stupidity. He didn't reply.

"And get me a doctor on the line Stiff Neck, or a nurse at least. I need to hear that you're OK from someone who actually knows what they're talking about."

Fortunately, Scheefnek's charming young nurse had just finished increasing his blood pressure and she was happy to explain.

"Your friend was lucky," she said. "From what we understand he threw himself across the room at an armed man. The single bullet that the man had time to fire hit your Officer Scheefnek's skull at a shallow angle. It knocked him out and left a deep furrow across the side of his head. He was unconscious for several hours and he has mild concussion, however our tests indicate there was no brain damage. Also, a flap of his right ear was torn away, but it was retained by the woman who accompanied him in the ambulance. We have been able to sew it back in place. It should heal nicely, and the scarring will be minor."

"Thank you," Zoya said simply as she deflated.

"Are you OK?" Scheefnek asked.

"Better," Zoya said. "Now take me through it again, step by step."

Scheefnek explained how he had figured out the tattoo artist and the sculptor were married. He had already suspected they knew where Anna was, and were lying to protect her. When he realised neither of them had left the building, but were also not in their studios, he had guessed they might also share a place to stay somewhere in the building. Which, he had thought, would also be a good place to stash Anna. He had known his conjectures involved a lot of guesses and assumptions, but when he had seen the man on the stairs with the old bullet wound in his hand he had also known he couldn't take any chances. He mentioned the sculpture he had taken as a weapon, and described the scene he had found in the top-floor apartment. He reported that the tattoo artist's leg wound wasn't too serious, and that he was twenty metres down the corridor in a separate room with his wife at his side.

"What about the gunman?" Zoya asked.

"I didn't actually see the result," he said, "but they tell me that he has a crater in his face the exact size and shape of the bronze statue's head."

Scheefnek paused and gulped. The words had been enough to release a wave of doubt and pain inside. He clenched his fists. He knew he had done what he needed to do. He knew he had saved at least one life. It would have to be enough.

"And yes, he's dead, in case you were wondering," he said.

"Which means we don't know who sent him?" Zoya complained.

"Which means that Anna Vries is alive and well," Scheefnek replied, which Zoya accepted was a fair point.

By now Scheefnek's face was drawn and haggard. Zoya could see that, despite his smile, he wasn't doing too well. And nor, to be honest, was she. So, she told him not to do anything else stupid. And she told him to rest.

*

Then it was the German's turn. He too called her back, and it turned out he wasn't at the park. He was at work, just like she was.

"I have everything you asked for," he said, and proceeded to give her a brief summary.

Zoya had learnt to expect the unexpected, yet even so she was surprised by the extent of what he had discovered. At least now she knew the truth.

"I sent you the relevant files," he concluded. "Guaranteed one-day delivery."

"Maybe I'll see you in Odesa again someday," she replied. *Goodbye, until I need you again,* in other words.

*

Reliable Robin was the next to call, making it three drakes in a row. Zoya explained what had happened to Scheefnek, and was surprised by the urgency of Robin's response.

"We need to speak with her. With Anna. She could be the key to all of this. I'll set it up and get back to you."

And he rang off without waiting for Zoya to argue or to agree. Which she thought was encouraging. Her defenceless little pupa had transformed overnight into an equally defenceless but rather more beautiful butterfly – or maybe a moth, given Robin's apparent aversion to sunlight. Although hopefully with a longer life span.

And since her butterfly-moth was busy setting up whatever it was that he had decided, Zoya moved her keyboard out of the way and buried her head in her hands on the desk. She began to walk through every detail of everything that had happened since she had first flown into Manchester: sequencing, cataloguing; looking for things she had not seen before and connections she had not made.

Dead Dutchmen and the fact that one of them had been killed close by, when the Hunter's men must already have arrived in Manchester.

The mugger's question – "What's the Ukrainian woman doing here?"

The photo of the man Zoya thought was the Hunter, and why he didn't seem to care if his face had been seen.

The calling card; and was that a man's head silhouetted in the rifle scope, or a woman's?

A dead ex-Stasi agent tortured both before and after death.

The vexing question of who in the Visser family Zoya could really believe.

Radiation in her hotel room.

Which was as far as she had got when Robin called again.

"I decided we should meet Anna in person," he said. "I never liked conference calls. Grab a taxi to the airport, I'll meet you there."

It was a novel experience. For once Zoya did as she was told.

*

And regretted it. They had missed the direct flight, having to connect at London Heathrow, and there was no one to meet them at the other end. They arrived at the hospital just before six p.m., and were greeted at the door to Scheefnek's room by a truculently armed Dutch policeman. But at least the greeting inside was warm.

"Thank you so much." Anna Vries sighed as she enveloped first Zoya then Robin in a long, perfumed embrace. "Officer Scheefnek told me everything. You saved both me and my friends, and I am forever in your debt."

Zoya's tilt as she entered the room had as always been towards professional scepticism, until it turned out that Anna was wearing denim dungarees over a six- or seven-month pregnancy bump. It was an unfair tactic, Zoya thought, even as Anna moved back to her starting position by Scheefnek's bed and beamed her petal-blue eyes in Zoya and Robin's direction from beneath her innocent jet-black fringe. She sealed the fate of Zoya's misguided attempt at suspicion by lowering herself awkwardly onto her chair with a slight groan. Zoya forced herself to inspect the tidy stitches on Scheefnek's reattached earlobe, then she watched his eyes for a moment. He nodded reassuringly. Zoya turned to Anna and began.

"You're a forger," she said.

Pitched between question and statement, her words were met by a rapid flutter of eyelashes – *remember, Zoya, she's a criminal even when she's pregnant* – and a quick glance towards the closed door, then a jangle of the bangles on Anna's wrist as she stroked a slim hand through her hair. *A smart woman, then, thinking how much not to say.*

"Whatever I did before, I've stopped now," Anna said in heavily accented but fluent English, as she braced a protective hand under her belly.

"You don't really need to tell me, since I already know," Zoya said. "The whole reason why I asked Scheefnek to find you so urgently was that I saw something in your Instagram photos that shouldn't have been there. Passport stamps set out in a neat row on your workbench, and the sheet of paper you'd already used them on – to check the colour, or maybe the dates. And the Dutch police will, I'm sure, find plenty of similar evidence in your studio."

Scheefnek helpfully and regretfully added a long stream of what Zoya understood to be references to the Dutch penal code. It sounded intimidating and it might even have been accurate, so Zoya pushed on.

"I understand that you don't want to incriminate yourself," she said. "But at the same time, you must realise that you and your baby will need ongoing protection. Whoever killed your fiancé and his friends, he was after you too. You have no guarantee that they won't try again, and I imagine the Dutch police has no reason to help you unless you give them something useful. That is something you will need to figure out; but in any case, I suggest we keep it simple for now. So, speaking hypothetically, Anna, if someone like you – a successful artist, and I have to say that I really like your work – was to have a sideline in forging passports and other documentation, how do you think that would have come about?"

Anna's eyes drifted upwards as her mind chased down a memory, then she smiled.

"My grandfather was a remarkable man," she said. "He ran a small printing business in Berlin. He was Jewish and when the war started the Nazis shut him down, but he never stopped working. He used the knowledge and the skill he had accumulated over the years, and he began to prepare fake documentation – anything from birth certificates to passports and visas; complete sets of everything an individual would need to escape Germany. Thousands of people – mainly fellow Jews, but also a number of escaped prisoners of war – evaded the authorities, survived, and went on to live happy lives, all because of him.

After the war he taught his son, my father, everything he knew, and then they both taught me. Even as a kid, although I had no intention of ever becoming a forger, I loved the process. Carving the stamps – out of hardwood, the old-fashioned way; or out of whatever else you had to hand. What types of ink to use, and how to mix them to get the perfect colour. Everything you needed to know about paper: how to make it from scratch if you needed to, techniques to age or adapt existing paper samples, the best ways to introduce watermarks. Not that I am admitting anything, you understand, but if I had ever wanted to become a forger, I'm sure that education would have allowed me to become a very good one."

"How did you meet Jan, your fiancé?" Zoya asked.

"Through our parents," Anna replied. "His parents knew my father. Maybe they worked together, hypothetically, maybe not. But my father's dead now, and my grandfather too of course, so they have nothing to do with whatever is happening now."

"Anna," Robin said, "we started off with our investigation, which eventually led us to you, after we identified a number of Dutch citizens who had died in suspicious circumstances. We discovered that they were all friends of your fiancé, who of course was also the victim of a tragic accident. And then you were attacked. Do you, hypothetically speaking, have any suspicions regarding who could have been targeting you all? Could this have been a business conflict, perhaps an unhappy client or a competitor?"

"Jan was always careful," Anna said a little hazily. "I never even met any of his clients."

She looked like she was going to say something else, but she cut herself off abruptly.

Robin didn't follow up with the obvious point: that Anna would at least have seen her clients' photographs and known the aliases they were given in their new documents. Instead, his voice had ladled out sympathy and commiseration, leaving Zoya to marvel at men's collectively excessive sense of care for expecting mothers. In her experience, and she had no reason to think Anna was any different, pregnant women were as tough as nails for the simple reason that they needed to be. But then again, "good cop, bad bitch" worked for her too.

"What about his friends?" she asked. "It would be a pity if you never got to meet any of them, because they're all dead now, Anna. Killed because of whatever it was that you and Jan and your friends were doing. You need to remember that when you tell us what a good man your grandfather was eighty years ago. Or how about Jan's father? He was sixty-eight years old, he was tortured and killed; and to be honest we don't really care at this point about forged passports – we just want to catch whoever murdered them all."

That got a reaction.

"Jan's father was a good man," Anna said fiercely. "I never liked his mother: I thought she was hard and controlling, and I know she didn't like me. But his father was kind and gentle. He didn't deserve what happened to him."

"What about Jan?" Zoya asked. "Was he a good man too? Your fiancé, the father of your child. Who you say was careful, but who I think brought someone into your life who got everyone killed."

Anna had to have thought about it. Surely over the past weeks – as she hid out at her friends' apartment, pregnant and alone – she couldn't have been saintly enough to avoid blaming him entirely. Zoya watched Anna's face and waited.

"He was ambitious," Anna said finally. "Sometimes that was a good thing, but it could be a problem too. And I don't think his friends always agreed with him. I know from Jan that they had been arguing about something to do with the business.

Which maybe is connected with what happened; but you have to believe me – I never knew the details. To be honest I never wanted to know the details. So no, I don't know who has been doing all this; and if I did, of course I would tell you. But now all I can do is beg you to find them, because unless you do, I know we will never be safe."

Anna clutched again at her belly. *We, meaning me and my baby? Or something else?* The light in Zoya's head was suddenly bright and harsh, her thoughts spinning towards a split-second decision. Should she ask, or should she leave it there?

Not so split-second after all. The silence in the room grew. Zoya glanced at Robin, whose face said he was searching for the next question, or maybe for a way to ask the same questions a little more compassionately. Zoya looked at Scheefnek and realised she needed to speak with him alone. Normally she would have asked him to step out into the corridor, but that wasn't an option today. She would have to call him later, she realised, and tell him what she wanted him to find out.

She blinked and looked back at Anna. At her laughter lines that were unused today, at the bangles and the dungarees. Her eyes were misted now and a little lost. She was pregnant. For a moment Zoya felt sorry for the woman – she had a feeling that Anna was holding onto something that didn't really exist, and that there was absolutely nothing Zoya could do to change her fate. Then she was overtaken by anger at Anna's many compromises and her bad choices, even though Zoya knew that her anger was directed just as much at her own compromises and bad choices. And, finally, she thought she was relieved that she would soon be leaving Anna alone with Scheefnek, since the only thing she was sure about was that Anna would be needing a wide shoulder to cry on. Perhaps they all would.

"I promise you we will find them," Zoya said.

And to Robin's surprise, she pulled him from his chair and hurried out of the room.

*

"It's going to be a rough flight, so buckle up tight," the pilot announced after take-off, and when Zoya spotted the jagged streaks of lightning lancing towards them she thought the warning was entirely unnecessary.

"What just happened?" Robin asked with the despairing tone of someone who just spent the last hour trying to figure it out for himself.

Zoya turned towards him and thought that what had just happened was that Robin had now lost his belief in happy endings, even if he didn't know it yet. But there was no point spoiling the surprise, so she set him a riddle instead.

"There are two things we need to understand," she said. "The first is how the killer or killers tracked down their victims. The second is this bloody Visser family. Everyone's protecting someone from something. We need to know how and why, and we need to know who started it all, and who plans to finish it."

Their plane bucked and jolted through storm clouds that were devoid of silver linings. Zoya said nothing else for the rest of the flight.

CHAPTER 29

No moon, no stars. Polished needles of rain, stabbing at the brittle black sky. The shredded wind shrieking its protest at the ocean, and riven waves that thrashed froth-white tendrils over the granite boulders of the breakwater. The weather that Sunday night in the grim port of Grimsby was perfect.

In the white panel van, only the driver was visible. The Hunter and three more men huddled in the back: out of sight, but ready for the worst; weapons loaded, waiting for the command. Jittery, because the Hunter didn't like this – not one bit. He had always insisted on two principles, and over the years they had served him well. First, that if a job was big enough to involve more than three or four men – and by now most of his jobs were – then the team had to split up when the time came to leave. Second, that no exfil route should be used more than once. It was that part that, this time round, had become an unexpected problem. The Scout had been entirely responsible for logistics, and, inconsiderately, he had not thought to pass on details of his plans before his own untimely bullet-through-the-head exfiltration to a better world. They had no maps, no contact names, not even the password for his laptop computer.

Given time measured in weeks rather than days, the Hunter could undoubtedly have organised something new. However, he knew that long a wait was something he could not afford to risk. Therefore, he had taken the only other option. He had abandoned rule number two and placed a satellite phone call to one of the four men who were busy puking up their guts in the hold of the Danish trawler somewhere in the storm-driven North Sea. The man had confirmed there had been no sign of surveillance when they had left port, and that they were now safely in international waters. He had relayed the skipper's forecast of approximately two more hours' travel until they reached waters that were sheltered enough to launch the trawler's inflatable for their drop-off on a sandy beach in the secluded Vadehavet national park. Then the man had passed on the Hunter's new instructions to the skipper. Once he had delivered the men to the agreed spot, he was to return to Grimsby for a double-fee extra cargo. The skipper had confirmed his agreement, and had made good speed: forty-eight hours later reporting that he was once again safely tied up alongside Grimsby's North Quay. He had said that he and his crew were going below to grab some sleep, and that he would need to load his new cargo within the next twelve hours in order to make the night tide.

In the back of the van, the Hunter's gut spasmed. It was getting worse. He had suffered through two days of pain already, and two nights without sleep, but he couldn't allow his men to suspect his weakness. He balled his fists and studied the map on his screen as he instructed the driver. He guided the van into a figure-of-eight loop of the harbour area. The driver chanted the street names in confirmation – Lockhill Road, left onto Eastside, then left again at the roundabout onto Gorton Street, back down to Murray Street – and he also listed the local sights as he drove (municipal car park on the left, a yacht marina, Offshore Renewable Services, something called Fastline Fish). The Hunter already wanted to tell him to shut it, but he knew it was all that was keeping the man calm. More importantly, the driver ended his recital by reporting that there were no pedestrians braving the three a.m. storm and that he had spotted a few CCTV cameras, but nothing unusual. So far so good, but not yet good enough.

The last street before the quayside was Humber Bridge Road. They paused in the shadow of a storage shed on its corner, just long enough for the van's back doors to open and for the sniper to slip into the night. They drove on, finding an alley next to a metal panelled building called Best Seafood, where they waited. A few minutes later the sniper reported in. He had climbed a fire escape onto the building's rooftop; he could see the trawler tied up a hundred metres away. He was already soaked to the bone, he complained, and visibility was terrible. The men in the van smiled grimly; the sniper's unwavering pessimism was a running joke. But they knew it was an attitude that made him good at his job, and they knew to trust him when he said "No signs of life, all clear". He reported lights on the trawler, but no movement, and described two small warehouses opposite the trawler at right angles to the quay, also with no movement. There was no one out for a walk, and no bored guards taking a cigarette break. There were a few parked cars, with no one inside.

"Thirty minutes", the Hunter said.

On twenty-nine, he asked for an update and was told the same as before. The van exited the alleyway and drove slowly back towards the quay: past the sniper's position (he would be the last onboard), past water to their left and storage facilities to the right. The Hunter climbed into the passenger seat. He made out the boat through the rain – fifty metres, then thirty – and he told the driver to stop. A minute later a crewman appeared on the deck of the trawler, then everything went wrong.

"Movement on your right," said the sniper's voice in the ears of the men in the van. His tone was usually calm, but not now – because whatever it was, whoever it was, he had missed it before, and he thought he might just have got his friends killed.

In the same instant, night was transformed into harsh day. A line of spotlights dazzled and blinded from high up on one of the warehouses, then more flickered into life at street level. A man's voice boomed through a loudspeaker.

"Armed police. Maintain your position. Turn off the engine. Do not exit the vehicle. We are authorised to open fire if necessary."

But the shooting had already begun, it was just that no-one could hear it. The sniper's rounds were silent to everyone but him as they pierced through the rain and wind. Then the arc lights on the warehouse wall began to shatter – spitting and hissing, glass shards littering the tarmac – and the police got the message.

"Two vehicles approaching from behind my position," the sniper shouted out. "They're going to cut you off. I'm engaging, but you need to get out of there. Fast."

He was outgunned, he knew it. His Vintorez rifle was a precision weapon when tonight he needed a grenade launcher. He didn't give up: he shattered one car's windscreen, he managed to burst a tire, he did everything he could to impede the approaching threat at the same time as the Hunter's van reversed at speed down the quay. Two of the police marksmen had emerged from their warehouse position. Their rounds battered at the van as it swayed and swerved. The Hunter yelled "Take a left here!" and they spun round the corner on two wheels, then made a right turn onto the parallel street, and it was quiet for a moment inside the van with just the jets of water pounding at the metal roof.

One of the incoming police cars skidded to a halt. Two officers exited their vehicle and raced to intercept the van. They ran towards the corner, automatic rifles at the ready, and the sniper could already see they would make it. They would cut the van off and rake its engine and its tyres, and he knew he had no choice. He forced his heartbeat slower. Even with the rain he had a perfect view, and the gusting wind wouldn't be a problem at this range. The sniper went for a leg shot, because he had no earthly chance to escape and because he knew that killing a police officer would guarantee him a life sentence. He held the top of his breath. He fired. The black-clad figure in his scope collapsed and there was a swirl of blond-ponytailed hair as her helmet was knocked from her head. The sniper watched as the second officer abandoned the chase and dived to his partner's side. And by then the van had passed, and the sniper could see the woman was alive, and so he laid down his weapon.

"See you on the other side," he said into his mic, and he thought that someone could at least have said goodbye.

*

They had their own problems. One man dead, one badly wounded. A single burst of fire had done most of the damage. One side of the van had been exposed as they had taken the fast left turn, and its thin metal skin had been no protection at all from automatic-weapon fire. The Hunter panted as he crawled back from the passenger seat into the cargo space. There was blood everywhere – spatters and arterial sprays, and a growing pool under the wounded man's body – and the Hunter was relieved because the awful choice had already been made for him. The man was as good as dead already, and all the Hunter could do was cradle his head as his life ebbed away.

"First car park you see," he shouted out to the driver. "We need to ditch the van."

It didn't take long. Five minutes later the driver hotwired a black Ford pickup that stank from a lifetime of hauling fish to market, and they stood for a moment next to the van and watched as it burned. From there they traced through a maze of unlit country roads – north first, then west – inscribing a long, jagged arc back to where they had started, with three less men than when they had left.

The other man didn't say a word, but he didn't need to. The Hunter knew what he was thinking. That he had messed up. That he shouldn't have killed the Scout, at least not before they were out of the country. He was right of course. Something was throwing off his judgement. He had let his obsession with the Ukrainian woman get to him, he knew that much. But how could he not, when she kept on reappearing in his life and screwing up his plans? And it wasn't only that – she was only part of the problem. There was the nausea, too, that never left him; the pain in his gut that kept him from sleep, the weakness he couldn't shake off.

He had to pull himself together. Four of his men had left, they were safe. His new, second team was secure too. For now, it was only the man at his side in the pickup's cab who needed him. He was the Hunter's responsibility; he had a family to return to. The Hunter had to find a way out. Ireland perhaps, he thought. Heading east hadn't worked out. Now they would try the west. He thought there had to be gunrunners and smugglers operating out of Liverpool. Back in the day they would have supplied the IRA, and after years of unprofitable peace they would have turned to anything that paid the bills. He didn't know yet how to contact them, but it was worth a try.

The Hunter slumped back. He had no idea if his thought made sense. His mind was misted and numb. Maybe Ireland would work, maybe it wouldn't, but all he knew was that he shouldn't have killed the Scout without first finding out every detail of his exfiltration plans. It was too late, he had done it, and he couldn't change it now – yet then he remembered perhaps the only useful piece of information the Scout had left behind. An address, a location. It was a thought that sparked something inside him; something far off, but glowing bright and hot. Because the Hunter knew what the real problem was. It was that he no longer really cared about escape: not for himself, not for his men. There was only one thing he truly yearned for, only one thing that could pierce the fog that had invaded him.

And he thought the Scout, loyal even in death, had just shown him the only way left to get what he wanted.

CHAPTER 30

Monday morning, 12 April. It was habit more than anything that got Zoya out of bed, and it was coffee that kept her going. It was only once she had walked down to breakfast that she had realised she wasn't hungry. That was a bad omen. She caught another taxi into the office, she said another "Dzien dobry, Janusz" at reception and she set off towards the stairs. Her upwards journey started uneventfully, but by the time she reached the third floor everything had descended into chaos and panic.

Lovell emerged from her office shouting orders. Zoya caught a glimpse of the man who had just banged a fist on Lovell's desk – burly, dark-haired, wearing black tactical gear. He was what she had learnt that the Brits called an authorised firearms officer, but right now he was without his weapons as far as she could see. Which made him an angry unarmed authorised firearms officer, to give him his full and current title. Then Zoya spotted tight-crotched DC Johnson as he scuttled past, and she grabbed him by his arm.

"What's going on?" Zoya asked.

"There was a shooting in Grimsby early this morning," he said. "We've got one officer in hospital with a bad leg wound, but I understand she's out of surgery and doing well. Also, there are two burnt bodies in a van, and we have one of their guys in custody. Right now, we're coordinating the manhunt for the rest of the gang."

Zoya thought for a moment. It was little consolation that Lovell's plan had been the right one. They had an officer down, a brace of dead bodies, plus an unspecified number of live ones had escaped. Since Zoya couldn't see that there was anything she could do to help, except stay out of the way, she released Johnson's arm and carried on up to the Interpol floor.

*

When she arrived, Zoya found access to her desk blocked by two large cardboard boxes covered with red and yellow stickers that shouted in German block capitals about the urgency and confidentiality of their contents. Her maybe-friend had done what he had promised, aided and abetted by the expensive miracle of an overnight courier service.

Zoya's desk was too small to lay everything out. She lifted the first box and carried it into the nearest meeting room. From an unknown colleague's desk drawer, she liberated a pair of scissors that he didn't seem to be using and sliced the packing tape from the top of the box. She was met by a single sheet of A4 that stated rather more reservedly than the external labels: "*Oberleutnant* Harald Bergmann. AKA Dietrich Visser. You're Welcome". The next layer in Zoya's excavation revealed a tourist guide to Berlin, followed by a small bubble-wrapped glass jar labelled "Authentic Sauerkraut". *German humour really does exist,* she thought – and maybe that meant friendship had a chance after all. Sadly, the initial joke was followed by an uninspiring stack of dusty cardboard files and the crumbling, yellowing mass of their contents. Zoya fingertipped the first file from the pile and began to read.

Her initial suspicion had been that her maybe-friend's despatch of entire boxes of disordered documentation was a form of revenge for Zoya's overly persistent requests for information. She soon realised she had underestimated him. To be sure, there was plenty of bureaucratic padding in what she read: layered in the peculiar Stasi form of ass-covering that recognised that every word and every report would be reviewed not only by multiple levels of internal management but also by the real bosses – the local KGB "liaison" officer and, if it was deemed necessary, by far-off Moscow too. But Zoya had to admit that there was a story in the files that couldn't have been captured in a neat executive summary. And, once she had forced focus on her wandering mind and learnt to peer through all the obfuscation, Zoya began to sketch out in bold charcoal lines the life and career of Harald-Dietrich Bergmann-Visser.

First, and presumably deemed most important, there were the operational reports. They described the tracking of dissidents, and the occasional arrest of low- and mid-level agents. Alongside the successes, there were other investigations that tailed off and pursuits that went cold. It was difficult to understand if the successes outnumbered the failures; and of course, quantity was no guarantee of quality. Overall, Zoya's impression was that Harald Bergmann was no star. He had bumbled along, doing his work; without catastrophe, but also without glory.

Next came the details of Bergmann-Visser's scientific work. Equipment had been developed and improved, and new techniques for the selective use of radioactive isotopes in espionage activities had been theorised, implemented, reviewed and corrected. Here the assessment was more clearly positive, at least in terms of the eventual results, even if there was also a consistent underlying mood of impatience at the slow pace of Visser's work. He was a scientist who was reliable and steady, yet incremental rather than inspirational.

Zoya paused for more coffee. She still wasn't hungry, which almost never happened.

As she sipped, she was surprised to realise she missed Robin's company. She wondered if the emotional strain of his previous day had worn off. She called him. There was no reply. Probably he was sleeping in, yesterday had been a long day after all.

She returned to her work and discovered a file with transcripts of the various disciplinary proceedings Bergmann-Visser had faced during his career. The pickings were slim, but they punched hard. Over the years, three complaints had been filed by three different KGB officers describing his disrespectful attitude towards both the KGB and the Soviet motherland. Which automatically lifted Visser in Zoya's estimation. She could only sympathise with his emotions, although she knew such criticism would undoubtedly have been a serious issue at the time.

She forced herself to read on, completing the disciplinary file. She discovered a document that catalogued Bergmann-Visser's love life, and dived in with a hope of finding something more scandalous. She ended up floundering in the shallows and marvelling that its notes had managed to render a forbidden and presumably passionate romance in precisely the same tedious and bureaucratic language as the rest of the files. The man had loved, he had lost, he had been punished. Again.

Operations. Science. Disciplinary complaints. A thwarted love life. And then that box was empty.

Zoya carried the second box into the meeting room. She stared at it unenthusiastically, then decided she should go down and see how Lovell was getting on.

Stretching and yawning, she heard a ringtone from her phone. It was a sound she didn't recognise. She unlocked the screen. It was the Telegram messaging app, which she never used.

She answered the call.

The howl of anguish that sounded out was followed by the dull thwack of a fist against flesh. Zoya's body froze with shock, then flooded with adrenaline. Forced to her feet, she stood ready to pounce. Then she heard a tortured, mumbling voice. It was Robin.

"Don't do it Zoya," he said. "Whatever he wants, don't do it."

Followed by a different voice.

"You know who this is?" he asked.

Zoya pressed record at the same time as she replied.

"What do you want?" she asked, her voice gentle and solicitous through tight clamped lips.

"I have your friend," the Hunter said. "But it's not him I care about. I want you Lieutenant Zoya Zozulya."

In the background, Robin's voice burbled unsteadily. Zoya filtered out the sound. She knew her emotion would only get in the way, and that in any case she would be able to play back Robin's words later.

"I give you my word that I won't kill him," the Hunter continued. "I won't even hurt him too badly, as long as you do as I say. Therefore, I have to ask you not to take this next part personally. It is simply a minor demonstration of what will happen if you choose to defy me. But first you must imagine that your friend is chained like a dog in front of me and that I am holding a knife. Then I want you to imagine me reaching forwards to grasp the little finger of his left hand."

And from the phone's tinny little speaker Zoya heard a long-drawn-out screech of agony that left no doubt in her mind about what the Hunter had just done.

"No police," he said. "Wait for my call."

PART 4

The Spy

CHAPTER 31

Zoya's body vibrated like a tuning fork to the fading echo of Robin's scream.

"What the hell was that?"

The deep voice came from behind Zoya's back; she wasn't alone after all. She turned and saw Tahiri standing in the doorway of his office. He was casually dressed, in jeans and a crumpled linen shirt. South of France in the north of England. She hadn't seen him arrive – *he must have come in early to catch up on his all-important paperwork*, Zoya thought numbly – and now she faced her first choice.

The Hunter had told her *no police*. He had proposed a swap. He wouldn't kill Robin; he would swap him for Zoya instead. She knew the only reason to take her was to kill her – and after seeing his previous handiwork she even knew how the Hunter would do it – but in return he promised he would let Robin go free. Zoya would have agreed in a heartbeat, but there was one problem. She didn't believe a word of it. For starters, the Hunter had no reason to let a witness go free. But there was more to it than that. The man's rasping words had oozed bitter venom, and even if Zoya's mind didn't understand exactly why, the spasms in her gut told her that he had reserved a special kind of revenge for her. Which would without doubt end with his well-rehearsed routine of prolonged stabbings and break-out-the-petrol barbeque burning. But the first course in his feast would surely be Robin. Because the Hunter would know that the most unbearable form of torture for Zoya would be watching her friend suffer.

The conclusions were unavoidable. As long as the Hunter believed he could use Robin to get to Zoya, he would not kill his hostage. If he came to believe that Zoya was not coming, Robin would die. And if Zoya surrendered herself, they would die together. Therefore, Robin's only chance of survival was if Zoya took out the Hunter first. For that she needed help. And she needed to be sure no one would get in her way.

It had only taken a few seconds. She blinked. Then she told Tahiri everything.

And for the first time she saw a different man. Her boss blazed. The suave bureaucrat he had become over the years of self-polishing and step-by-step advancement was replaced by the ghetto street fighter he had started out as.

"Fuck Interpol rules," he snarled. "You have my blessing, Zoya, to do whatever it takes to get Robin back. We lie and we cheat, we make a deal with the devil if that's what it takes. We fight, and if necessary we kill."

Which was what Zoya had been planning, since that was pretty much how she always operated. But it was good to hear that, for a change, someone else felt the same way.

*

Next, Zoya briefed Lovell.

Not because Lovell or her team needed any additional encouragement to pursue the Hunter. Lovell had her own motivation, and Zoya was already convinced of her ruthless professionalism. If anything, Zoya's concern was exactly the opposite. Zoya had pictured the firearms officers: who would likely lead any eventual assault, and who had seen one of their own gunned down that same morning by the Hunter's men. They all had to understand that a hostage was now in play.

Lovell got the message, but her response was action first, then words. She had an urgent trace put on Robin's phone. It didn't help. The last time the phone had connected with the network had been at his home just before nine a.m., and now the phone was either switched off or smashed and discarded. Next, Lovell organised a review of CCTV coverage around Robin's house and sent over a forensics team in case they could identify anything that would help their search. Lovell knew it was unlikely, but she wanted to cover the bases.

After she had issued her instructions, Lovell searched Zoya's face with troubled eyes.

"I already feel like I know you reasonably well," she said. "Tell me you're not even thinking of doing what this psycho wants."

Zoya confirmed that she wasn't. Even though she knew, if all else failed, that was exactly what she would do.

Which Lovell seemed to understand without being told.

"We'll get him back," she said. "It won't come to an exchange; I promise you we won't let it get to that."

*

Then Zoya called Scheefnek. Not because she thought he could do anything particularly useful from his Amsterdam hospital bed, surrounded by his charming Dutch nurses soothing his neatly cross-stitched Dutch ear. Just because she wanted, needed, someone to talk to.

To her surprise, their conversation turned out to be productive rather than simply reassuring.

Because ten minutes after they finished talking, Scheefnek called her back.

"Anna's here too, she spent the night under observation at the hospital," he said. "I just spoke with her, and I think she can help."

He moved his phone and Zoya saw that Anna was sitting straight-backed next to Scheefnek's bed. There were dark stains under her bright eyes, she looked tired and stressed, and right now Zoya didn't care about either her fatigue or her feelings.

"Help with what?" Zoya asked.

She wasn't getting it. Maybe it was the concussion still clouding his mind, but didn't Scheefnek understand that solving the mystery of the dead Dutchmen was no longer Zoya's top priority? That, dead or alive, the Dutchmen no longer even made the list that, after all, now had only one item on it.

"I know what you're thinking," Scheefnek said. "But trust me on this. Listen to Anna."

"I didn't tell you everything yesterday," Anna said. "I was afraid. But none of that matters now that your friend has been taken. I can help you. Because I know all about the man who took Robin."

Zoya groaned from the almost painful sensation of cogs turning and pieces falling into place; and from the definitely painful realisation that, in this puzzle, she seemed to be condemned to playing catchup.

"Anna, how do you know about the Hunter?" she asked with a brittle calm.

"You're right that I was a forger," Anna said, "but it was wider than that. Jan's group helped people who needed a new start, a new identity. I was responsible for preparing documents, the rest of his team provided logistics, moved money, helped with altering people's appearances. Somehow the Hunter found out about us. Jan met him many times, and it was us who gave him a new appearance and a new identity."

Zoya's sense was that Anna was still being extremely careful with what she was and wasn't saying. There was also a quaver in her voice that she was controlling with great effort. *Pain perhaps,* Zoya thought, *or fear*. But Zoya knew there was no longer time left for prevarication and half-truths. She asked the question she had decided not to ask the previous evening – the question she had left with Scheefnek to pursue.

"He's alive, Anna, isn't he? Your fiancé Jan didn't die in a car accident, and it wasn't his body that was burnt. He's been hiding out somewhere, just like you were."

Anna nodded silently.

"You were right," Scheefnek said. "He's alive. Which is very good news. For him of course, but also for us. He knows how to track the Hunter."

Zoya remembered one of her last conversations with Robin, and her whole body ached with the realisation of how much she wanted to be able to give him an update. She could picture his shy smile when she told him that his doubts about the car accident had been proved right; she could hear his excitement as he began to work forwards from the new information. At the same time, she saw that Scheefnek had moved the phone's camera back to his own battered face. He was grinning, and for the first time Zoya noticed that a large triangular chip had been knocked off one of his front teeth, and she hoped that he hadn't lost anything else that he hadn't told her about.

"This time it's your turn to meet and greet at the airport," Scheefnek continued with a repeat of his chipped-tooth grin. "Anna spoke to Jan a few minutes ago. He's been close by all this time, and he headed straight to Schiphol Airport. He's booked on the same Manchester flight you guys took, and it should be leaving any minute. You'll recognise him easily enough. Just use the before photo, not the one where he's burned to a crisp."

*

Zoya was almost out of the door when she remembered one last thing. She returned to her desk and connected her phone to her desktop PC. At the same time, she dialled Lovell's extension from the landline.

"I'm sending you an audio file," she said. "I recorded the Telegram call from the Hunter. Robin was talking in the background, but I couldn't make out the words. He was in pain, so he was kind of garbled, and I needed to focus on what the Hunter was saying. Can you get someone on it? To figure out if there was anything useful in what Robin said, or any background noise that might help us with a location?"

She pressed send and put down the phone without waiting for a reply.

*

The traffic was heavy, but Zoya arrived at the airport with minutes to spare. Or so she thought. It turned out the flight had arrived early, and Jan Visser hadn't checked any luggage. He was standing off to the side of the arrivals hall, his back to a pillar. They spotted each other at the same moment. He was medium height and blond and dressed unremarkably. Everything about him was unremarkable, until she focused on his eyes. Their gaze, which had been scanning the crowd, was now tunnelling towards her. They were green, but that wasn't the point. They were wary and fierce, but immensely calm – hypnotic almost – which was why it took a moment for Zoya to realise that Visser was already advancing towards her. And why she didn't find a way to avoid the first thing he did, which was to drag her into a tight embrace.

"Thank you for saving Anna's life," he said as he pulled back. "We should find somewhere to talk, but let me give you one thing first."

He blinked and now he had dialled it down, his eyes instead aiming for soothing reassurance. He delved into his roller and pulled out a single sheet of paper. It was a photo, with three names written below it.

"This is what the Hunter looks like now," he said. "And the names are the aliases he uses. The ones I know about at least."

Zoya read the names and stared at the picture. She didn't recognise the aliases. And she was absolutely certain that she had never seen the man in the photo.

*

They walked towards the exit. Then Zoya swivelled on one heel. She mumbled at Jan that she needed to use the ladies room, then called Scheefnek from inside one of the pine-scented stalls.

"Are you alone?" she asked in a defiantly loud voice.

"Yes, Anna just went to check on her friends," Scheefnek replied.

"And are the doctors ready to let you go?" she asked.

"I think they wanted to keep me another day. But I'll discharge myself now if it's important. What do you need?"

"I asked Robin before to find out about the father's grave. Now it's urgent Scheefnek. I need you to go to where he's buried."

She told him why, then she left the stall. With no sins to hide, she didn't flush; and she didn't wash her hands, or pause in front of the long, smudged stretch of the wall mirrors to apply lipstick, or eyeshadow, or even to run her fingers through her tousled hair. She simply marched back towards Jan and quickstepped him out of the terminal to the nearest taxi rank.

CHAPTER 32

Zoya told Jan she wanted to return to the Interpol office, since she knew that from there it would be easier and faster to act on any new information he provided. However, Jan flatly refused.

"Somewhere neutral," he said. "And no police. You'll understand why."

Grudgingly, Zoya directed the taxi driver to her hotel and used the ride as productively as she could. She unlocked her mobile and scanned the page Jan had given her, then forwarded it to Lovell. A few minutes later she followed up with a call, because an important question had occurred to her.

"You remember our discussion about damaging the Hunter's business?" Zoya asked. "Is it too late to stop the information flow? I was just thinking about the Hunter's reaction if he hears what we've done. Robin warned me at the time, now I'm thinking he was right."

There was a suck of air down the phone, a pause, and then Lovell said there was nothing she could change. The requests had already gone out to dozens of sources and snitches right across Europe. All with the same basic story about the Hunter's incompetence, rashness and treachery. The problem was that some had already reported back that they had begun spreading the dirt. There was no way they could reverse it now.

For the first time in many years, Zoya wanted to cry. *Provoke a reaction and deal with the consequences,* she thought. It was one of her favourite tactics, but it was very different when she provoked and someone else had to deal. Especially when the reaction involved a sadistic torturer with a knife and all the time in the world.

*

Dry-eyed, holding it inside, her and Jan arrived at the hotel.

Zoya had no wish to take a man she had just met up to her room. Not today, not now. Instead, they walked across the lobby into what the Edwardian called its Library Champagne Bar. It was too early for the evening crowd and the place was almost empty. Zoya occupied as much of one of the long black sofas as she could, and Jan took the adjacent blue velvet armchair. His roller bag was at his side, and he wedged one foot against it so that he would know if it moved. They were passed a menu that proposed something called Mexican small plates for English large prices and the waiter also boasted that their afternoon tea was the best in town. In response, they both ordered a medium-rare burger with fries, and when Zoya glanced at the bar's name on the menu she asked for their cheapest bottle of fizz, since desperate times called for desperate measures and she wasn't in a reading mood. Then she fixed her own eyes, brown and angry and ready to tear the world apart, into Jan's.

"My partner, who is also my friend, will die if I don't get this right," she said. "So don't even try and bullshit me Jan Visser. I need to know everything, and I need it fast."

"I understand," he replied. "And I know I'm in your debt. I tried to protect my Anna, but it didn't work out too well. You came along and you did what I had failed to do."

Zoya blinked rapidly. His implication was clear, but she let it go. He was right after all. She had failed too and maybe, just maybe, this was the man who could help put it all back together again.

"I also know time is short," he said. "But I think I should start at the beginning. It won't take long, I promise."

The waiter returned and popped his cork ceremoniously as waiters always liked to do. He leaned over the table and poured out the bubbles. There was no celebratory or commiserative toast to give, so Jan began his story.

"When I was fifteen," he said, "my father told me what he used to do."

He gulped at the champagne, maybe wishing he had ordered something stronger.

"And you have to understand," he continued, "that there had always been something about him that I didn't understand. Sometimes he was this jolly and gentle guy, the dad who took me camping in the local forests and read me bedtime stories. But he could be a hard man too. If you said or did something wrong, even the smallest thing, he could suddenly fly into a rage. With me, and with my mother too. It always felt like he was standing near an edge, like there was something inside him that he didn't know how to control. And then there were days when he disappeared inside himself. He didn't shout, he didn't cry, he didn't show any emotion at all. It was like he wasn't there. But the thing was, even if he wasn't perfect, he was the only father I had. I was afraid of him, but I loved him too, and I would have done anything to earn his approval."

Jan paused, gathering his thoughts.

"One day my mother sent me to fetch him for dinner, and I found him sitting in his barn in his favourite armchair, drinking. He had already downed almost a whole bottle of schnapps, and to be honest all I wanted was to turn round and leave. But he wouldn't let me go. He made me sit with him, and that was when my father started to tell me about his real life before he moved to the Netherlands. He said that he had been an agent with the East German secret police. That he had run a department responsible for surveillance of people the government considered dissidents or suspected of spying. He spoke slowly, like he was stumbling, and I could tell that he was struggling to find a way to explain everything that would make sense to a fifteen-year-old kid who had grown up in a different country and a different system.

He talked about the propaganda that had been such a big part of their lives, about how they had all been brought up to believe the West was a threat and the Soviet Union was their friend. He said they believed they were guarding against enemies inside the country who threatened their way of life. And he said everyone did it: that everyone in East Germany spied on each other, informed on each other, denounced each other.

Then, finally, he began to talk about how they did it, I mean the practicalities. Especially about his own specialty, which I think you already know."

"Scandium-46 and the whole radioactive tracking thing?" Zoya half asked, half confirmed.

"Exactly. Which became an obsession for him, as you saw for yourself when you went in the barn. And the obsession only got worse after we had talked, I guess because then he didn't feel any need to hide what he was doing. In any case, he talked about Scandium and a host of other stuff, then he finished his account by falling asleep in the armchair. And that was that."

"Except it wasn't," Zoya said.

"No, it wasn't. I had suddenly seen my dad in an entirely new light. I was young and I had no basis to understand or to judge the political side. What I did have was a teenage boy's mind that was fascinated by any kind of adventure. Murder mysteries, thrillers, spy books. To me, what he had described seemed impossibly glamorous. My father, the spy!"

"Do you think that was deliberate?" Zoya asked.

"Absolutely," Jan said with a calm smile. "I've had plenty of time to think about it over the years. About how everyone packages up all their conflicting beliefs and motivations inside their heads and their hearts. And about spies specifically, and how the good ones have a natural ability to work on multiple levels, and how that characteristic is identified then trained and developed. Because I'm quite certain my father was like that. I'm also sure that he wasn't just confessing to me that day, he wasn't simply trying to get something off his chest. He was trying to provoke my interest. He wanted me to see him as not just another dad like all the local village dads, but as something different, something special."

"It sounds like he succeeded," Zoya commented.

"He did, at least at the time. Now after everything that's happened, I admit that I've gone off the whole spying business. But it took the death of my friends and the near death of Anna to change my mind. Back then I was curious, I was excited. I pestered my dad to show me stuff, how it worked. The Scandium, since that's what he loved – but everything else too. All the surveillance and the counter-surveillance techniques. Dead drops and switch passes, communication protocols, codes and code-breaking. How to recruit agents, and how to run them. All the tricks and techniques of this endless game of cat-and-mouse."

"You were being groomed," Zoya said factually. "But for what? East Germany no longer existed. Why would an ex-Stasi agent want to create a spy?"

"It took years before I understood. We kept on playing these games that were really training for something that I hadn't yet understood. Eventually – and this was in the summer after I finished high school – I came to realise that, although I liked everything about what we were doing, there was one part of the overall picture that I enjoyed the most. Now I think it was exactly what he had been pushing me towards, but back then I assumed it was my own brilliant idea when I went to him with a proposal. We would set up our own business that would focus on a specific part of the spy trade. We wouldn't work for a government or any of their agencies, we would be private, freelance. We would offer a specialised service; we would be the best. And, of course, since I was only eighteen when I had this idea, I also had a big priority. Which was that I wanted to become rich."

The waiter delivered their burgers and a haughty expression. Zoya looked around and saw that the bar was gradually filling up. She shifted over so that none of the beautiful people would be tempted to commit the dangerous error of sitting down next to her on the sofa. They began to eat, and Jan continued talking.

"In everything that we had studied, the part that I really loved was the possibility of one individual being able to swap between multiple different identities. That you could be one person one day, and a different person the next. Or several people at the same time. More than that, I enjoyed all the work behind the scenes that went into creating those different identities. The documentation, the backstopped legends, new languages and accents, new locations, changing appearance. And that, essentially, was the core of my idea. We would avoid all the dangerous stuff that gets people killed and concentrate on the interesting part that could make us money."

"You weren't concerned that people who need a new identity, and can afford to pay for one, are usually criminals?"

"It's a fair question – but no, not really. We had a policy that we didn't ask about our clients' backgrounds, but it was true that with many of them you could make a pretty good guess what they did just by looking at them. And sometimes clients told us about themselves even when we asked them not to. Which led, admittedly not very frequently, to hearing something we didn't think was acceptable and then taking a decision to refuse to work with a specific individual."

A thought occurred to Zoya.

"What did your mother think of all this?" she asked.

"Nothing really," Jan replied. "We were quite vague about what we were doing, and my mother lives in her own little world. I told her we were consulting, I told her it was a family business, and that seemed to be enough to keep her happy. That and the money of course."

Zoya found it interesting that Jan seemed to have such a gaping blind spot in regards to his mother. It was something she would need to return to at some point. After they got Robin back safe and sound. For now, she needed Jan to get to the point he was gradually leading up to. Preferably before she finished her burger. Or at least before they finished the bottle of champagne.

"And presumably you figured out that this couldn't work with just the two of you?" she said. "When did you start to get more people involved?"

"We began with no team and no clients, just a concept," Jan said. "Our first big break came when we identified an experienced forger. He was also ex-Stasi, he was living in Amsterdam, and, like my father, he had nothing particular to do now that he had retired. We worked with him for just over a year, quite successfully, until his eyesight began to fade, and he needed to retire. Fortunately, he already had someone he could pass that part of the business on to."

"His daughter, Anna Vries," Zoya said, even as she wondered how the daughter's positive view of her father tallied with Jan's comment that he too had been with the Stasi. And why Anna hadn't mentioned it when they had talked.

"That was how we met," Jan said. "Anna's an artist, a genuinely talented individual, as you have seen. But the prints she loves to make were actually an evolution of the craft her grandfather and her father had trained her in. So, it was natural that we started working together; and then, over time, our relationship developed into something more serious."

"You should tell her to be more careful," Zoya said. "I figured out her role because she was careless. In some of her Instagram posts there are photos of her studio workbench. It's covered with equipment that a woodblock printer would use, but you can also see a selection of border crossing stamps – the kind you would add to a forged passport to give it a convincing back history."

Jan sighed as if this was a discussion he had previously had with Anna.

"She has an artistic spirit," he said by way of explanation. "In her defence, the situation with her was different, which was why she wasn't perhaps as careful as she should have been. There was no obvious link with me, and we kept our relationship secret. That was the reason we never got married. Also, she never met any of the clients – she hasn't even met the other members of our team. I was responsible for getting whatever she needed: photos of the client, details of what documents they needed. She did the work, then I passed the end product on to the client."

"And talking about your team, that brings us to your friends," Zoya said.

"It does. And based on your questions to my mother, I know you've figured out the truth, more or less. We started off preparing fake documentation and establishing background legends. At that point it was just me and my father, working with Anna's father and then with Anna. After a while we started to discuss other services we could provide. The first thing I did was to look at my own group of friends, since I knew they were people I could trust. Not surprisingly, many of them were working in careers that had no particular relevance to our business – my best friend went on to manage his family's dairy farm, for example – but there were a few who fitted the profile. One friend had become a banker. He hated both his job and the bank he worked for, so he was easy enough to recruit. His knowledge enabled us to piggyback on his employer's financial infrastructure to move our clients' assets wherever they needed, in line with their new identities. Without leaving a trace, of course. Another guy had set up a travel agency, so we put him in charge of transport; both the straightforward stuff – commercial travel, air-tickets and so on – and more discreet transportation methods. Off-the-book private flights, for example, or contracting with cargo operators to transport people as human cargo in planes and ships. We even had contacts with two people-smuggling groups, who were more than happy to be referred high-paying VIP clients. Finally, there was the class nerd who had gone into medicine. He had trained as a general surgeon then specialised in plastic surgery. Obviously, that was something that was extremely useful to us. And the best part of it was that all three of them could continue in their normal day jobs, which gave them a perfect cover and a stable income. We just brought them in when they were needed, and paid them very generously for what they already knew how to do."

"A one-stop shop," Zoya said. She ran through her mental list of dead Dutchmen and found one who wasn't yet accounted for. "How about the soldier?"

"Yes, Hans the soldier. Ex-Dutch special forces, with a talent for violence. He hadn't been our favourite at school since he was the class bully, but we forgave him once we started running into trouble. As you pointed out, some of our clients were not particularly nice people, and some of them either tried to renegotiate our fees – which we always insisted on receiving upfront for obvious reasons – or threatened us with all kinds of bloody consequences if anyone found out what we had done for them. Hans's job was to provide security for our client meetings and to ensure they went smoothly. Or, if there was any trouble, he would be the one making sure we came out on top."

"It all sounds very cosy," Zoya said. "Your dad, you and your girlfriend, and your school pals, working together in harmony. Until it all went wrong."

Jan nibbled through his last fry and washed it down with a grimace and the rest of his champagne.

"Until the Hunter came to see us," he said.

CHAPTER 33

By now the hotel bar was buzzing with bright young things – the kind of women who glowed in little black dresses, and the kind of men who stared in Gucci shirts. The kind of partygoers who didn't need to be told that the colour-coded books on the library's shelves were purely for show, and wouldn't be caught dead with burger sauce oozing over their manicured hands. And the kind who couldn't be allowed to overhear a conversation about spies and killers. So, Zoya charged the bill to her room and they rode up in the lift, as she warned Jan not to get any smart ideas.

Zoya sat on the bed, because it was her bed and because she wanted to stretch out her legs. Jan pulled up a chair.

"Let's cut to the chase," she began. "The Hunter. When was this exactly?"

"The first time we met was about two and a half years ago. Perhaps closer to three. I can look up the exact date if you need it. What's more important is why he came to us."

"For a new identity, I assume."

"Yes, but more specific than that. He came because of you, Lieutenant Zozulya. It was pretty much the first thing he told me, in far more detail than I wanted to hear. This whole chain of events, which had led to him needing not just new documents but also a new face. And about why he hated you. Obsessively, even by his own admission."

"Because of Odesa? I don't really get it. I was just doing my job, investigating a murder."

"All I can say is that it had become a symbol for him," Jan said. "This is a guy who has suffered immensely over his life. And I say that not to make excuses for him, just so that you understand. He's a Kosovo Albanian, who saw his family and his friends murdered by the Serbs. Then he started hunting the culprits. He saw people he loved tortured and killed, and he tortured and killed in revenge. That would damage anyone, and I don't think he was particularly stable to begin with. Eventually the war ended, and he had to attempt to start a new life after everything he had seen and done. He tried moving to Russia – I don't know why exactly – and while he was there he got this idea of becoming a player in the production of input chemicals for the synthetic-drugs trade. He thought it was something relatively low-risk that offered relatively high rewards. But first he decided to take out the competition. He attacked some factory in Saratov and got it closed down, then there was the one you know about in Ukraine. Which is where it all started to go wrong."

"Because I had his photo?"

"Exactly. You had his photo and, in his view at least, you were excessively persistent in making sure it was distributed everywhere. He told me he had even bribed one of your bosses to stop the investigation, but you wouldn't let it go. He seemed to find that quite offensive: that you wouldn't go along with what someone else had already been paid to do. In the end, he had to leave Ukraine – and he also couldn't go back to Russia. To make matters worse, you sent his photo to Interpol, and he wasn't safe anywhere anymore. That was when he came to us. He wanted the complete package. New documents and a new face. Which is why we saw him so many times. Because he wanted to change everything about his appearance. His nose first, then the shape of his ears. There was a birthmark over one eye that needed to be removed. He had a facelift to alter his jawline, and he had his cheeks filled out to hide the shape of his cheekbones. That meant multiple operations, which would have taken months even in the best-case scenario. Though this definitely wasn't best-case. Which was his fault – in the gaps between the surgeries he kept on working, and he also kept on drinking and snorting coke. Some of the skin grafts didn't take properly; he kept getting new infections, and the alcohol and the drugs interfered with the antibiotics the doctor gave him. Each time he had to come back for treatment. It was a difficult process."

"His motivation doesn't make a lot of sense," Zoya said, "but if I'm getting this right, he blames me for having a photo that ruined his Russia or Ukraine plan, although the only reason I had it was because of his carelessness. Then he blames me because he decided the only solution was to get a new face?"

"He also blames you for all the problems he's had *with* the new face. Even though the problems were his own fault."

"What else can you tell me about him? About his character, I mean?" Zoya asked.

"He's a sadist with a taste for torture," Jan said. "I don't know if he always was, or if that's what the war turned him into. Probably the reason doesn't matter, as much as the end result. And he's what I would call a schizophrenic. I'm not a psychologist, so that's no kind of formal diagnosis, but I've seen the two very different sides to his personality with my own eyes. It's like he's trying so hard to create some new version of himself, but he keeps getting pulled back into the old version. He loves to talk like a businessman, like some kind of fancy MBA consultant. Market research, business niches, future trends, even the lessons of historical analysis. But of course, the business he's describing actually involves killing whole groups of people without a second thought. And by the way, because of all that strange mix, his men are terrified of him. They say he's brilliant, but totally unpredictable."

Until now Jan had been studiously calm. For the first time, Zoya heard the emotion creeping into his voice and saw the anger that blazed from those stabbing green eyes.

"This is personal for you too, isn't it?" she asked.

"He killed my friends," Jan said. "That's probably the part you didn't know – that it was the Hunter. For a long time, our relationship had seemed to be going well. Not perfectly, but in the sense that even with the surgery the Hunter seemed to have accepted that it wasn't the surgeon's fault and that the guy was doing everything he could to help. Then everything changed. The Hunter got this idea into his head that he wanted to take over our business. As I said, he liked to talk in corporate terms, so he sat my father and me down and he phrased it as a merger opportunity. We would come into his existing organisation, which he was already beginning to expand. We would get fancy titles, and we would work with clients both inside and outside the business. We would grow as they grew, and everyone would prosper."

"What was your reaction?" Zoya asked.

"The idea had some merits of course. Even so, right from the beginning I didn't think it would work. Mainly because I had big doubts that the rest of our team would accept the idea. So, I was cautious. I said I would have to talk with everyone, that I needed to take their views into consideration. But then I turned to my dad and straightaway I knew a slow refusal wasn't going to work. My dad was sitting there, and you could see him swelling from all the anger that was building up inside. And he lost it completely. He went mad. He started yelling at the Hunter, he threatened him, he said he'd expose him and his new identity. It was crazy stuff, which I don't think my dad would ever actually have done, but it was still stuff that he said. I did my best to quieten him down, and all the time I kept looking back at the Hunter. Unusually for him, he was completely calm. He didn't respond to what my father had said, and the meeting ended there. But it was obvious what was going on in his head. He was just taking a little time to figure out his options. Whether it made sense to try and continue our negotiations, whether he believed my father's threats, and what he should do about it."

"Then, a week later, there was an attack on one of our team, just outside Amsterdam. It was a car bomb, and the only reason you won't have seen anything about it is because the attack failed. For the stupidest of reasons. This guy had a vintage Porsche sportscar and he'd been having problems with the battery, but he'd never got round to replacing it. His delay saved his life. It was a freezing January morning, and the battery didn't even spark when he turned the ignition. He opened the bonnet to jump-start the engine from his neighbour's car, and that was when he spotted the wires leading to a block of plastic explosive. We got the message loud and clear, and we didn't wait around. We had contingency plans in place, so the team scattered across Europe using the escape routes and the documents we'd prepared. Except for my father, who refused to go. And Anna – since, like I said, we thought she was safe. And she was pregnant too."

"Then everyone started dying," Zoya said.

"One by one. Although the timing was slightly different. First, the team scattered. Then my father was taken and tortured. He must have given away the identities the rest of the guys were using, and their travel arrangements. Then they started to die. The last was the guy you know about in Liverpool. With my dad dead, that leaves only me and Anna. And now that he's taken your partner, Zoya, you have to understand that this is a man who will stop at nothing. You won't be able to negotiate or bargain with him. He was trained to kill, and that's what he enjoys doing. The only way to save your partner is to kill the Hunter."

*

Zoya felt exhausted. Jan had mashed together two worlds that until then had seemed to exist entirely separately. On the surface everything made sense, but Zoya couldn't shake the sensation that not everything fitted as perfectly as Jan's neat account suggested.

He had described a father who was prone to anger and possibly to violence. A man he had been afraid of. Mrs Visser had implied the same thing. Yet Anna had described him as a good man, kind and gentle. And what about the files Zoya had reviewed? There had been no psychological profile, yet still her impression had been of a man who was happiest in his laboratory and had never been a particularly successful or enthusiastic agent. True, it could have been that very lack of success that had made him bitter and angry, that had given him something he needed to prove, but for now Zoya simply wasn't sure what to believe.

As she stared at Jan, Zoya remembered a rainy afternoon from just after she had turned eighteen. A blaze of hormones had taken her to her then boyfriend's apartment, where he had led her into his bedroom and confessed to an unexpected passion. Jigsaws, he had said shyly: all sizes, all shapes, the more complex the better – and would she like to try? She had been young; she had forgiven him. And the two of them had spent the next three hours assembling his latest find: a rare, thousand-piecer Mona Lisa. Zoya had rushed at the puzzle almost in a frenzy, for the simple reason that she had far more interesting designs on this handsome lad's strong and nimble fingers than watching them slot together deviously similar scraps of cardboard into a picture she had already seen a few too many times. Finally, the jigsaw was complete; or at least that was what Zoya had claimed.

It was true that they had accomplished a smooth surfaced portrait – those eyes, that smile – but if you peered closer you could see the areas in the background where the tabs didn't fit the blanks, and further inspection would have shown that poor Lisa's smooth jawline had been fractured in three places. The two of them had sat there for a long moment, and they had both pretended not to notice – Zoya because she didn't care; and the boy because, better late than never, he had figured out that if he attempted to correct Zoya's mistakes, he'd be doing it on his own with those strong and nimble fingers.

None of which was an experience Zoya could afford to repeat this time. Too much depended on getting it right; there could be no gaps, and no inconsistencies, in today's picture – not when Robin was out there somewhere in the hands of a sadistic schizophrenic, diagnosis unconfirmed, with a bizarre grudge against Zoya that was based entirely on his inability to take responsibility for his own actions.

Zoya shrugged and remembered her priority. Whoever's description of events was correct, she needed to focus on freeing Robin.

"In the airport you gave me the photo," she said. "Which I sent straight to the police team. But how does anything else you've told me since then help us find him?"

Jan bent and unzipped his bag – which, Zoya realised, had never left his side.

"Because of these," he said.

And, one by one, he took three identical black-boxed devices out of the bag and laid them out on Zoya's bed. Devices that she recognised immediately, because they were so similar to the Geiger counter Zoya had left behind at Professor Mulligan's laboratory.

"The one you have from the barn is an earlier version," he said. "I had already taken these three before you visited – they're the final version my dad developed before he died. There's a small increase in range, but that's not the main change. The big improvement is that they integrate with a map tool on my laptop, which plots every second of signal. In the right hands you can build up the track in real time. Where the radioactive source has been, how recently, and you can predict heading and distance going forward. That's how we can track him – if you take me with you."

*

Zoya picked one up and switched it on. She didn't know what she was expecting. Maybe she was hoping this particular device, new and improved, would react somehow differently from the previous one. It didn't. For the moment it wasn't linked to its mapping function, and so all she saw and heard was the same flickering needle, the same clicking and buzzing, as she pointed it around her. The same hotspots in the room; the same cold spots on her own body, and on Jan's body too.

For a moment Jan looked a little shocked. Then he figured it out and looked more shocked.

"He's been in your room," he said. "It's the only explanation."

"Why?" Zoya asked. "Not why has he been here. I mean, why is the Hunter leaving a radioactive signal behind him?"

"Because my father poisoned him," Jan said. "My mother told me afterwards what he was planning to do. The Hunter had arranged to meet after the unsuccessful car bomb in Amsterdam. He said he wanted to give my father one last chance: to apologise maybe, to agree to a deal. But my father didn't believe him. He saw the Hunter as a threat to all of us, so he decided to spike the Hunter's drink with a dose of Scandium-46. The day after that my father disappeared, and you know the rest."

"And that's why the guy who was murdered in Liverpool left the Serbian photo as a clue?"

"Correct. Although it wasn't just him. Each of my friends had the same picture with them, but it looks like you were the only one who found it. Or perhaps you were the only one who figured out what it meant."

Suddenly it hit Zoya. The timing. The night after the Scout's exploding-head trick, Zoya had gone drinking with Robin then spent the night on his couch. It had to have been then. Everyone, including her, had assumed the Hunter had fled town, but he had stayed. And the next day, when the police presence had dispersed, he had walked into the hotel. Front entrance, back entrance, it didn't matter. He had a face no one was looking for, and he had gone into the hotel and let himself into her room. It had been part two of his shockingly arrogant plan. The Scout's death had not only been a necessary precaution to protect the Hunter and the rest of the team, it had also been a diversion.

And Zoya's original assumption had been correct. The Hunter could have had his sniper take a second shot, he could have had her killed in the street, but such an impersonal approach wouldn't have satisfied the festering need he had nurtured over the years. So, the Hunter's plan had been to capture Zoya in her hotel room and take his time. Zoya looked across to the window, and yes, there was the radiator he would have fastened her to. And it had been a good plan, she thought, which had only failed for one entirely unforeseeable reason. That Zoya had taken the simple, idiotic, decision not to seduce Robin that night, but to take him drinking instead.

She had blamed herself before for not figuring out that the Hunter would be ruthless enough to kill his own friend. Now she was realising she had underestimated him again.

She switched off the Geiger counter and stared at Jan.

"So how do we do it?" she asked.

"I'll come with you and help," he said. "As long as you don't expect me to repeat anything I just said to your police colleagues."

CHAPTER 34

Even with Jan's help they still needed a search area, and the more they could narrow it down, the faster their search would be. Fortunately, late on Monday night, Lovell's team was finally making progress.

Everything had changed with the new information they had received about the Hunter. They had aliases; better still, they had his face now too. Zoya's addition – that the Hunter had been in her hotel the night after the Scout's assassination – gave the team a starting point for their search. They quickly began to get hits.

The hotel's CCTV showed the Hunter exiting from the rear of the building early the following morning. He had walked east along Windmill Stret. The team lost him for several blocks, then found him again as he entered a multistorey car park on Chepstow Street just before seven a.m. The next step was straightforward – since most of the activity at the garage at that hour was the arrival of commuters from the suburbs, grabbing a parking spot at the beginning of their working day. Exits were rarer, and only two cars left the multistorey in the twenty minutes after the Hunter had entered it. The camera image quality wasn't sharp enough to distinguish the faces of the drivers, but the team did have numberplates, and having just two targets to investigate made it an easy day at the office. At least until they hit the next stumbling block.

The first car was a silver Ford registered to a woman who lived in Rye – a small town on the coast near Brighton. The team had tracked it leaving the city and joining the M6 motorway heading south. They called the Ford's owner, who confirmed she had just returned home – tired after her long drive, but happy – from visiting her daughter who was a student at Manchester Uni. They moved on.

Car number two was a black Toyota SUV. Again, they contacted the car's registered owner. He stated that even though he lived nearby, in Sheffield, his last visit to Manchester had been at least four years ago. And yes, he was sure where his car was since he could see it on his driveway through the living-room window. In theory, the man could have been lying – and with more time they would have checked – but, given the circumstances, it seemed more likely that someone had simply copied his numberplates.

The team found several sightings of the suspicious Toyota. It was caught by a speed camera on the northbound carriageway of the M60 motorway. A traffic-flow camera filmed it transitioning onto the M61. The last sighting showed it turning off the motorway at junction nine, heading east towards Blackburn. Then it disappeared. Which meant they had a starting direction – roughly northwest from Manchester – and they had a spider's web of country roads with not a CCTV camera in sight that could have taken the Toyota anywhere within an area of countryside, dotted with multiple villages and small towns, that measured thousands of square miles.

*

It was good, but not great. The process was like using bloodhounds to hunt through a thick forest. There had been a burst of speed as the dog's noses picked up the scent, and as they had bayed and dragged their handlers behind them. Then water blocked their rush – a stream or a lake – and the trackers had paused anxiously to sniff at the air; running along riverbanks, splashing through mud and undergrowth, processing the signal scents, coursing for new direction.

In that pause, Zoya returned to her cardboard boxes. But with a new, wild energy this time – with the sudden conviction that there was something else she needed to understand if all of this was going to make sense.

In the second box, she found an entirely different situation. These files contained none of Bergmann-Visser's diffident mix of praise and criticism. There were no complaints about a lack of motivation or speed, no transcripts of disciplinary hearings, and no hint of disloyal thoughts. Instead, this was the story of an officer who had risen quickly through the ranks. Of a star who had shaken off an early moment of scandal and never looked back. Zoya saw political dedication overtly displayed. She saw multiple successful operations carried out in the most complex of situations. She reviewed lists of agents recruited from the most unlikely of backgrounds and run productively over a decade. This officer was a Stasi wet-dream – an individual who possessed in equal measure an aptitude for insightful analytical work and for the perilous cut and thrust of fieldwork.

When she was finished, Zoya knew which of the two Stasi agents she preferred. She also finally knew what had been bugging her ever since she had started working the case.

Which was when Anna called. Her face on the screen was damp, and Scheefnek wasn't even there to cry on. Anna was home, she said, in her apartment. The police had come by and checked everything out. They had removed all the hidden cameras and the microphones before they had let her back in. For now Anna had been assigned a guard, and they were discussing a deal for her to pass them details of all the passports she had forged – allowing the police to track down the users in return for continuing protection and immunity. Which was wonderful, Zoya thought, an inspiring example of justice in action; but it didn't help her right now. Until Anna finally got to the point.

"I didn't want to agree to the deal at first," Anna said. "But when I got back home, I found this."

She held it up, proof if proof was needed. A letter on thick, creamy paper; five pages of loose-looped cursive script, smudged by Anna's tears.

"It's from Jan's father," Anna said. "He was an old-fashioned guy, he liked to write. Maybe he also thought it was more secure than using email or phones. It was posted weeks ago, but I haven't been home as you know, and today was the first time I've seen the neighbour who was picking up my mail for me whilst I was gone. And now you need to listen to what he had to say."

Anna read through the letter: slowly, each sentence in Dutch and then in English. (Not that Zoya really needed the translation, but she was happy to hear everything twice.) It was a man's confession to his almost daughter-in-law – his confession and his warning. A dying man, doing the right thing.

Faster and faster, the pieces were snapping into place, gifting Zoya the sense of enthralling absorption that she had never felt with her teenage boyfriend's jigsaw puzzles. Those had been fragments of card and a picture she already knew by heart, but these were the fresh and unexpected fragments of real lives and real people to assemble. Until there it was: a whole new view – one that had been marshalled and gathered, shifting each time that she realised a piece was wrong, that it needed to be turned, reversed, slotted in somewhere else. It didn't matter if her fingers were strong and nimble or hesitant and clumsy, and she knew some pieces would never fit and some would always be missing.

But in the end all the *your truth* and *his truth* and *her truth* – those that everyone these days seemed to like to discuss and advance and develop – they all slipped away into irrelevant distance, until finally there was only one image left to stare you proudly in the face and proclaim the charmingly antiquated concept that it was not yours or his or hers. That it was simply *the* truth.

An assistant passed by at a high-heeled, flute-skirted dressage trot, bearing summons. The sound technician had finished cleaning up Zoya's recording of the Hunter's call. They gathered in Lovell's office – Zoya, the technician and Lovell – where they perched around her desk; their eyes all staring down, casting their spells of hope at the sleek black cube of the sound technician's speaker.

With a dry, staccato voice, he explained how he had split the recording into different frequency ranges and isolated each section as a separate track. The first track they would listen to had been stripped of human voices, leaving only what was happening in the background. The technician's face – lean, unshaven – was strained, and Zoya could understand why. She had heard Robin's screams just once, and that had been more than enough. This young guy must have listened to the recording, amplifying and analysing it, hundreds of times over the last few hours. For a moment Zoya wondered what a knife slicing through flesh and tendon, and maybe even bone, sounded like when played at high volume through doubtlessly top-of-the-range headphones. Then she realised this was one of the rare situations where not all knowledge was good knowledge, and that her eyes were flickering and her mind was racing, and she forced herself to slow down and breathe as the technician pressed play.

They heard wind and the rustle of trees. They heard a clink of metal on metal. They heard something they didn't understand, but that the technician assured them was rainfall on a stone surface. All common sounds, adding little to guide their hunt. Which, the technician said, was why he had started there – to get it out of the way. Zoya understood the logic, but wished he hadn't bothered if he had known it wasn't going to help.

"The next track is where I've isolated the hostage's voice," the technician said. "The high tone and the vibrations in his voice are consistent with pain and fear. However, he is coherent, it sounds like he knows what he is saying, and I believe there is some kind of message in his words. It's just that I haven't been able to figure out what it is."

He pressed play again. They listened from burbling beginning to screaming end without comment. Then again.

"Don't do it Zoya. Whatever he wants, don't do it."

Next, less clearly:

"I've been abandoned. I've been abandoned."

Robin's voice tailed off. There was a pause in the recording, which was when the Hunter was talking, followed by:

"Ireland's revenge. That's what this is, you *durna suka*. Fokking Ireland's revenge."

Lovell raised an eyebrow. Zoya buried her face in her hands and struggled to piece it together. Time that had been rushing past so fast had stumbled and slowed.

"He hasn't been abandoned," she said fiercely. Then, more calmly: "And he knows that perfectly well. So, it must mean something else. And that's also the first time I've heard him swearing. In English, and in Ukrainian too".

She thought some more.

"The second part. After the stuff about being abandoned. It's all from the night after the Scout was killed. I went drinking with Robin. I had this strange idea that I wanted to drink Guinness, and Robin told me to be careful. He called it Ireland's revenge. And then the part about *durna suka*. It means *stupid bitch* in Ukrainian. He teased me about it in the morning – he said that's what I kept on calling myself when I was falling asleep on his sofa. Which didn't surprise me at the time, since I was pretty upset at myself that my plan to catch the Hunter had gone so terribly wrong."

"Let's assume he wasn't just trying to insult you," Lovell said. "He's pointing to something to do with Guinness, or maybe something related to that evening as a whole. But it would make no sense for his big clue to be that he's being held in some bar somewhere that serves Guinness. There must be literally hundreds of them in and around Manchester, and if he's smart enough to try and tell us something he wouldn't waste what might be his only opportunity by giving us something that doesn't take us any further forwards. However, one thing that comes to mind is that there is a Guinness Road somewhere near Old Trafford. We'll check it out, but even that doesn't really convince me – it would take us to south Manchester, inside the city limits, which doesn't tie in with the car with the false numberplates we've tracked heading north and out of town."

Nothing else occurred to Zoya. Lovell tried to encourage her.

"Tell me about that evening, Zoya. Walk me through what you did. Where you went."

Zoya traced through the sequence. They had taken a taxi from the office into the city centre. They then hadn't gone into the hotel, with Robin suggesting they walk to an area of the city he liked, where he said there were plenty of good restaurants and bars. There was something to do with coats in the name. Ancoats, that was it. But they hadn't made it that far. When they were still passing through a different area – Robin had called it the Northern Quarter – he had started complaining that his feet hurt in his office shoes. Typical man, Zoya had said, but the reality had been that she was tired too. Although she hadn't admitted it to Robin. And they had stopped two minutes later at the first bar that looked halfway decent.

"The Chapel," Zoya said. "That was the name of the place we ended up. Where I drank the Guinness."

"I've been abandoned," Lovell said. "He's not saying it about himself. He means the place he's being held."

"An abandoned chapel," Zoya said triumphantly, accelerating again. "It has to be."

"Let's not jump to conclusions," Lovell replied. "We'll still check out Guinness Road, especially since it's close by. But your version makes more sense. We know the Hunter's car headed northwest out of the city. He took an eastbound exit off the motorway, but from there he could have diverted in any direction. Luckily, even if he did a U-turn and headed west, he would just have run into the coastline – so that leaves an arch. from northwest to northeast as our priority. If they had just the one base, then they've been there and back several times. They drove there after the original attack, they returned to town a couple of days later, then they drove out again after killing the Scout. It's possible there were also other trips we don't know about. I think it's a reasonable assumption that they wouldn't want to travel a huge distance each time. So, we'll start with an arc with a thirty-mile radius from the city centre and take it up to fifty if we don't find anything relevant. And within that area we're looking for abandoned chapels or churches."

"And we have these," Zoya said, pointing to the three Geiger counters she had laid out on Lovell's desk.

"Indeed, we do," Lovell replied. "I'll get people researching chapels and churches in the search area. We'll use the Geiger counters once we have possible targets. And we'll give one to the team we send down to Guinness Road."

Zoya sat for a moment, trying to figure out if there was any other way to confirm the abandoned chapel theory.

"I want to see the sniper," she said.

"You're welcome to," Lovell replied. "But we've had multiple people in with him and he hasn't spoken a word for two days. What makes you think seeing him will help?"

"Because I don't care if he says anything or not," Zoya replied. "I just need him to listen."

*

It took thirty minutes to set up. Too long. The sniper was moved from his holding cell to an interrogation room. The sign on the door called it an interview suite, which Zoya thought sounded cosy. When she entered, he was already sitting un-cosily on a metal chair, and handcuffed even more un-cosily to a metal table.

"You know who I am?" Zoya asked.

Silence. But an upward lift of exhausted eyes licked over her face and was followed by the faintest twitch of his lips. She took that as a yes.

"It's good to meet you at last," Zoya said. "Especially after your impressive shooting the other day outside the hotel. And don't worry, I respect your silence. After all you've come a long way together with the Hunter, so I understand your loyalty. I'm also guessing you don't want him to die."

Silence, and a stare of defiance this time that said the Hunter could take care of himself.

"The Hunter's down to one or maybe two men," Zoya said. "We now know where his base is, and we're about to surround it with an army, and he won't have a chance. But that's not the worst of it. Your boss is sick. He's been given a massive dose of radiation poisoning and he doesn't even know about it. If he doesn't get treatment he will die. So, you really are his only hope. Which is why we want you to come with us. You can talk to him, he'll trust you. You help us persuade the Hunter to surrender, and you have our word that he'll get the specialist attention he needs. It's his only chance to survive."

The sniper's eyes had lifted again when Zoya mentioned the radiation poisoning, and this time they had stayed on her face: examining her, struggling to understand if she was speaking the truth. Whilst at the same time Zoya was holding herself still, hoping desperately that the sniper would have seen at least some indication of the Hunter's sickness over the past few weeks.

"Nausea," she said, "and stomach cramps. He must be weak by now, maybe he has problems with his vision. He would have difficulty sleeping, and all of that would lead to paranoia and mood swings. And there'll be the hair loss of course, he'll be shredding clumps of hair. Does any of that sound familiar?"

Now she was sure. The sniper's eyes had blinked rapidly; he was seeing his boss's face, reviewing for the symptoms Zoya had just listed and understanding something he hadn't understood before.

"You know I'm right, don't you?" she continued. "You already knew there was something wrong, that he was hiding something; you just didn't know what. Nor did he, for that matter, not the cause at least. And now you know I'm not lying, and you know your only choice is what to do about it. Or maybe you still think the other part of what I said was a bluff. Maybe you think we don't actually know about the abandoned chapel he's hiding in."

He couldn't control it. At the mention of the chapel, the sniper had flinched his head slightly to the side as his body had instinctively attempted to avoid the jab of her words.

And she couldn't help herself either. What was it that Tahiri had said? We lie and we cheat, we make a deal with the devil if that's what it takes. She grinned with the clean sensation of victory. She left the sniper alone to figure it out whilst she ran back up four flights of stairs to tell Lovell the good news.

CHAPTER 35

It was early morning and Zoya thought there were worse places to die. Admittedly she had selected her preferred option long ago. It was a small village she had visited as a child in the foothills of the Carpathian Mountains, west Ukraine, north of Odesa. Mountains how they should be: green and verdant in the summer, deep snow in the winter, wolves and bears all year round. But as she stared into the distance, Zoya thought this place would do. There would be less snow no doubt, and tamer wildlife too, but apart from that . . .

Ahead of her a sinuous stream burbled innocently, almost as if it hadn't spent the last few millennia chiselling its own private valley millimetre by millimetre through the rock. There was heather on one slope, a spruce forest on the other; and a series of green-clad hills climbed straight ahead, their faces shaded then illuminated in shifting patches by the rising sun. And there, inside the tree line, was the reason she was here. A small and solitary building, fashioned from the same pale-grey stone as the surrounding crags and roofed in darker slate, with a gravel track that angled in from the left and pointed the way.

Zoya took one last look and decided she had waited long enough. She told Jan to stay where he was and slammed the car door behind her. She set off. Her feet crunched in the gravel, not loud enough. She didn't want her arrival to be a surprise. She began to sing – Okean Elzy again, her favourite song – at the top of her voice as she marched towards the enemy.

*

Guinness Road had been a no-show. Lovell had insisted on checking, even after the sniper's involuntary confession, and Zoya had known it was the right thing to do. The prudent thing. The team had been accompanied by Jan and one of the Geiger counters. They had driven in the dark of night through the surrounding streets. They had found nothing. They had searched every building they could access. They had found nothing.

Which had left them with a lot of work to do – with an intense bout of research, and the small issue that they had several Geiger counters yet Jan was the only one who had access to the integrated mapping tool. They could use any of the counters as a normal detection advice, but only Jan could take full advantage of its real-time plotting and prediction capabilities. And he couldn't be everywhere at the same time.

They had identified three possible sites. Two were on a straight line drawn roughly north from Manchester. The first of these was fifteen miles out, on the edge of the descriptively named market town of Ramsbottom. News reports said the building had been damaged in a fire, then a few months later the lead had been stripped from its roof by scrap metal scroungers. The cost of repairs had been too high to contemplate for a small and poorly attended parish church. The second was ten miles further on. This one had been built on a wooded hilltop in the middle of nowhere for reasons no one had been able to identify. Unsurprisingly it too had had few visitors, and the ever financially minded Church of England had decided they had other priorities. The third possibility was further off to the northwest: three miles inside the perimeter of the forest of Bowland, where it had been built a couple of centuries ago by the local Lord of the Manor – his whim or his folly until successive generations of inheritance taxes had chased his family into the nobility's version of destitution, which involved retaining the luxury Knightsbridge townhouse but allowing the country estate to crumble under the encroaching brambles and weeds. Rewilding, as they liked to claim at their fashionable London dinner parties; lazy entitled gits, as the locals called them when they walked past the manor house's fenced-off ruins.

The detail in this irreligious realm was that the Geiger counters, according to Jan, had a maximum range of two kilometres and a reliable range of one. Depending on the strength of the radioactive signal of course. They had debated using a helicopter to fly over the three targets. It would speed their search, but they would have to be close. They would need to hover at various points and make several passes. Therefore, they would be noisy and conspicuous. It was bad enough that they would disturb the burrowing badgers and puzzle the caterwauling foxes, though they would also risk spooking their target. They had decided they didn't want to tempt their target to put a knife into his hostage. They had decided to use cars.

They didn't have the manpower to tackle all three targets simultaneously, and so they had headed due north since that gave them quick access to two of the targets in close proximity. They had set off at four a.m., with their tactics agreed in advance. An unmarked car would go ahead with two armed plainclothes officers. One would drive, the other would hold one of the three Geiger counters and try not to worry. They had decided that they would stop as soon as they received even the weakest of signals and bring in Jan's support. Until then they would be on their own. The car had approached the first target. Closer and closer, with no evidence of radiation. A kilometre away, they had paused and allowed the rest of the team to catch up. Then they had set off again, creeping slowly through the empty town streets. Two hundred metres out, there was still no signal.

But the team hadn't taken it for granted. They had established a perimeter. They had sent in a drone, which had seen nothing in the dark even as it hovered over the gap in the stripped roof. They had used thermal cameras, which had detected a single heat source in the building. They had double-checked the Geiger counters and conferred with Jan and agreed that whatever was inside wasn't radioactive. They had debated, then they had sent in a tactical team, which had advanced cautiously through the rubble, automatic weapons at the ready, and ended up scaring half to death the town drunk, who had chosen to spend the night on a mouldy, rain-soaked mattress in what was left of the church's nave.

Nearly two hours had passed. The team had moved to the second site and repeated the same process, with approximately the same result – except that here the view was better, and there was no one, drunk or sober, sleeping inside.

And there had been one more difference. Which was that Zoya had decided not to wait around. Despite her general fondness for watching the balletic displays of an armed response unit entering a derelict building, this time she had departed as soon as the lead car had approached within five hundred metres of the hilltop chapel without detecting any radiation signal. She had headed towards the third site – in Robin's car, with Jan at her side and her pedal to the floor, and wondering if Robin was ever going to get round to cleaning up the egg and sausage stains since, to be frank, there was already an unpleasant smell emanating from the fabric upholstery. She had followed the GPS, and most of the time she had remembered which side of the road she was supposed to be driving on. The rest of the time she hadn't cared, since the next place had to be her target. Because if it wasn't, they were back to square one.

*

And here she was, singing along to Okean Elzy in the early morning with worse places to die.

Jan was in the car; he had spent the drive hunched over his laptop, and he had told her everything she needed to know. A signal, growing in strength, pulling them in. Jan had pointed directly at the chapel, and there was nothing more he could give her except for his last warning, which was still ringing in her ears.

"He won't negotiate, Zoya. You have to take him down, or he will kill you and Robin."

She had taken the Geiger counter from him and carried it in one hand, switched off for now. It was a prop, or a demonstration if she made it that far. Her steel-wire tactical whip was sheathed safely down her thigh, and that was it. Walking into a gunfight, and she hadn't even thought to bring a knife. Her throat was dry, but she kept on singing and she kept on walking forwards.

Forty metres out, the wooden door of the chapel opened with a sound of unoiled protest. At last. There he was. There they were. Robin first: the top of his head reaching the Hunter's chin, a poor shield for the bigger man; pushed forwards, with an arm clenched hard around his neck.

Zoya inspected her friend. He was alive, that was the main thing. On his own two feet, but hobbling. Dirty and unshaven, but he still managed to hold up his head and meet Zoya's gaze, even if his spectacles hung broken over his face. His left arm was cradled in his right over his chest, and his hand was bandaged. His left foot was bare, and what the hell had the Hunter done to him? Zoya felt the anger swell inside, she gulped and swallowed. This was not the time for emotion. For now her only task was to seize the Hunter's attention and keep him listening and talking.

Twenty metres out and she focused on the Hunter. On the machine pistol in his right hand. An MP5. A good choice. He could use it one-handed – he could spray her with a full magazine within a couple of seconds and she would have exactly zero chance of surviving. She lifted her eyes to his face. She didn't like what she saw. His eyes were wild, darting and angry. There was a seeping scar at the edge of his forehead, and his mouth twisted as he spoke.

"How did you find me?" he asked.

"I got tired of waiting for your call," she said. "And your sniper friend gave most of it away. He didn't seem happy that you abandoned him on the rooftop. Then when I got close, I used this."

Zoya held up the Geiger counter.

The Hunter's gaze scanned the empty skyline behind her, then focused on her hand.

"What do you mean?" he asked.

Zoya turned the counter on and pointed it towards the Hunter. It gave out a furious signal, battering at the still morning air.

"You hear that?" she said. "It tells me that you are a major source of radioactivity. Of Scandium-46 specifically. I'm sure you remember Dietrich Visser?"

The Hunter nodded numbly.

"Well, old man Visser took a strong dislike to you. And for once that's something you can't blame on me. In fact, I really don't understand how you blame any of this on me. You were careless enough to leave your photo behind in Odesa. After that, I did my job – no more, no less. And ever since you arrived in England you've been adding one screwup after another, with no help from my side at all. Not controlling the Scout, getting him to follow me, then letting him send two men after me. It's all been your fault."

She watched his face as she spoke. She seemed to be having the desired effect. His mouth was spasming, his eyes blazing. His grip had relaxed, and he almost seemed to have forgotten he was holding Robin in his arms. *Provoke a reaction and deal with the consequences*, she thought. *Just don't do it too fast.*

"Anyway, I don't know what exactly you did to piss Visser off, or maybe he was just crazy to begin with. But in any case, you upset him enough to slip you a double dose of Scandium in a tumbler of schnapps and now it's killing you. And it's also what enabled me to track you here."

The Hunter moved one hand up and stroked it over his head, through what was left of his moulting hair. Now it made sense. As he raised his arm, for a moment Robin was free, and Zoya held her breath. Then the Hunter realised what he was doing. His hand moved back down; his arm wrapped back around Robin's neck.

"I don't understand why he would do that," the Hunter said. "I had nothing against the old man – he was the only one I liked in their rotten family. He was nothing like the mother or her son. But that doesn't matter anymore. If what you say is true, then I have nothing left. You've taken everything away from me. My first business that I tried to start. Then you left me with no choice but to change everything about myself. My name, this face that I don't even recognise in the mirror. And now you've destroyed my new business with all the slander and the lies that you've spent the last week spreading all the way across Europe."

Zoya cursed silently. He had found out, somehow, and it didn't really matter how.

"I've lost everything I built. I've lost the men who were my friends. And now you tell me that I am dying from radiation poisoning. So, tell me, Lieutenant Zoya Zozulya, what exactly are you expecting me to do?"

When he put it like that, Zoya thought, it really didn't sound too good. The Hunter was definitely a glass-drained-to-the-dregs kind of guy. But his voice was dark and stripped bare, and Zoya knew she had to offer him at least a scrap of hope, some small hook for his mind and his desire to hold onto.

"I expect you to keep your word," she said. "I expect you to let Robin go and to take me instead. He walks, and you get to spend as long as you want doing whatever sick torture shit you want to me, and we'll see which of us dies first."

Robin's hands clenched over his chest in protest. He opened his mouth, but no sound came out. And all Zoya could do was hope that it was not too late.

The Hunter's right arm came up. The MP5 found its aim. Centre mass; and now she was scared, even if there were worse places to die.

"Why would I do that?" the Hunter said. "I have you both now, and I have absolutely nothing to lose. I may as well enjoy myself, since I'm dead one way or the other."

But Zoya wasn't listening. Because, at last, she heard what she had been waiting for. The voices in her earpiece.

Jan first: "You have to take him down Inspector Lovell, there's no other way out of this".

Then Lovell: "We have you Zoya, but you're in our line of fire. Take two steps to the right".

And she had run out of options. She stepped to the right, and the Hunter's expression was puzzled and his gun tracked her movement. And then Zoya heard the boom of the rifle and, one way or the other, the Hunter died.

CHAPTER 36

Robin sagged to the ground as Zoya ran forwards. A loudspeaker sounded out from behind her, ordering the remaining man in the chapel to lay down his arms. Sirens sounded out, engines revved, and she heard none of it.

Zoya reached Robin's side and gathered him in her arms. He was sweaty and dusty, his gaze flickered and jumped. Zoya was crying and he was dry-eyed, and she was apologising and he was silent as she lifted him and carried him out of danger.

Then he was safe, and he was shouting at her – not angrily, just trying to get her attention.

"Zoya listen to me," he said. "We spent a lot of time talking whilst he was holding me. He told me everything. I know what he did and why he did it."

He looked into her face, and he started laughing. Rather hysterically, she thought.

"But you already know everything, don't you?" he said as Zoya hugged her friend who didn't know how to give up tighter and tighter, until he groaned in protest. Then she let him go, and grinned at his dazed expression and stroked a hand over the long cut on his forehead.

"Don't worry," she said. "While you were having your little manicure spa-break in the woods, we've been working. Now I get to show you some of the results."

*

Zoya needed a quiet space, and Robin needed medical attention. There was an obvious solution. The paramedics over-solicitously wrapped Robin in a rustling metallic survival blanket and walked him slowly back to the tree line where their ambulance awaited. They lifted Robin up the step, sat him down on the edge of their stretcher bed and began to inspect his wounds, whilst they enjoyed what seemed like an overly long discussion about their patient's blood pressure and whether or not he needed oxygen. When their conclusion was that he needed to lie down and rest, Zoya's patience ran out. She jacked up the bed's backrest, propped Robin on its pillows and told the medics not to make such a fuss. Robin still had nine fingers and nine toes left, she pointed out, which was more than enough to do the only thing he needed to right now – this being to hold a bottle of water in one hand and Zoya's telephone in the other, and watch the screen.

First she dialled, then she passed him the phone.

Scheefnek's face appeared, too close for comfort. He was framed by foliage; he seemed to be hiding in a bush.

"We have Robin," Zoya said. "You're good to go."

"Then I'll switch to my headcam," he replied. "Enjoy the film."

Zoya and Robin's view changed. As Scheefnek glanced left and right, they saw brief glimpses of heavily armed black-clad men. They heard Scheefnek's voice passing on Zoya's message – in Dutch, she translated for Robin – and the men immediately began to advance over a neatly tended lawn. Scheefnek went forwards with them, but stayed out of the way. He was looking directly ahead now, and Robin's breath caught in his chest as he recognised their target. A few seconds later the breach team was at the door, but they didn't bother to ring.

A heavily built man swung a black battering ram at the door's lock. Once, twice, then the door exploded off its hinges and the team poured inside.

"Who are they?" Robin asked. His voice was numb, but his eyes didn't move from the screen.

"We tried the police first," Zoya replied. "Unfortunately, the judge decided he didn't have enough for a warrant. But the spooks seem to have lower standards, and they were very intrigued when they heard about Mrs Visser's Stasi past. These guys are a combined unit from the Dutch DISS and British MI5. Luckily, we have complementary interests. Even if Mrs Visser's spying days were a while back, they're still keen to figure out if there are any leads on Stasi agents or contacts who might have moved on to other roles in public life. We on the other hand are looking for something rather different."

The view was confused now. They caught a glimpse of a wildly screeching Mrs Visser being escorted out of the house. They saw more thronging bodies, and understood that the breach team had been joined by a larger group of men and women in civilian clothes.

"It'll take a while," Zoya said. "They'll need to do a fingertip search of the whole house. I'm afraid I didn't have time to get popcorn, but you keep watching Robin, tell me what they find. In the meantime, there's one more thing I need to do."

*

Zoya left the ambulance doors wide open to give Robin a view: of nature, and of what would happen next. She sauntered back along the path to the bare space in front of the chapel. It was quiet again. The second gunman had surrendered and been led away. As she watched, a small team of armed officers moved into the chapel, making sure it was clear so that the forensic team could begin their work.

Zoya stood at the Hunter's side. He hadn't moved. His fall had been cushioned by pine needles and he felt nothing. His sightless eyes pointed up at the sky and saw nothing. His mouth gaped, and he had already said everything he had to say. Zoya thought for a moment about the long chain of events that had brought him to this place. It didn't change anything; it was just how it was.

Lovell finished speaking with one of her team. She spotted Zoya and walked over to join her. She raised a questioning eyebrow and Zoya nodded in reply.

Then they saw Jan walking towards them. His steps were slow in the gravel, hesitant maybe, and he stopped short and raised his hands with a gesture that looked like a question. He called something out, but not loudly enough that they could hear the words. It didn't matter though, because his meaning was clear – he was a humble onlooker, checking that it was OK for him to approach. Lovell waved him on.

When he arrived, he stood next to Lovell and Zoya and stared down at the Hunter's corpse. He paused; reflection perhaps, or relief, but about what?

"It's over at last," he said. "We're safe now."

Zoya felt the exhaustion of the past few days flood over her. But she knew she wasn't finished yet. She moved a little closer to Jan. She too looked down at the Hunter for another last, long moment. She remembered his confusion at the thought that Dietrich Visser had poisoned him. She thought that his reaction had been unfeigned, sincere, but she still wasn't sure regarding what she was about to do. So, she turned to Jan and tried to read his hypnotic green eyes as she summoned the last of her strength. She bent her knees; she flexed her complaining muscles. She jumped as high as she could, springing forwards and upwards, and with the scything hard dome of her skull Zoya headbutted Jan full in the face.

"Now we're safe," she said.

And although over the years Zoya had come to savour the moment in each of her cases when weeks or months of painstaking investigation culminated in the metallic click of her cuffs around a suspect's wrists, today she thought that, if it couldn't be her, she was entirely content to stand exactly where she was, her head a little sore, and watch Lovell do the honours.

*

Zoya turned back towards the ambulance. She heard a shout. She ran.

Robin was leaning forward, gesturing wildly for Zoya to join him. She jumped up into the ambulance.

"They found something," he said.

Some things never change, Zoya thought, *just a little more specific would be nice.*

"What did they find, Robin?"

"A cache of documents, which everyone sounds very excited about. Apparently their search was much faster than they expected, because once Mrs Visser calmed down she told them where to look. She said she knew they would find everything eventually, and she didn't want them to tear her house apart in the process. But in with the documents was what I guess you were hoping for."

"So, tell me," Zoya said.

"I'd rather you saw for yourself," Robin said, then: "Scheefnek, can you hear us?"

A moment passed, then they heard Scheefnek's voice. His confirmation was followed by a few seconds of disorienting movements as he paced towards his goal, after which Scheefnek's eyes and his cam focused down.

They stared at the screen and saw a plastic evidence bag, sealed already, set on a polished wooden tabletop. And inside was the possible answer to Zoya's impossible dreams.

"It's a SIG Sauer P938," Scheefnek said.

"Nine-millimetre rounds," Zoya confirmed with a smile of satisfaction.

"We'll expedite the ballistics tests," Scheefnek said, "and keep our fingers crossed that it's the right weapon. The only bad news is that I can already tell you it's been wiped down. But we'll see what we can do."

"We'll be there as soon as we can," Zoya said. "Isn't that right Robin?"

And she waited a moment for Robin's reply, then looked across when she didn't hear it. Only to see that his eyes were closed, and his head had slumped to the side.

"What's wrong with him?" Zoya asked, suddenly panicked.

One of the medics checked the monitors and bent close to Robin's face. He straightened with a smile.

"He's asleep," he said. "Not surprising after everything he's been through. Now, if you're done with overexciting him, let's get him to the hospital."

Zoya thought the man was being a little unfair. She was sure that if she had been overexciting Robin, the one thing he wouldn't be was asleep. But then the engine turned, and they drove slowly over the rutted track until they reached the tarmac. They accelerated, the sirens blared, and through the window Zoya took a last look at forested slopes that she was happy to be leaving behind, even though she still knew there were worse places not to die.

CHAPTER 37

Robin was back in the same hospital. Maybe they had even been considerate enough to reserve the same room, since he was clearly destined to become a regular – one who would return slightly more damaged with each successive visit. His wounds were dressed, his brow was soothed, and for the next two days and two nights Zoya stayed at his side. Her initial request to wheel in an extra bed had been politely refused, until, late the first evening when Zoya stole one of Robin's pillows and laid herself down to sleep on the well-scrubbed floor – at which point the hospital staff had politely relented. She stayed, and Zoya wasn't even sure if her presence was helping. The truth was that she simply didn't want to leave.

She felt guilty. She knew that Robin's first beating had been almost nothing to do with her – after all, she had only just arrived in the country. Even the severed finger couldn't really be considered her fault, since it was down to the Hunter being an essentially deranged and damaged human being. But when it came to the missing toe, Zoya had no choice but to accept its verdict. She had consciously set out to infuriate the Hunter, to trash his reputation and his business. Which he had discovered when, according to Robin's account, the Hunter's replacement scout had called in to report that their latest contract had been cancelled before it had even been finalised. This by a nervous client who had heard from several different sources the rumours Zoya and Lovell had spread. It was Robin who had warned her, and it was Robin who had paid her price.

And when she looked into his eyes, she saw it all. The flashes of horror as Robin watched again and again the knife slicing at his flesh, as a previously unquestioned part of his body was severed and fell away. The persistent terror of captivity, which he admitted he had not expected to escape. The recollection that had haunted him of how the Lee End man had died, petrol poured, and matches thrown. And last, but in no way least, his fear for Zoya, who he was sure would try to rescue him and end up leaping from her frying pan into their joint fire. Which was the point he reached when, as he did at the most unexpected moments, Robin closed his eyes and he slept again. The doctors confirmed what the paramedic had said – that this was a normal reaction to the trauma Robin had experienced; his body and his mind shutting down, fleeing pain, leaving everything behind. Until he woke and it began again. His wounds would heal, yet it was his mind Zoya was concerned about.

She avoided talking about death and destruction, and instead filled the resulting awkward silences by trying to joke. "What can you do after all?" she had said, "it isn't as if there is anything left to sew back on. Not like Scheefnek, with his disengaged ear flap," she had commented. "What has fallen has disappeared," as she had told him, the Ukrainian expression putting it so presciently. Robin knew what she was trying to do. He smiled gently, and worst of all it was him that clasped four-fingered comfort around her outstretched five-fingered hand. So, when he pointed out that he was simply happy to be alive and that Zoya seemed far more upset about absent digits than he was, she pretended to be persuaded, and she celebrated his survival by eating most of his evening meal, even though the risk of poisoning seemed to have passed. If it had ever truly existed.

On the morning of the second day, Lovell dropped by. She spoke gently with Robin, then furiously to Zoya: berating her for her stupidity and rashness, for her blind rush into danger without the benefit of backup. Or of any form of communication for that matter. It was a reaction that Zoya interpreted as Lovell's convoluted expression of concern and relief. However, the Inspector's anger abated fast when Robin reminded her of the successful outcome of Zoya's tactics. This was how it usually worked in life: do something stupid and succeed, and your stupidity will immediately be forgiven; do the same thing and fail, and you know what happens next.

And if you were balanced somewhere between success and failure, there was always flattery to fall back on, so Zoya added that she would never have put Robin's life and her own in danger unless she had complete confidence in Lovell's ability to figure out what she had done and to get her team in place in time to take the shot when the opportunity presented itself. These were words that Lovell clearly appreciated, and which had the virtue of not being flattery at all, but the plain and simple truth.

On the third day Zoya did what she could put off no longer. She went shopping. She made liberal use of the money she had confiscated from the Liverpool curtain-hung stash, and prioritised time over cost. Which in practice meant she swerved and dodged in and out of the shops as fast as she could, tried nothing on, and bought whatever took her fancy. She returned to the hospital and placed one of her five shopping bags on the bed at Robin's side. In it were clean men's clothes, since his were covered in bloodstains; plus, since he wouldn't be wearing shoes for a while, Zoya had even compromised on another of her principles and purchased him a pair of sandals.

"You can hobble, or we can get you a crutch," she said. "Hell, I'll even carry you if I need to. But there's someone we have to visit."

On the fourth day, they flew. It felt like a commute already. The same airport to negotiate, the same duty-free stores to ignore, the same flight that hummed and vibrated its passage through the same drifting clouds. A slightly reduced Scheefnek met them, and they drove south with a little more variety along the way. The tulip fields had finally started to do their thing – swaying their wide, flat stretches of green and red and yellow under the wide, flat sky, nodding their still closed-petalled heads in the breeze. And although they had headed in the same direction as before, today their destination was different. No white-painted woodlap house, no overly equipped barn. All that was in the past, and it was a plain, white-on-black sign on an arched metal gate that informed them that they had arrived. *Begraafplaats Vredehof*, it said. Vredehof Cemetery.

Scheefnek already knew the way. He led them along a brick-laid path that meandered up a gentle slope. Robin limped, Zoya supported. They branched off across a freshly mowed stretch of grass, through the shade of ancient trees – maybe oaks, maybe poplars – and past the bright clumps of flowers. Neat lines of headstones, modest and plain, stretched ahead of them. Some were weathered and worn; then the years passed as they advanced, until they caught up with the more recently deceased. Here were mounds of earth, wreaths piled up, fresh-carved marble capping the loss of loved ones. It was respectful and quiet. Zoya was not generally a fan of neatness and order but, if they had a place, she admitted that this was it. They stopped.

"Why are we here?" Robin asked. He seemed dejected at the sight of the grave.

"I thought it was time you met Mr Dietrich Visser." Zoya replied. "Since he did as much to solve this case as any of us."

Robin thought it was a strange thing to say, even for Zoya. But by now he knew better than to ask. He rubbed a hand down his aching leg and waited as Zoya stared at the headstone.

She stared, but she didn't see at first. Instead her imagination heard. From the silence that surrounded, the sounds of an old man emerged – the slightest scratch of a fountain pen's steel nib, its passage over thick paper smoothed by the spread of Indian black ink. Then the smells: the soot of the ink, of course; then a hint of pear from the tumbler placed on the beeswax of his oak desk, their recipe stirred by the drift of night air through the barn doors behind him. Next his hand came into her mind's eye – neat-clipped nails, mottled fingers still strong – then his face. It held the features of a man Zoya had never met, so it was the mortuary that guided her: fittingly, she thought, given the pain he must already have been facing as the cancer chewed its way through his body. But she knew he would have fought, and so she watched as he straightened his back, as he pursed his lips and forced calm into his muscles, whatever the effort cost him. Alone, at the end, but aren't we all.

"Scheefnek," Zoya said, "give him the letter."

It wasn't the original, and Zoya thought it was a little sad that Robin wouldn't see what she had seen. But Mr Visser had written in Dutch, so it was a pragmatic translation that Scheefnek handed over, and it didn't matter, not really. It was what he had written that was important, not where he had sat or the tools that he had used. Those words that Mr Visser had addressed to Anna Vries: the daughter of the man who had been his oldest friend; the woman who should have become his daughter-in-law, but now never would.

"Pages two and three are the important parts," Zoya said, even though she knew already that Robin would read slowly and attentively from beginning to end. She stood and watched him and forced herself to remember that he had earned her patience.

Robin reached the end. He looked around, a little lost.

"It doesn't seem fair," he said finally.

"Don't forget that Mr Visser was already sick," Zoya said. "I'm sure he thought it was worth it."

She paused, and she wished she had thought to stop and gather a bunch of flowers as they drove – because they would have been no use to the dead, but they might have helped the living. Then Zoya remembered what had truly been of value to Mr Dietrich Visser and she took the letter from Robin's hands, and she watched him again at his desk as she began to quote, selectively this time, from passages that she already knew almost by heart.

"Dear Anna, it is with a heavy heart that I write to you. I have done a terrible thing and it is important that you understand why.

"Both your father and I hated everything about the Stasi, even though neither of us ever found the strength to leave. However, of the three of us, only my wife was ever a successful agent. I believe the work must have answered some need in her – for adventure, for intrigue, or perhaps for the power and prestige her successes brought her. And it was my wife, once the political need for her work had dissipated, once her own network of agents had scattered or died, who had the idea to establish a new business. She ignored all my objections, and she brought Jan into her organisation. She blackmailed your father to begin working again. And, when your father's vision deteriorated so much that he was no longer able to work, she told Jan to persuade you to replace him.

"I comforted myself with the thought that the risks were limited. Your team helped clients with documentation, helped them change their appearance or move their money. But you were never involved directly in the many other repellent activities of the spy business – the assassinations, the seductions and blackmail, the theft and passing on of secrets. Therefore, I allowed myself to follow the logic of the weapons dealers who tell the world that it's not the guns that kill, it's the people who use them. I refused to be involved myself but beyond that I simply closed my eyes to what was going on.

"Until the day when the Hunter appeared on the scene. And the strange thing, Anna, was that I liked him. We spent many evenings together talking and drinking Schnapps, and I came to understand how terribly damaged he was. I could see that he was straining with every fibre to pull himself away from his past, that all his efforts and his ambitions were an attempt to mould the violence within him into something more positive. I can't explain it exactly and maybe it wouldn't have been important; he would have been just another client who purchased your team's services and then moved on. Except that he started talking with Jan.

"Now I must be careful. Jan is my son; he is your fiancé and the father of your future child. But I must tell you the truth – you deserve that much. Anna, whatever the good you see in him, Jan is a ruthless and ambitious man. Perhaps he takes that from his mother, he certainly does not take it from me. Jan had come to believe that in its current form, his business had reached its natural limits. Neither his friends nor even his mother were ambitious enough for him. He had outgrown them, and he had also come to despise me – this weak old man pottering around in his barn. In contrast, when he spoke with the Hunter, he glimpsed excitement and opportunity. And so, at some point, Jan began a discussion with the Hunter about combining their businesses. He didn't tell anyone, not at first. He wanted to be the hero, to negotiate an agreement himself and present the completed deal to his team and to his mother, so that they would have no choice but to accept his terms. But it didn't work. Jan and the Hunter had a completely different understanding of their relationship. The Hunter certainly saw the advantages of being able to offer a wider range of services, but he viewed it as a minor add-on to his grand plans. Jan on the other hand believed he was the equal of the Hunter and tried to insist that he should be a full partner in the combined business. And when Jan finally spoke with his mother and his friends, he discovered that no one supported what he was trying to do. His friends had no wish to become the full-time employees of a single, particularly violent, client. My wife hated the idea from the beginning. She saw herself as the founder and the boss of their business. She was furious that Jan had gone behind her back, but worse than that she had understood immediately that there was no place for her in any version of Jan and the Hunter's future organisation.

"Then there was you, Anna. Your father was my friend and, before he died, I had promised him that I would do everything I could to look after you. In one big way, I had already failed. You began to work with Jan, and even if you were distanced to some extent from their operations, there would never be any way to remove the risks entirely. What your group did, after all, was illegal, and you worked for dangerous people. But that was nothing compared to what would happen if the Hunter took over. Pregnant or not, there was no way he would ever allow you to sit off comfortably to one side of his business.

"I tried to talk with the Hunter, but it didn't help. And each time he and Jan spoke, they ended up in a furious confrontation, with Jan continuing to make demands that made no sense at all to the Hunter. One day it all came to a head. The Hunter stormed into my workshop, shouting and cursing. When he had quietened down a little, he told me very simply – Dietrich, he said, you must persuade your son to accept my terms. Or I swear to you that it will end here. Your son and his people, they know me. They know my identity; they gave me this new face. If I cannot trust them, if I cannot come to an agreement with them, then I must kill them all.

"Then, Anna, I confess that I did a terrible thing. I went into my study, and I took a bottle of the schnapps we used to share, and I dosed it with my beloved Scandium-46. I poured out equal measures for each of us, and we carried on drinking until we had finished the bottle.

"Now, I do not have much time left. One thing remains, and I have been putting it off these last two weeks. I will walk down to the village this afternoon and post you my letter, and then I must speak with my wife and with Jan. My wife will perhaps not be too upset since one way or another the Hunter will be removed from her life. My son is a different matter. I have killed his dream and I know he will never forgive me. But it was worth it Anna. I did what I believe is right, and I will live, and die, with the consequences."

Zoya looked up from the paper. She was just in time to see Robin stagger at her side, and Scheefnek catch him with an arm around his waist. Robin's body was limp and trembling, and his forehead was beaded with sweat. Together they walked him to a nearby bench and lowered him down. He slumped, he closed his eyes and his breathing slowed.

"Is that normal?" Scheefnek asked.

Zoya shrugged. She was worried too; even if, over the last few days, she had grown accustomed to Robin's unexpected stops and starts. For now, all they could do was to prop Robin and his demons between them and sit in silence as they dozed in the soothing sunlight.

CHAPTER 38

Robin started and opened his eyes into a panicked gaze. Ten minutes had passed. He shook himself like a dog emerging from the waves, and his eyes sought the reassurance of his bookending colleagues. Then he pushed himself to his feet and stood, swaying slightly, as he stared at the cemetery ahead of him.

"Did you figure something out?" Zoya asked.

He swivelled abruptly towards her, looking down and wiping a hand over his forehead, and his eyes suddenly blazed into hers.

"Why the hell do you think I would have figured anything out?" he said with a bitter, rough voice, unlike anything Zoya had ever heard from him before. Then, crestfallen, his eyes fell towards the ground. At least he hadn't apologised, Zoya thought. That was progress. And now she had one simple priority: she needed to get Robin talking. She needed to get his mind working again.

"Begin with what you know," she said gently. "What the Hunter told you. And the gun."

"So, there are two pieces," he began hesitantly, numbly, "that I don't know how to join together. The Hunter didn't just tell me what he had done, he was boasting to me. That he had decided the Dutchmen had to die, so that no one could reveal his new identity. That he had personally taken part in one of the murders – the man they threw out of the window in Valencia – and tried to make it look like a suicide. That the poisonings and the heroin overdose were the work of the new team he had recruited a few months back. That it was the Scout who strangled the man in Liverpool. That much is clear, it makes sense. But then there's the gun they found in Mrs Visser's house, which ballistics have now confirmed was the weapon used to kill her husband – which makes it very likely that either she or her son shot him. And if that's true it just takes me back to your question from before."

"How the Hunter tracked down the Dutchmen?" Zoya confirmed.

Robin closed his eyes for a moment, but not to sleep. His hands lifted in front of him; flexing, moving, trying to shape something he couldn't see. Zoya thought he probably didn't even know he was doing it.

"That's the key, isn't it," he said. "And there's only two real possibilities. First that it was Mr Visser. One of the first things we discovered was that he was tortured and killed. We added two and two to make five and assumed it was him who had the information about the team's locations and gave it up. Mrs Visser hinted at that version too, and you told me that Jan supported it as part of the story he told you in Manchester."

"But," Zoya said, "if what Mr Visser wrote in his letter was true . . ."

"Then Mr Visser had no involvement in the whole identity-forging business, and therefore he was unlikely to have known the details of the team's aliases and locations. Plus, of course, it means Jan was lying to you. But how do we know which of them was telling the truth?"

Robin's face was furrowed, and Zoya realised there was one sauerkraut-flavoured box of information that she hadn't yet told him about, since he had already been taken by the Hunter when she had received it herself. However, she didn't want to spoil the surprise; and besides, she saw a small opportunity for revenge for the times she had endured Robin's own statistically overlong explanations. So, the aperitif she started with was a different German specialty.

"There was a small detail that made me curious about Mrs Visser," she said, "apart from the whole lost old woman routine. It was the Echter Aromatique liquor she drank. It's revolting stuff, which I know because my father kept a bottle in our apartment in Odesa that one of his colleagues had brought back from a work trip. It's produced in the town of Neudietendorf, in what used to be socialist East Germany. That caught my attention, and it was in my head when I called my policeman friend in Berlin. So, as well as giving him Dietrich Visser's real name, I asked him to see if there was anyone in the records who could meet Mrs Visser's description. Which is how I discovered that she was also with the Stasi."

"That confirmed that both husband and wife were spies," Robin said, a little more calmly now. "But it doesn't tell us which one of them was in charge."

"No, but there's a part I didn't have a chance to tell you," Zoya continued. "On the same day you were taken hostage,

I received two boxes of files with Mr and Mrs Visser's service records. They gave me a pretty clear picture. On one hand there was Mr Visser. He never progressed very far in his spy career, he didn't play the Stasi's political games, and he made no secret of his feelings about their KGB bosses. In fact, all he seemed to care about was his laboratory and his scientific experiments. Then there was Mrs Visser, who was the exact opposite. When she worked in the field she was responsible for at least three assassinations, and there were also multiple examples of military and industrial espionage. Not surprisingly, she was promoted fast; and then she went on to set up a network of spies that, as far as I can tell, has never been detected.

Without doubt, she was hard-working, ambitious and extremely successful. For me, that looked like the profile of a person who would be keen to make use of her old skills and her old contacts, and would be ruthless enough to bring her own son into her world. But I saw absolutely nothing in Mr Visser's profile to suggest that he would want to have anything more to do with the spy trade. All of which tallies with Mr Visser's letter."

Robin paced – limped, really – as he thought it through.

"So, we assume it was Mrs Visser who was in charge of the business, working with her son. So it's likely they would have known how to contact their team. But why would they, one or both of them, have betrayed everyone else to the Hunter? I mean, we know the Hunter threatened them – that's confirmed by both Jan and by Mr Visser in his letter. In theory I can imagine them making some kind of deal. But Mr Visser wrote that he was about to tell his wife and son that he had poisoned the Hunter. If they knew that, why wouldn't they just tell the team to stay put wherever they were and hope that they survived until the Hunter died a few weeks later?"

Now Robin was entirely still: his hands at his sides, his mind focused somewhere inside. Zoya was happy to wait. This was one puzzle she knew he needed to solve. Then she changed her mind and decided to give him a helping hand.

"Remember the first file we looked at together," Zoya said. "The one with the round glass top on the rectangular coffee table. Now think about the letter again and look for the inconsistency. There's something out of place in Mr Visser's letter too. It tells you the reason."

"The timing," he said finally. "Mr Visser waited two weeks before he told his wife and his son what he had done. Jan didn't know about it when he betrayed his friends."

Zoya smiled proudly.

"It's the only explanation that fits," she said. "Jan told me that the Hunter planted a bomb in a car belonging to one of their team. I think that part was true, and that it happened before Jan found out what his father had done. The team immediately scattered, and by now Jan was certain they would never agree to work for the Hunter. But the Hunter was still planning to hunt everyone down, which would have included not just Jan's friends but also his mother and Anna – who were the most vulnerable members of the team, and also the two who were closest to Jan. So, Jan made a deal. He agreed to give up his friends, and in return the Hunter agreed not to touch Anna or Mrs Visser, or Jan himself. And going forward, they would presumably all be forced to work for the Hunter. And it was only after they made the deal that Jan's father told him what he had done, and that both he and the Hunter were dying."

"Which brings us full circle," Robin rushed on, excited now. "As his father wrote, Jan must have been furious that his father had destroyed all hopes for a merger with the Hunter's organisation. He might even have blamed his father for forcing a decision on him to betray his own friends. That would explain him killing his father with the gun we have in evidence. But it doesn't explain why he would torture him. The only explanation I can think of is that he was trying to create a false trail for us, or anyone else who came looking."

"And that's the part I missed for a long time," Zoya said. "I've been a homicide cop nearly ten years now, and I've seen some pretty depraved stuff. But I still couldn't figure it out, because I couldn't imagine a man who would treat his own father like Jan did. I mean, murder is one thing – but torture of a dying man is something else entirely. Of course, Jan could just have left everything as it was and hoped no one would fit the puzzle together. He had already learnt that the Hunter and his father were dying from radiation poisoning – they would soon be out of the picture. It must have seemed unlikely that anyone would link the deaths of a series of apparently random Dutchmen scattered across Europe. And, even if they did, they would at worst find his mother – the only survivor – and just see her as a tragic victim. But when it comes down to it, Jan learnt his spying lessons too well – he's far too cunning for his own good. I think he decided to construct a backup story so that if someone started investigating, they would find that all the indications pointed at the Hunter and at Mr Visser. So he started with his father – some real torture, some post-mortem additions that he thought would make it look more convincing – then he killed him. Then, since we seemed to be making progress, he roped in his mother to help scatter a trail of breadcrumbs. There was the wedding photo that she used to hint about Mr Visser's spy background, and the other album that helped us identify Jan's friends, which in turn eventually suggested the Hunter's motive to kill them. Then the envelope I found, which I think Jan must have planted, with the cryptic reference to Scandium – another hint pointing back to his father. Like all good liars, Jan blended fact and fiction, and he almost got away with it."

She paused and remembered Jan's embrace when he arrived in Manchester Airport. She shuddered at the thought of his touch.

"And you're sure it was him, not his mother?" Robin asked. "You think she just went along with it?"

"Well, the gun has traces of both their DNA, so we can't be sure who pulled the trigger. But on balance I don't believe she went that far. Or maybe I just don't want to believe it. I'm pretty sure she loved her husband, on some level at least, and it's a stretch to think she tortured him herself or even agreed for him to be tortured. I think Jan took charge, and once he had killed his father Mrs Visser had no choice but to go along with it."

"What about Anna?" Scheefnek asked. "If Jan had made this deal with the Hunter, why was she attacked?"

"We know she was being watched," Zoya said. "It's possible that the Hunter never intended to keep to the terms of his own deal. He might simply have split his plan into two parts for his own convenience. First, he would use Jan's information to locate and kill the junior members of the team. Then, once he was sure he didn't need Jan's help anymore, he would take out Jan, Mrs Visser and Anna. Alternatively, the surveillance was just for insurance: to keep an eye on Anna and make sure she didn't do anything stupid, like talking to the police. And it was us – specifically you, Scheefnek – who inadvertently set the alarm bells ringing by turning up and camping overnight at Anna's apartment."

"Then the last question is why Jan took the risk of coming to England to help you take down the Hunter," Robin said. "He must have seen you were getting too close, and he knew that absolutely the worst thing that could happen was if by some miracle you took the Hunter alive. The Hunter would have exploded Jan's version of events, so Jan had to do everything he could to sell his story, and to make sure everyone believed the only option was to kill the Hunter."

"His words," Zoya confirmed, "were the last I heard in my earpiece before Lovell told her sniper to take the shot. It was Jan, urging Lovell on – supposedly to save you, Robin, but actually to save himself."

Robin thought everything seemed to fit together. But he also thought that, in his new world, *seemed* was no longer good enough. Zoya read the doubt on his face. She knew he was terrified, after everything he had gone through, of getting it wrong. She also knew he wanted to be convinced.

"There's one more thing you should see –" she said – "the original reason I asked you and Scheefnek to find out where Mr Visser was buried."

She stood and took Robin's arm, guiding him back to the graveside.

"Even before I read the letter, I knew that the Hunter had been irradiated because of the traces he left in my hotel room. But I didn't know who had done it. Mr Visser had already seemed to be the most likely candidate, then he confirmed it in his letter. But I wanted to be sure, which is why I asked Scheefnek to come here."

Zoya fished into the pocket of her coat. She showed Robin what she was holding in her hand. She held it over the grave and switched it on. The Geiger counter squealed and pulsed over Mr Visser's resting place.

"He was a good man," she said, "who sacrificed himself to protect someone he loved."

Zoya was about to switch off the device when an idea struck her. It was better than flowers, she thought. She bent and placed the Geiger counter on the dark, moist earth. And she stood with Robin, the pair listening listening in silence as the device clicked and whistled its condolences over the body of its creator.

*

They walked back to where Scheefnek was waiting and sat again: the three of them in a neat row. *Beauty and the two beasts*, she thought again – the roles this time reshuffled, since she was the only uninjured one; but there was always tomorrow. Zoya looked at Robin. He seemed steadier now, and she was glad they had come. She thought that perhaps she had been able to hem a silver lining to the dark cloud of Robin's captivity and suffering.

"What happens now?" he asked.

"The good news is that I'm told Anna has agreed her deal with the police. She'll give up the identities of dozens, maybe hundreds, of criminals across Europe in return for immunity. The Dutch spooks have Mrs Visser in a safehouse somewhere, singing for her supper. And the Netherlands has already put in a request to extradite Jan from Britain. They want to try him for the murder of his father and conspiracy to murder his friends. If that doesn't work out, he'll probably be passed to the intelligence services as well. One way or the other, both of them will be out of circulation for years to come. At the same time, Interpol is coordinating the search for the remaining members of the Hunter's two teams – not forgetting the sniper, who's already in custody. And most of that, my dear professor, happened because of you. Because you found a single, unlikely little thread, and you forced everyone to grab hold and follow wherever it took us."

Robin smiled gently at the praise, and also because that wasn't what he had meant at all.

"What happens to us?" he asked.

"Scheefnek gets to stay and look after his ear," she said, at the same time as she dug an elbow into his big, handsome flank. "Maybe he decides to look after Anna too. As for you, you still have plenty of digits left to lose, so there's nothing to stop us being partners. If that's what you want?"

"If we're going to be working together," he said, "you have to promise me something."

"What's that?" Zoya asked.

"No more eating in my car," he said. "Or driving it. Or parking under No Parking signs."

Which was three somethings really. But Zoya didn't mind, since the warmth of his words told her that, somewhere, somehow, the sun had managed to pierce through the dark bank of Robin's clouds. For a moment she was even tempted to agree to his terms, until she remembered it was a bad habit to make promises that she might not be able to keep.

"I think it's time to go home," she said.

And it was a strange thought for a woman whose country was so far away, but she liked the sound of it. She had left Odesa only three weeks ago, give or take a day or two, but already she felt something she had not expected – that somehow, she had managed to find herself a new second home with a new second family. And then Robin smiled again, and maybe he had even understood what she was thinking. Because this time it was him who stood, calm and perhaps even a little proud, and pulled Zoya up from the bench.

ACKNOWLEDGEMENTS

Writing a novel begins as a solitary pursuit; fortunately, the professionals then get involved…

It is this team of talented and committed individuals that I would like to thank for turning my drafts into what I hope is a polished and enjoyable read. They have done a sterling job and of course any and all remaining shortfalls or errors are solely my responsibility.

First and foremost, my thanks and respect go to Anne Hawkins at John Hawkins & Associates, Inc. in New York. Anne was the first person who picked up my work and believed in its publishing potential. As any first-time author knows, that is an inspiring sensation. Ever since, Anne has offered far more support than it would be reasonable to expect. Her feedback has always been insightful and constructive, and I am immensely grateful.

On copyediting and proofreading respectively, my thanks go to the son and father team of Richard and Robert Arcus. To Richard for adding clarity and for restraining my love of complexity and some of the more obscure attempts at humour, and to Robert for picking out my errors even after my many drafts and rereads. Also, a call out to Ramesh Kumar Pitchai for his typesetting skills and for taking the time to educate me on things I should probably already have known.

Next came the cover design. I hope you like it! I certainly do and all credit goes to Lisa Brewster at The Brewster Project for grasping so quickly what I was looking for (before I had myself) and coming up with such a stunning set of images. Please feel free to judge this book by its cover.

Finally, I am very grateful to marketing gurus Merle Bennett and Fergus Edmondson. Their expertise and experience are evident in every conversation. Best of all they are responsive, open, friendly and enthusiastic. No pressure, Merle and Fergus, but everything depends on you now! And the Champagne will be on me just as soon as we sell the ten thousandth copy!

TO THE READER

A message from L. G. Wilder

Thank you!

If you are reading this page, that means you have purchased my novel and read it to the end. I am very grateful.

Now that you have finished reading, I invite you to imagine, for just a moment, labouring away on a project for months or even years without ever receiving a word of feedback. Is the end product good; is it entertaining? Who knows… I love to write but that is sometimes how the process feels. It can be lonely. Until the moment when someone picks up my book and starts to read. Then everything makes sense, and I remember why I started out on this journey.

The best result I can hope for is that you have enjoyed the result. If you have, I have a favour to ask.

Please spend a few minutes to leave a review on whichever retail platform you used for your purchase, or elsewhere on social media. Let other potential readers know what you liked about Zoya and the Dead Dutchmen: the plot; the characters of Zoya and Robin; their relationship and their shared humour; or the supporting cast of characters both good and bad. Hopefully, your opinions will inspire others to give Zoya a try.

This book is planned as the first in a series of Zoya adventures. I am already working on the next instalment as you read the first. Let me know if you think that is a good plan and if you would be keen to see Zoya's return.

And, finally, I am always happy to hear from you. You can find my contact information on my author website:

www.lgwilder.com

Thanks again!
L. G. Wilder

Printed in Great Britain
by Amazon

54922893R00192